### *"Meet Ryan*

Marca said softly

Ian swallowed, his gaze riveted on his son. His jaw was set, his face ashen, breathing uneven.

Silence settled between them, broken only by the sound of Ry's breathing. Ian had drawn into himself, becoming aloof and distant.

"He's mine, isn't he?" he said finally, his voice quiet but distinctly rough.

Smiling a little, Marca rubbed Ry's back—to reassure herself as much as her child. She wasn't sure exactly what she'd expected in telling him, but she knew now she'd been hoping for the joy she'd felt when she'd seen Ry and his two brothers for the first time. "Yes, he's your son, Ian."

"Is he—" Ian broke off, his gaze riveted suddenly on the photograph of the triplets on her desk. The color that had begun to return to his face disappeared.

"Oh, God," he said. "Triplets?"

Marca smiled. "I'm afraid so. A ready-made gang." And family, she hoped....

Dear Reader,

Winter's here, so why not curl up by the fire with the new Intimate
Moments novels? (Unless you live in a warm climate, in which
case you can take your books to the beach!) Start off with our
WHOSE CHILD? title, another winner from Paula Detmer Riggs
called *A Perfect Hero*. You've heard of the secret baby plot? How
about secret *babies*? As in *three* of them! You'll love it, I promise,
because Ian MacDougall really *is* just about as perfect as a hero
can get.

Kathleen Creighton's *One More Knight* is a warm and wonderful
sequel to last year's *One Christmas Knight*, but this fine story stands
entirely on its own. Join this award-winning writer for a
taste of Southern hospitality—and a whole lot of Southern loving.
Lee Magner's *Owen's Touch* is a suspenseful amnesia book and
wears our TRY TO REMEMBER flash. This twisty plot will
keep you guessing—and the irresistible romance will keep you
happy. FAMILIES ARE FOREVER, and *Secondhand Dad*, by
Kayla Daniels, is just more evidence of the truth of that statement.
Lauren Nichols takes us WAY OUT WEST in *Accidental Hero*, all
about the allure of a bad boy. And finally, welcome new author
Virginia Kantra, whose debut book, *The Reforming of Matthew
Dunn*, is a MEN IN BLUE title. You'll be happy to know that her
second novel is already in the works.

So pour yourself a cup of something warm, pull the afghan over
yourself and enjoy each and every one of these terrific books.
Then come back next month, because the excitement—and the
romance—will continue, right here in Silhouette Intimate Moments.

Enjoy!

Leslie Wainger
Executive Senior Editor

---

Please address questions and book requests to:
Silhouette Reader Service
U.S.: 3010 Walden Ave., P.O. Box 1325, Buffalo, NY 14269
Canadian: P.O. Box 609, Fort Erie, Ont. L2A 5X3

# Paula Detmer Riggs

## A Perfect Hero

Silhouette®
INTIMATE™ MOMENTS®

Published by Silhouette Books

America's Publisher of Contemporary Romance

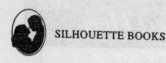

**SILHOUETTE BOOKS**

ISBN 0-373-07889-7

A PERFECT HERO

Copyright © 1998 by Paula Detmer Riggs

**Printed in U.S.A.**

**Books by Paula Detmer Riggs**

Silhouette Intimate Moments

*Beautiful Dreamer* #183
*Fantasy Man* #226
*Suspicious Minds* #250
*Desperate Measures* #283
*Full Circle* #303
*Tender Offer* #314
*A Lasting Promise* #344
*Forgotten Dream* #364
*Silent Impact* #398
*Paroled!* #440
*Firebrand* #481
*Once Upon a Wedding* #524
*No Easy Way Out* #548
*The Bachelor Party* #656
*Her Secret, His Child* #667
*\*Mommy by Surprise* #794
*\*Baby by Design* #806
*A Perfect Hero* #889

Silhouette Desire

*Rough Passage* #633
*A Man of Honor* #744
*Murdock's Family* #898
*\*Daddy by Accident* #1073

Silhouette Books

*Silhouette Summer Sizzlers* 1992
"Night of the Dark Moon"

36 Hours

*The Parent Plan*

\*Maternity Row

## PAULA DETMER RIGGS

discovers material for her writing in her varied experiences. During her first five years of marriage to a naval officer, she lived in nineteen different locations on the West Coast, gaining familiarity with places as diverse as San Diego and Seattle. While working at a historical site in San Diego, she wrote, directed and narrated fashion shows and became fascinated with the early history of California.

She writes romances because "I think we all need an escape from the high-tech pressures that face us every day, and I believe in happy endings. Isn't that why we keep trying, in spite of all the roadblocks and disappointments along the way?"

For Catherine Anderson and Alexis Harrington.
Friends, indeed.

# *Prologue*

Ian MacDougall wasn't quite drunk enough yet to pass out. In fact, he hadn't yet downed enough booze to work up a pleasant buzz. Though his rent was due and his money was low, he'd given serious thought to buying another bottle. A man had his priorities, after all.

So he'd walked to the convenience store on the corner to buy scotch. The good stuff, not rotgut. As long as he bought the good stuff, he wasn't a drunk, right? He still didn't know why he'd bought dog food instead. Hell, the damn hound could find better eats scrounging through the trash barrels on the beach. Now as forty-four-year-old Ian walked the familiar strip of sand and rock, his belly was on fire, and his head was one pounding misery.

He should have bought the scotch and let the dog do without. Dogs didn't have nightmares. Or memories that twisted and tore through a man's mind until he wanted to run himself into oblivion.

With the exception of the regulars who slept beneath newspapers or tarps or in cardboard shelters wedged between the rocks above high tide, Ian was alone on this stretch of coastline. Overhead the stars glittered like cold, hard chips of ice. Above the phosphorescent surf, fog roiled on the horizon, sending long, angry tendrils toward the beach. Below the cliff, the surf was a wild thing, angrily ripping and tearing at the land.

Pausing in the lee of a jagged chunk of ancient California granite, he lit another cigarette and drew in smoke. Spindrift dampened his face and chilled his bones. Behind him the funky Southern California community of Ocean Beach in San Diego had finally settled down for the night, only a few dimly illuminated windows salting the darkness.

Ian's eyes felt gritty as he looked out over the sand. The beach itself was empty.

No matter where he started or what direction he took initially, he invariably ended up at the cliffs. He knew why, of course. It was the place where he'd once decided to end his life. And the place where he'd met the woman who'd changed his mind.

After field stripping his cigarette butt, he dropped the remnants into the pocket of his windbreaker before settling his wired body onto a flat chunk of cold rock. As he fished another smoke from the pack in his shirt pocket, the mutt who'd appointed himself Ian's bodyguard settled down on the hard red dirt at his feet.

"Get a life, you miserable cur," he muttered, frowning. The ugly creature glanced up, growled a protest, then rested his scarred snout on his paws, closed his eyes and went to sleep.

Lucky bastard, he thought as he wearily lit his cigarette. His throat was raw from the pack-a-day habit. The cough that had driven him to quit when his twin daughters were born had returned with a vengeance. He'd started smoking again a few days after watching the matching caskets of his babies and his ex-wife being lowered into the ground. That had been almost a year ago. He'd been drunk every night since then—with one exception. A full-moon night, when the dog had come into his life.

Ian had heard the shouts first and then the furious barking, carried to him by the on-shore breeze. He still didn't know why he went to investigate. Habit, he suspected. The deeply ingrained response of a man sworn to uphold the law—like an old fire horse stirred to action by the sound of an alarm.

By the time Ian reached the spot where the shouting had erupted, the dog had been sprawled on the sand, battered and bloodied by a group of rampaging teenage hoodlums out for some fun. Only a tiny, prickly lady with black curls and snapping brown eyes had been keeping the gang from finishing off the poor beast. Before Ian could figure out what was going on, one of the little doper bastards had locked his brutal hands on her slender arms.

Though Ian had been at least two sheets to the wind, his twenty years in law enforcement had clicked in. Months of trying to drink himself to death had slowed him down a few steps, but he'd still had the moves—a right cross fueled by a simmering rage against bullies. Like all cowards, the mean little creeps had run away rather than fight a guy their own size.

"The lady saved your life, you ugly no-name mutt," he now muttered, glaring at the long-haired, floppy-eared canine clown at his feet. With the uncanny perception that annoyed Ian no end, the dog opened the eye that could still see and thumped his stubby tail.

Scowling to show his irritation, Ian knuckled the thick fur between Mutt's ears. Not because he liked the pathetic creature, he reminded himself. No way. Hell, what was to like? The dog was half-lame, ugly as sin, and had the appetite of a piranha. Worse, he had to be about as dumb as a post, because only the canine equivalent of an idiot would willingly hang out with the sorry likes of Ian MacDougall.

"She's not here, you sorry so-and-so. Hell, she probably forgot us both before her plane left the ground." Even as he said the words, he knew they weren't exactly true. The woman who'd sobbed against his shoulder in the vet's office wasn't the kind of cold-hearted bitch who would forget.

Ian took a deep drag and let the smoke trail out. He never should have touched her. It had been a stupid thing to do. The kind of idiot impulse he thought he'd overcome years before, when he'd signed on with Alcohol, Tobacco and Firearms. Two strangers on a beach, each driven by private demons, hoping to find comfort in one another. Thank God the woman had had the presence of mind to use protection, because he sure as hell hadn't given a damn.

He'd been a little crazy that night, full of rage and guilt and anguish. The trial had been over less than forty-eight hours. Hutch Renfrew had winked at Ian as he'd walked out a free man—and then laughed. The man who killed two innocent little girls and their mama—free to kill again. Renfrew was alive only because Ian had gone to the courthouse unarmed that morning.

Since then, the swastika-waving son of a bitch had gone to ground. Not even the vast resources of the various and sundry law enforcement agencies of the good old U.S. of A. had been able to find the leader of the New Aryan Freedom Brigade.

God knows Ian had tried.

Tomorrow his year-long leave of absence from ATF was officially over. His boss, Big Ed Stebbins, had warned him in his thick Alabama drawl that it was time to fish or cut bait. Agent Ian MacDougall was out of wiggle room. He was either in or out. Eddie wanted him in.

Ian didn't much care one way or another. But he was out of money, and ATF was the only home and family he had left.

He had another assignment waiting, Eddie had told him, when he'd called a few days back. A weapons-smuggling case in Florida. No more skinheads, the boss had also said. Ian was too personally involved.

Yeah, he was involved, he admitted, taking the last, bitter drag on the butt before stubbing it out on the stone. Involved enough to daydream, a little too often for his peace of mind, about gutting that white supremacist bastard with his own hunting knife. Staying with ATF would give him a pipeline to information that would someday lead him straight to Renfrew.

"Florida," he muttered, drawing another lazy look from the ugly beast at his feet. "I hear they have alligators down there. Probably eat poor dumb fools like us for breakfast."

Tail thumping, Mutt gave an eager bark. An answering "woof"

came from further along the beach, stirring Mutt to his feet. Head cocked, the mangy mongrel peered into the darkness, giving out with a pathetic whine every so often, as though he were pining for the lady with the angel smile and a big heart.

He had a wishing star up there in the skyful of twinkling lights, she'd told him. There was one for each soul that came to earth. He'd damn near laughed at her, but he'd kissed her instead.

Ian grinned a little as he rolled his shoulders. "Forget it, old son. The lady lives in Oregon, remember? Works in some college up there in the trees." Frowning a little, he reached into the pocket of his windbreaker and pulled out the business card that had been there since she'd given it to him eight and a half months ago. He'd meant to throw it away, but somehow had never gotten around to it.

Her name and title were embossed on expensive card stock. Classy and upscale, like the lady herself. Though she'd been dressed in button-fly jeans and an ordinary T-shirt, she'd worn diamond studs in her ears and her perfume had evoked images of priceless crystal and antique silver.

Marcella Kenworthy, Director of Public Relations at Bradenton College. Bradenton Falls, Oregon. Marca, she'd called herself. Had come down to San Diego for a conference of other academic types.

Try as he might to kick free, he kept wanting more of her. Another night in her arms. And another, until he no longer woke up with the sheets twisted like a shroud around his sweat-slick body and a scream trapped in his throat.

Stebbins was a decent guy. No problem to extend his leave a few weeks. For the first time in months, he'd felt something beyond the heavy pall of grief. Hope, maybe. A reason beyond the need for vengeance to get up in the morning.

And then what, ace? he demanded with the ruthless honesty that was damn near all he had left. Send her a bunch of daisies and walk away? Or stay and watch the light in her eyes dim when she realized he wasn't the hero she'd thought he was?

Hell, what he'd done was easy. She'd been the one putting

herself on the line. One lone, unarmed woman against a pack of crazies. He had no doubt she would have fought until she was unconscious—or dead—simply to protect a stray dog.

He'd been trained to fight. Once, maybe, he'd done it because he'd had some grandiose idea of making the world a better place. Some half-assed notion that he could right a few wrongs, protect the innocent against the bullies of the world. Now it was just a job he did because he was too uneducated and too tired to start over at something else. No, he wasn't anybody's hero. In fact, he was a pretty pathetic example of a man. A drunk wallowing in grief and guilt. A loser with nothing inside but emptiness.

"Forget it, Mutt," he said as he climbed to his feet. "The lady's way out of our class."

The dog with no name gave a mournful yip before falling in at Ian's side.

Pausing at a brightly painted and badly dented trash basket on the edge of the sand, Ian took a breath, then tore the card into pieces and let them sift through his long fingers into the basket.

"Goodbye, angel gypsy," he murmured, glancing up at the stars. She'd made a wish on one of them that night. He hoped it had come true.

It was almost dawn and the stars were fading. Marca was determined to get these babies born before her special star disappeared completely. According to the ultrasound, she was about to deliver three little boys.

"Ian should be here," Marca muttered as she felt the ominous tightening of her back muscles.

"It's not your fault, Marce," her Lamaze coach and friend, Carly Scanlon, assured her before calmly talking her through the rhythm of panting breaths that was supposed to ease the pain.

"He...doesn't...know," she gasped out as the agony took her.

"You did everything humanly possible to find him." Carly's voice dimmed as the pain surged through her.

Ian MacDougall. They'd made babies together, and she scarcely knew him. The private investigator she'd hired when she'd discovered her pregnancy had cost her a hefty slice of her savings, yet he'd come up with nothing. There'd been seven Ian MacDougalls in the San Diego phone book, but none had been her Ian. Ian with the haunted gray eyes and deep, blood-shivering voice. Ian with the coal black hair and lonely heart. A man with the look of a street fighter and the soul of a poet. A man who'd taken a filthy, flea-infested mongrel into his strong arms so gently the animal scarcely whimpered. Later, when he'd made love to her, she'd felt the gentleness in him. And a hunger to love and be loved that matched her own.

The pain eased off and Marca opened her eyes. Carly's green eyes were rimmed with weariness. She, too, was hugely pregnant, her due-date scarcely a month away.

"I shouldn't have asked you to be my coach," Marca told her wearily. "Mitch will shoot me if anything happens to you."

"I'm fine," Carly assured her, smoothing back a lock of Marca's sweat-drenched hair. "And Mitch loves you as much as I do, so stop worrying. As he told Tracy when she called last night to ask about you, bringing these babies into the world is a family project."

Marca closed her eyes, hoarding her strength the way the La-maze instructor had drummed into her.

Carly was more than a friend. She was the sister Marca had never had. They had met as freshmen roommates. Carly, as the only child of Bradenton College's president and a blue-blooded Virginia debutante, had been the closest thing to royalty the campus had.

Marca's background had been boringly ordinary. Also an only child, she'd grown up in a singularly unimpressive town in central Washington where her mother had been a bookkeeper for a mortuary and her father had worked in a mill, endlessly sharpening the huge saws that planed logs into boards. Neither had known how to relate to their changeling child who'd come into the world with a startlingly high IQ and boundless ambition. It had been those two God-given traits that had won Marca a scholarship to Bradenton.

After graduation, both she and Carly had gone east—Carly to

Rhode Island where she had taught social anthropology at Brown, Marca to Madison Avenue and a career on the fast track. Ten years later, when Carly had succeeded her father as Bradenton's president, she'd enlisted Marca's aid in changing their alma mater's stodgy image. With her marriage to a fellow advertising executive gone bust and her will to compete burned to ashes, Marca had come home to Bradenton for good.

"Whoa, here comes another one," she muttered, feeling the pincer-sharp cramp slicing her belly. But instead of easing off after sixty seconds or so, this one escalated, nearly bringing her off the mattress before it finally eased.

"I think you'd better page Dr. Mason," she heard Carly telling someone.

Minutes passed like seconds, yet paradoxically, telescoped into hours. Through it all, Carly's voice was her lodestar, leading her, encouraging her. But it was the image of Ian's tenderness when he'd held her in his arms that sustained her.

She'd fallen in love with a man she didn't know. A stranger with a stalwart heart and haunted eyes.

"Push, Marca. Now." It was the doctor's voice, and mindlessly she obeyed.

"Look at the shoulders on this little fellow," Dr. Mason marveled as he eased the infant into the world.

Marca opened her eyes and made a feeble gesture. Obligingly the doctor held the baby aloft, giving her a look at her firstborn. A tenderness unlike anything she'd ever felt before ran through her. It was a new kind of love, and so powerful she nearly wept from the joy of it.

"Oh, Marce, he's gorgeous!" Carly, exclaimed softly, her eyes glistening with tears above the mask. "Look at all that black hair."

"Ryan James," Marca whispered, then frowned as another viselike spasm squeezed her abdomen. Regretfully she allowed the nurse to whisk her son away, but only for a little while, she reminded herself, before the pain took over her mind.

"Quick, light breaths," Carly coached, wiping Marca's dripping forehead. "You're doing fine, sweetie. Wonderfully well. Be strong for just a few more minutes. Just a few more."

Exhausted and nearly numb, Marca turned her head and watched the nurse weigh her son while the doctor worked to deliver his brother. Simon and Garfunkel played on the boom box she'd brought with her, the same songs she'd listened to on the night of her fortieth birthday when Ian had fathered these babies.

*Ian. Ian. Ian.* His name was a mantra. A plea.

"Bear down now," the doctor said urgently, lifting his head to give her a quick, encouraging look over his mask.

"Push, Marce, push," Carly ordered, her voice calm and soothing, yet compelling. Nearly done in, Marca concentrated on her friend's voice, obediently pushing when she was told, relaxing on command.

"There's the head," the doctor exclaimed before ordering, "Push, Marca. Give me one more big push...that's it...aah, another bruiser."

Carly laughed and squeezed Marca's hand. "Son number two," she said, leaning forward to watch as the baby squirmed under the efficient ministrations of the nurses. "A tough little so-and-so," she said, grinning.

"Sean Mitchell," Marca murmured through numb lips.

"Number three is a little reluctant," the doctor said wearily, glancing up at the clock as a member of the birthing team swabbed his damp forehead.

Marca closed her eyes and listened to her two boys squalling their heads off. Lusty, angry cries that made her smile even as another murderous pain gathered in the small of her back.

"Daddy must be a big man," the older of the two nurses said as she swaddled baby boy number two. "These two are busters."

Marca concentrated on breathing into the pain, but the image of haunted silver eyes rose in her mind. Eyes framed with thick black lashes and swooping black brows. The rest of his face had been hidden behind a black beard, but she would never forget the slash of white teeth as he'd smiled at her.

"C'mon, little one," the doctor muttered as Carly urged her to reach for that last reserve of strength. "Yes, *all right*, here he comes."

Her third son let out a yell as soon as the nurse suctioned his lungs clear—a loud, indignant protest that had the doctor's eyes crinkling. "The smallest of the three. Looks like this one's making up for his lack of size with sheer volume," he said, laughing.

Trevor Allen had just arrived.

Marca met Carly's gaze and realized her friend was crying even as her eyes were soft with emotion. "Three adorable little boys," she murmured, leaning down to give Marca a hug. "You are so blessed."

Marca fought off the seductive lethargy of sleep and breathed a silent little prayer of thanks before rousing herself to open her eyes.

"Can I see them?" she murmured, looking toward the nurses.

"You bet," one of them said, grinning.

While the doctor finished, Marca opened her arms to receive three babies, now swaddled in blue with nubby blue stocking caps covering their perfect little heads. They were warm and heavy and sweet. Her breasts ached as she cuddled them close. Tears spilled over her lashes and slipped down her cheeks.

"I'm terrified I'll let them down," she whispered, glancing with brimming eyes at Carly, who'd raised her own firstborn for sixteen years before Mitch had come back into their lives.

Looking radiant in spite of her weariness, Carly brushed a finger over a silken cheek of one of the newborns. "You'll be a marvelous mom." She laughed a little before adding, "And a busy one for the first few years at least."

Marca smiled at that, but her attention was fixed on the three identical faces of her children. Sean and Ryan were already sleeping, their stubby lashes resting on cherubic little cheeks. Trevor was awake, his deep blue eyes fixed like dark pools of curiosity on her face while his soft mouth made greedy sucking motions.

Ian's sons, all with his face, she suspected, but not his mouth. His hard, bitter, angry mouth. He'd been intense and driven and hurting, a big man with a terrible pain burning deep in his eyes. A gentle man who kept himself apart and solitary. And yet, when they'd made love, he'd been tender and sweet and loving. From that love had come three perfect miracles. His birthday gift to her.

"Dear, Ian, I'll teach them to love you," she whispered, her eyes filling with tears. "I promise."

There was a window in the birthing room. Beyond the window was her star, the one she'd watched that night as she'd laid sated and blissfully happy beneath Ian's powerful body. She'd been lonely and sad that night. A woman who had thought the best years of her life were behind her. Ian had changed that.

A part of him would always be with her. Let him be as happy as I am at this moment, she wished, closing her eyes. And wherever he is, let him find peace.

# Chapter 1

*Twenty-two months later.*

The air-conditioning was busted again.

By the time Ian had climbed the stairs from the lobby of the federal building in Miami to ATF's second-floor offices, his T-shirt was plastered to his chest, and he felt as though he were breathing through a wet cloth. Even the usual sounds of clattering keyboards and ringing phones that greeted him as he walked through the door seemed muffled by the heavy air.

"Don't you dare say a word about the temperature, you hear me talking?" the middle-aged African-American receptionist warned, as he opened his mouth to ask her about the progress of the repairs on the air-conditioning.

"No, ma'am. Not a word."

Sherry Sue Jackson scowled up at him as she handed over his messages. "Cut the meek act, MacDougall," she drawled in the honeyed Alabama accent that fascinated him. "A man as mean-looking as you, it gives me the willies when you come across all soft spoken and sweet-like. Like one of those gators laying in the saw grass, just waitin' to get him dinner.''

Ian did his best to look hurt, which won him another snort, followed by an impatient wave of Ms. Jackson's hand.

''Get on out of here. You've bothered me enough for one day.''

''Yes, ma'am.'' He glanced around, saw that no one was watching, and leaned down to plant a kiss full on Sherry Sue's cheek.

''Boy, you do that again and you're in for a real jaw bruising from Charles Lee.''

Ian grinned. He played poker with Sherry's fireman husband every Thursday night, and he'd been invited to dinner on Thanksgiving and Christmas this past year. He suspected they felt sorry for him, a man without family and no steady girlfriend. Hell, no girlfriend of any kind. A damned charity case. It rankled, but not enough to keep him from turning down a chance to gorge himself on Sherry's cooking.

The truth was, he was restless and itchy inside. He figured that was because he hated Florida. He'd been miserable every day of the twenty-two months he'd spent in this sweatbox, and for the past six months he'd been angling for a transfer back to California. Last month he'd gone so far as to threaten to put in his retirement papers if Stebbins didn't pull the right strings.

The weather was part of the reason. A kid raised in the desert just naturally felt smothered by the ever-present humidity in the deep South. He was also bored out of his skull, riding herd on gunrunners and dope smugglers.

The case he'd just wrapped up had been a no-brainer. His elderly landlady could have hidden the contraband Uzis a lot more cleverly than the Habib brothers. Smart, they weren't. Or loyal, apparently, since Yusuf had ratted out his little brother, Tarif, in exchange for a lighter sentence. As an extra-added bonus, he'd given Ian the names of both his supplier and the client who'd placed the order.

Dade County Assistant D.A. Federico Smith had sent Ian a case of scotch as a thank-you for gifting him with the high-profile case.

Ian planned to pass the booze along to his boss as an early Christmas present. Real early, it being only the end of August. But, hey, a man angling for a favor had to take his shot when it was presented.

As he walked through the crowded bull pen toward the corner where his desk was situated, he glanced at the glass cubicle where Stebbins usually hid out when he wasn't hassling his field operatives. Eddie was actually seated behind his desk, a rare occurrence for a man almost as addicted to action as Ian himself. At the moment, however, the boss had his big, flat feet propped on his desk while he jawed into a phone receiver clamped against his shoulder by his too-prominent chin. At the same time he was shooting rubber bands at a fly on the ceiling.

Ian was on his way to his own desk when his attention was snagged by the office's resident computer guru, Juan Carlos Ortiz who was beckoning to Ian from the computer cubicle tucked into one corner of the bull pen.

Short, balding and disgustingly good-natured, J.C. was sending his oldest daughter through the University of Miami on the money he won playing poker with Ian and a half-dozen other Miami-based agents. Although Ian was a better-than-average player, he'd long since stopped trying to bluff J.C. out of a pot.

"I think I've got something for you, Mac," Ortiz said when Ian stuck his head inside the cramped airless box that passed for J.C.'s lair.

"I'm listening," Ian told him, masking the sudden spike of excitement behind a laconic laziness. One night, over a plate of oyster shooters, he'd given the easy-going Cuban-American a brief rundown on the years he'd spent in deep cover, acting as Hutch Renfrew's second-in-command of the New Aryan Freedom Brigade. He'd asked J.C. to keep an eye out for anything that crossed his path about the wily bastard who'd apparently gone to ground. Somewhere in Idaho, according to the whispers in the drug-running underground.

Deep in the marrow of his bones, Ian knew Renfrew had to surface sooner or later—probably with a different name but undoubtedly with the same MO. Hutch was far too regimented and arrogant to change the methods he'd labored so hard to perfect.

He would quietly move into a new area, recruit a cadre of hatemongers and misfits and train them to roam through the streets like a pack of rabid dogs, attacking unsuspecting members of minority groups and religious communities. Invariably one of the NAFB "soldiers" would carve a swastika into the flesh of the helpless victim. Consequently, Ian had had J.C. looking for a pattern of violent beatings with that vicious behavior as part of the attack. If anyone could find a needle in a cyber haystack of databases it was Ortiz.

J.C.'s fingers danced over the keys. Faster than even Ian's marksman's eye could track, lines of text scrolled down the screen. When the blur of letters stopped, Ian scanned the lines quickly, his excitement growing.

"Well, I'll be damned," he muttered as he reached past Ortiz to hit the down arrow, reading as fast as the text scrolled into view. One after another, a series of wire service articles detailed a pattern of attacks over the past two months on minorities in a small Oregon town, all related to a nearby college.

The first had been the middle-of-the-night burning of a cross on the lawn of an African-American professor, followed at regular intervals by others—lurid splashes of red paint thrown at the house of a Jewish fraternity, a young Ethiopian exchange student forced off the road into the ditch by two young men in a pickup truck, then beaten senseless. A swastika had been carved into his cheek. It had been this fact that had triggered the system to spit it out.

"It's Renfrew, all right. I feel it."

"There's no mention of his name, which is why it took me so long to put it all together in any of the articles. Or of the NAFB for that matter."

"It's him. I feel it."

Ortiz leaned back and exhaled noisily. "The man might be a prize sleazoid and a criminal, but he's no dummy."

"Anything but. In fact, if his mind wasn't all twisted up with hate, he would have made a brilliant politician. He told me once he'd studied every film of Hitler's speeches he could lay his hands on. Even learned German so that he could understand the pacing and nuance.''

J.C.'s eyes narrowed behind his glasses. ''Didn't Hitler go after the students, too? Called them the Hitler Youth?''

''Yeah.'' Absently rubbing at the spot on his belly where he'd taken a 9 mm slug early in his career, he scanned the last article again, more slowly this time. His breath hitched as he stared at the name of the college. *Bradenton.*

He drew a slow, careful breath, his mind clicking through the events of that night in San Diego, two and a half years ago. The short, sweet tussle with the dopers, the rush to the vet in his Jeep with the mutt's bloody head cradled in the lady's lap, the wait to find out if emergency surgery would save the mangy animal's worthless life. And then, when the mutt survived, holding Marca while she'd soaked his last clean shirt with grateful tears.

He'd taken her back to her rental car, only to find out the bastards had trashed it. What else could he have done but stay with her while the police took the report, then wait for the rental company to bring her a replacement?

They'd had a drink. The first round had led to another. She'd talked. He'd listened—and wondered what it would feel like to bury his face between her soft breasts. Damn his randy hormones to hell, he thought now, raking a hand through his hair.

''Mac, you okay?''

Ian scowled at the screen. ''Print that out, will you, J.C.? I'll need hard evidence to take to the boss.''

Ortiz clicked the mouse button, and moments later the laser printer on the desk began slipping out pages. ''I'm with you all the way, you know that, buddy. But no way is Stebbins going to let you anywhere near Hutch Renfrew.''

Ian lifted an eyebrow, the one with the scar he'd gotten in a knock-down, drag-out as a scrawny kid with too much temper and not enough muscle. ''Do you see Renfrew's name anywhere in those reports?''

"I don't have to. His stink is all over them. If I can see that, Eddie can see it."

"I have an ace or two I haven't played yet," Ian said, his mind already on the argument he planned to lay out for his old friend. "Thanks, Jace," he said, swiping a paper clip from the container at Ortiz's elbow. "I owe you."

J.C.'s dark eyes turned serious. "You can pay me back by staying alive, buddy. This old world's always going to have scumbags like Renfrew, but we ain't got all that many good guys."

"No, damn it!" Stebbins exploded, slapping both palms on the desk as he leaned forward, his expression fierce. Ian realized he'd never seen Eddie's face turn quite that shade of red. "Not only is it a possible conflict of interest and against Bureau policy, but it's also tantamount to suicide. You're a pain in my ass, but I'd miss your ugly mug if you weren't around, hassling me about something or other."

Ian leaned back and braced the worn sole of one ratty sneaker against the edge of the brown metal desk. He grinned a little as he eased his chair back on two legs.

"Doesn't sound like you have much confidence in my ability to do my job, boss."

Stebbins snorted. "The bastard swore to see you dead in front of his whole frigging Brigade. To show the rest of those cretins what happens to traitors. Planned to drop you off in the wilderness someplace and hunt you down in some twisted idea of sportsmanship is what I heard from that wanna-be storm trooper who turned state's evidence."

Ian thought back to the attacks on the USC campus a few months after the bombing. Renfrew had skated on that one, too. Not enough evidence linking him to the perpetrators.

"Lance Peavy is an opportunistic weasel. He'd turn state's evidence against his own mother if it suited him."

"He passed a polygraph, Ian. You're alive now only because Renfrew's too smart to try anything so soon after the trial. But if you go after him, he's got to make good on that threat or lose face."

"I can take care of myself."

"In a fair fight. Renfrew doesn't even understand the word."

"He had an edge last time. This time he doesn't. No one to threaten or bully or hurt to get to me."

Stebbins patted his shirt pocket for the smokes he'd carried there until two weeks ago when his wife threatened him with grievous bodily harm unless he quit.

"Damn that woman," he muttered, casting a hopeful look at the outline of a soft pack in the pocket of Ian's T-shirt. "Give me a smoke, will you?"

Ian allowed himself a small smile. "You can't smoke in here. Government regs, remember?"

Stebbins uttered a blistering oath before opening his bottom drawer to pull out an ashtray fashioned from the bottom of a five-inch shell casing.

"I won't tell if you won't."

Ian eased his chair to four legs before tossing the pack and matches onto the desk. Reaching behind him, he shoved the door closed, and Eddie grunted his thanks.

"Look, Ian, I understand how you feel," Stebbins said before lighting up. "I even admit you're good at what you do, maybe the best I've ever known, but even a man with your street smarts loses a step when he's emotionally involved."

"So I'll get uninvolved."

Stebbins drew in smoke, let it out slowly, a look of reverent pleasure on his face for a moment before a frown took over again. "You don't even know if Renfrew is in on this." He tapped the printouts in front of him with a stubby forefinger. "There's no mention of him or the NAFB in any of these articles. It's probably just a local gang of skinheads on a rampage. Sooner or later they'll make a mistake and get busted."

"Fine," Ian said with a casual look through the glass barrier at a woman with a mane of black curls weaving her way through the rabbit warren of desks. For a split second he couldn't breathe.

His gypsy angel had hair that shone with the same ebony shimmer. Though his memory of the night they'd shared had dimmed, he'd never stopped thinking about her.

"Assign me temporary duty attached to the Portland office for a few months. Let me check it out. If you're right, I'll spring for dinner for you and Gretchen at any place you say."

Stebbins drew in smoke and held it long enough for his eyes to water before letting it out in a narrow stream. "If you think I'm gonna buy that quick Persian rug you're not as slick as I figured, hotshot."

Ian resisted the urge to push to his feet and pace the office's narrow confines. Stebbins would take that as weakness and bore in. Deliberately, consciously, he balanced his chair on the two back legs again, rocking a little. Concentrating on the flex and give of his thigh muscles. Taking his time.

"Eddie, you remember the department shrink you strong-armed me into seeing after the trial?"

"Yeah? So?"

"He had this thing about closure. Kept telling me I had to accept what I couldn't change and move on."

"Told you that myself more than once, as I recall."

Ian shifted, uncomfortable with the memory of those tense sessions in the psychologist's office. The well-meaning head doctor had kept encouraging him to let go of his rage. To cry instead of hate. Little had the man realized that the hatred was all that was keeping him from spiraling off into madness.

"Yeah, well, maybe this is my chance for some of that closure."

Eddie flicked his ash into the tray. "Not if that chance includes blowing Hutch Renfrew's head off."

"And deprive the bastard of due process?" He shook his head. "Not my style."

"I know your style, Ian. You're tough and savvy and as tenacious as they come. In the fifteen years you've worked for me you've closed more cases than anyone else. Before that you were the best there was at rooting out 'shine in the hills."

Ian scowled. He'd hated his time in Kentucky. Two of his fellow agents had died in those hills, lured into traps by rosy-cheeked youngsters trained by their fathers and uncles and big brothers as Judas goats. Ian had been lucky. Living with his half-crazed uncle for ten years had taught him never to trust anyone but himself.

"Because I know you, I know that hard shell of yours covers a damn soft heart." Stebbins took a quick drag. "If I had a brother, I'd want him to be just like you. But damn it, Ian, re-venging yourself against vermin like Renfrew is not worth de-stroying your future."

Ian felt a painful tightening in his throat. He'd had a brother once, with the same face as his. The same genes. Kieran had been five minutes older. Kier had been with their parents, flying back to their home in Santa Barbara in Rourke MacDougall's Cessna after a trip to Disneyland, when the plane had gone down in a freak windstorm over the Pacific. Ian had been saved only because an ear infection had kept him home with a baby-sitter.

He'd been two days shy of his sixth birthday when he'd been taken to live on his uncle's ranch outside of Fresno. He remem-bered with crystal clarity the confusion he'd felt when the social worker had led him up the dusty stone steps of a wide porch to meet a strange man with big rough hands and the stench of cow manure clinging to his dirty jeans.

At first Ian had thought it was his daddy waiting for him in the strange place and had broken free to run into the man's arms the way he'd always done when his father came home from a day in court or his big office downtown. Instead of enfolding the crying little boy against his chest, however, Angus MacDougall had held Ian at arm's length, eyes the same gray as Ian's own, studying him as though he were breeding stock up for auction.

"Trust Rourke to breed him an ugly little runt," he'd barked to the embarrassed social worker before passing Ian off to the overworked, whey-faced woman he'd later learned to call Aunt Thea.

Ian had been fifteen before he'd learned that his aunt and uncle had only taken him because of the money his father's will had left him. Money they'd spent to put their own three children through college, leaving Ian to pay his own way.

"Remember who we're talking about, Eddie. The man is a monster, a worthless excuse for a human being, who preaches hatred and violence to kids who are looking for a father figure." He took a breath. "Someone to love them and make them feel special—but it's all a con. A sick manipulation to recruit disciples he can twist into mirror images of his own evil soul. If he had his way, he'd annihilate anyone who's not white Anglo-Saxon Protestant, which, given your Jewish ancestry, makes you one of the first he'd back up against a wall. Or march naked into a gas chamber."

Stebbins sat back, his shoulders slumping. "You're going to do this no matter what I say, aren't you?"

"Guess I am."

Stebbins took a long drag, dribbling out smoke in a lazy stream. With narrowed eyes, he regarded Ian thoughtfully through the haze now filling the small space.

"I admit that was a hard one to lose."

"Look, I'm due for a vacation, anyway," he said, deliberately keeping his tone on the lazy side. "Oregon is as good a place as any to get in a little R and R. If I just happen to stumble onto one of Renfrew's schemes, no one could fault me for following up."

Eddie had changeable eyes. When he was amused, they twinkled like every kid's image of Santa. When he was angry they bored like an ice blue laser beam into a man's very core. Ian had seen them filled with tears when Eddie had stood next to him at the funeral of his twins and their sweet mother. Rarely had he seen them dark with fear.

"Ian, if you play this wrong, you could be the one spending the rest of his life in a cell."

# Chapter 2

Marca definitely needed a vacation. A nice long one. Starting now.

The new semester was only two weeks old and already she was feeling the pressure of a brand-new year. Coming up with new ways of creating excitement about the college she loved was always a challenge. Generating alumni donations was part of the package. However, attracting quality students was the part she liked best. Her current project was a mailer showcasing the various scholarships Bradenton offered to so-called fringe students. She'd been going great guns until Friday, when the hard drive of her computer had gone to the great electronic junk pile in the sky.

She'd been holding the wake between frantic calls to the purchasing department when Carly had called to invite her and the boys for a swim in the presidential mansion's indoor pool on Sunday.

Spending time with Carly and her family was always a treat, and the mansion had become a second home to her and her boys. In spite of the creaking floorboards and old-fashioned radiator pipes that clanged endlessly in winter, and the constant fear that her boys on a rampage would break something irreplaceable, Marca had always liked the huge, granite monster that had been built by Bradenton's founder and first president, Artemus Alderson. No one but Aldersons had ever lived there.

Carly had been born there, and she'd lived in Alderson House most of her life. Her mother, Felicity, had continued to live there after the death of her husband, serving as Bradenton's official hostess until her marriage six years ago to Mitch Scanlon's former coach and mentor, Pete Gianfracco.

The older couple now lived in a Queen Anne cottage they'd built overlooking the first tee of the Bradenton Hills Country Club, leaving the five Scanlons, their housekeeper, Tilly O'Neill, and an Australian au pair named Lulu to rattle around in the place alone.

At present, however, Lulu was on holiday back home in Brisbane, and Tracy Alderson Scanlon, Carly's twenty-three-year-old daughter, was attending graduate school at Brown. Tilly had complained that the house was as empty as an Englishman's heart when she'd admitted Marca and the boys twenty minutes or so earlier.

Now, dressed in shorts and a tank top that should have been consigned to the rag bag ages ago, Marca was seated across from Carly on the tile-lined terrace of the mansion's indoor pool.

Of all the beautiful rooms in the turn-of-the-century building, Marca had always liked the pool area best. Added twelve years ago after Carleton Alderson's first stroke, it had always reminded her of a Roman bath, with its handmade tiles lining the long, narrow lap pool and lush greenery.

The lovely perfume of the dozens of potted roses Felicity Alderson had placed around the tiled terrace clashed with the stinging scent of chlorine and suntan lotion. The smell seemed even stronger in the saunalike heat of the glaring, mid-afternoon sunlight, which poured through the narrow, tinted windows that stretched from floor to vaulted ceiling.

Marca shoved her sunglasses over the bridge of her nose to shield her eyes, then rubbed at the ache in her temples that had started during the drive from her place in the country and now seemed to be getting worse with every breath she took.

She knew why, of course. Earlier that morning, Richard Hartson, the man she'd been dating for the past six months, had asked her to marry him. Before, he'd always called before stopping by, but today he'd surprised her by showing up at her house with the fixings for a picnic brunch in a wicker basket over one arm and a huge bouquet of long-stemmed red roses in the other.

Knowing that she and the boys would be spending the afternoon at the mansion, she'd planned to work this morning. Somehow, though, Richard had managed to convince her to play hooky. She and the boys had ended up having a wonderful time playing wiffle ball in her backyard and gorging on fried chicken and potato salad.

No doubt about it, Richard was wonderful with the triplets. The boys were increasingly at ease with him. But then, with his golden hair, engaging grin and congenial manners, Richard was good at winning friends. In fact, he was the most charismatic person she'd ever met. The perfect man.

"Will you marry me, Marca?" he had asked.

No one had actually said those words to her before. Her ex-husband had simply handed her the ring box, taking her acceptance for granted. Richard never took anything for granted. He seemed to want nothing more than to please her.

Two years shy of fifty, he was originally from Seattle—and sick to death of the fast lane. So just over six months ago he'd moved into a spacious log cabin tucked away on wooded acreage in the hills above her converted barn.

A true Renaissance man, Richard seemed to make a very comfortable living restoring and selling antique weapons in a workshop he'd had constructed on a section of his property. Flintlocks and dueling pistols were his specialty.

They'd met when Marca had noticed a small ad about the opening of his shop located in the front of his workshop. She had immediately called about buying her father a pistol for his collection.

From the first, Marca had been attracted to the passion Richard brought to his work. His blond, Greek-god looks and his perfect smile hadn't hurt, either. Still, she'd turned him down the first three times he'd asked her out. Gentleman that he was, he'd been sweet and charming, but persistent. Perversely, she'd found that even more appealing than his looks.

They'd been seeing each other at least once a week for the past two months now. Still, his proposal had taken her by surprise. Though she always felt a pleasant little zing when he kissed her, she'd remained reluctant to begin a sexual relationship despite his expert coaxing.

"I've waited a long time for a woman with your qualities, Marca. Your breeding, your intelligence, your strength. We would make a perfect team."

She liked the man a lot. But enough to marry him? That was the question that had niggled at her since they'd said goodbye five hours earlier. Hence, the headache.

Desperate for some relief, she fumbled in her tote bag for the bottle of extra-strength aspirin that was part of her trusty "mom's emergency kit."

"Another headache?" Carly asked, frowning her concern over the crystal goblet of lemonade cradled in her hand.

"What else?" Marca muttered, all but melting in relief when her fingers closed around the slick bottle. Gritting her teeth, she wrenched off the lid and shook out two tablets, considered the pain level, then grimly added a third.

"Can you spare a couple of those?" Carly asked, holding out her hand. "I get a sick headache myself every time I think about those horrible bullies beating Ted to a bloody pulp simply because his ancestors came from a different part of the world."

The campus had been in uproar since Friday night when the Dean of Asian Studies, Dr. Theodore Matsuda had been attacked while out jogging near his home.

Though small in stature, Ted had a huge heart which he'd opened to countless foster children over the years. He also had a wickedly droll sense of humor and a formidable backhand. Marca and Ted often played as a team in the college tennis tournaments, and she'd come to consider the gentle, soft-spoken professor a treasured friend as well as a respected colleague. When Marca had stopped by to see Ted yesterday evening he'd been surprisingly chipper, even pugnacious, which was unusual for the laid-back professor.

"What did the cops have to say? Have they got any suspects?"

Carly shook her head. "Nothing concrete yet. According to a witness, who was too far away to make a positive ID, it was a gang of young Caucasian males that jumped him."

"I refuse to believe it could be students. Not *our* students, anyway."

"The board of trustees blames me, of course." Carly sighed. "They want to make Bradenton into a darn prison, with metal detectors and armed guards. I hate the idea. This place was founded on an open-door policy. Until my grandfather's day, the only requirement for admission was a desire to learn."

Marca tried to wash away the taste of disgust with lemonade. "You can't really blame them, though. Protecting our students from that kind of insanity is part of the unwritten contract of any educational institution."

"I don't know what Father would have done, but my great-grandfather would have hunted down the assailants and used his buggy whip on them."

Though she looked more like a coed in a worn T-shirt and baggy shorts, Carly Alderson Scanlon could be as tough as any of the three hard-headed, granite-faced Alderson men who'd sat in the president's chair before her. Maintaining Bradenton's exemplary reputation for the quality and class of its faculty and the excellence of the educational experience was a sacred trust. Protecting its students from bigotry and hatred was part of the Alderson legacy.

Marca knew all too well how heavily that responsibility lay on Carly's slender shoulders. At the moment, though, there was little she could do to help her friend except act as a sounding board.

Which was one of the reasons she'd accepted Carly's invitation this afternoon.

"Seems to me you had a headache last time we were together," Carly mused as Marca returned the painkillers to the tote. "Maybe you should see a doctor."

"I already have. She told me to cut down on coffee and sign up for a cruise. One-way, preferably."

Carly groaned, but her moss green eyes tilted up at the ends in an engaging smile, eyes she'd passed on to the two little girls in the pool. "Sounds great to me. Well, not the coffee, but the cruise part anyway."

"Not to me," Marca declared emphatically. "I get seasick."

More's the pity, she thought morosely. The chance to insulate herself from ringing phones, soggy diapers and rampaging minimales, even for a day, sounded darn near irresistible. Though her babies were her life and she adored them utterly, she sometimes felt as though the mommy track she'd embraced so eagerly had turned into a hamster's exercise wheel.

In spite of the fact that she had a part-time nanny and someone to clean, Marca was still a hands-on mom, and her hands were definitely full from the predawn hour when she rolled out of bed until the wee hours when she dropped into it.

"Mitch and I have kicked around the idea of a cruise a few times," Carly confided in her, before treating herself to another of Tilly's angst-numbing, soul-soothing brownies. "I don't even care where the ship's headed, since we'd probably spend the entire time in bed."

"Go for it. I'll watch the girls." Smiling a little at the thought of the noise and confusion she'd just invited, Marca washed down the aspirins with a slug of lemonade. Glancing up, she caught Carly's incredulous look. "No joke. The little guys and I would love the company."

"I have to admit I'm tempted. Maybe when things settle down."

"You two never did have an official honeymoon."

"I'll give it some thought—after football season."

Carly shifted her gaze toward the pool and the big man with the silver-dusted blond hair and massive chest patiently teaching Ryan Kenworthy how to open his eyes under water. The two youngest Scanlon daughters and Ryan's always-rambunctious brothers sat on the edge of the lap pool, watching.

Though Mitch had lost the use of his legs years earlier and used braces and crutches in order to drag his artificially stiffened legs from place to place, he managed to look powerfully male no matter what he did. Buoyed by the water, he was able to move almost normally, which is one of the reasons he grabbed at any chance to strip off the heavy steel and spend time in the pool.

"You could always highjack him," Marca suggested, a familiar feeling of envy licking at her. Carly truly had it all—worthy work she loved, three beautiful daughters and a remarkable man who adored her.

"Now there's a thought. I—"

"Mommy, Auntie Marca, Ryan's swimming," four-year-old Letty Scanlon shouted as she jumped up and down on the steps leading to the lap pool. Sure enough, Ryan was dog-paddling in a circle, held afloat by one of the miniature life jackets Mitch made all the children wear when they were in the pool area.

"I see, darling," Carly called.

"Go for it, Tiger," Marca chimed in, then winced at the sharp jab of pain in her temple.

Hearing their shouts, Mitch glanced their way, his highly telegenic grin flashing white against his sun-bronzed skin. An innately shy man in spite of the fame garnered during his years as the quarterback of the then Los Angeles Raiders, Mitch had slowly and quietly become one of the most respected coaches in college football.

"We're talking Olympic gold here, Mom!" Mitch said, brushing back his hair with the big square hand that had once worked magic with a football.

"I thought Ry was the designated quarterback for this Scanlon-Kenworthy dream team you have planned," Marca tossed back.

"Hey, the kid has to have something to do in the off season," he said before returning his attention to the dark-headed toddler who was churning the water with his strong little arms, his little face alive with pride.

"Thank God for Mitch and that marvelous patience of his," Marca said in a quiet voice as she, too, reached for another brownie.

Carly's smile was soft and loving. "He's crazy about the little hooligans."

"They're crazy about him. And I'm so grateful they have a strong male role model." She grinned. "Sometimes, though, Mitch seems more like their big brother than an honorary uncle."

"Time out, buddy," Mitch said, lifting Ryan with strong arms to the lip of the pool where the little boy sat dripping and grinning, still kicking his chubby feet in the warm water.

"Me next," Trevor shouted, jumping up from his place next to Mitch on the steps. Instantly Sean protested. Diplomatic as always, Mitch settled the argument by pulling his two-year-old daughter, Nan, into the water for her turn.

Mollified, the boys sat down again and began shouting encouragement as best they could to their honorary sibling while Letty hovered next to her daddy, keeping a watchful eye on her little sister. Now and then Mitch would give her a little hug.

"Mitch doesn't say much, but in light of these stupid attacks, I think he's worried about something happening to me or the girls," Carly said quietly, her face pinched with concern. "Most of the time he handles the frustrations of his limited mobility pretty darn well. But he has this thing about needing to feel he can keep us safe." She sighed. "I've tried to talk to him about it, but he just closes up. Tracy says it's a man thing."

Marca shifted, stretching out her bare legs. "Richard's trying to talk me into buying a gun for self-protection. In fact, just this morning he brought one to show me. A cute little nickel-plated thirty-eight or thirty-two. I forget the caliber, but small enough to carry in my tote."

"Much as I hate the idea, I think Richard may be right," Carly said as she poured herself another glass of lemonade from her mother's Limoges pitcher. "The sheriff strongly suggested that we hire more campus policemen—and arm them." Carly grimaced. "I hate the very idea, but if we really are a target for terrorists, I don't see a choice."

"Perhaps not, but I for one am not going to have a gun in my house. It's barbaric. Besides, with three toddlers running around, I'd have to hide it on a high shelf somewhere, which means that it would take forever to get to it, then put the bullets in. By that time I'd probably be dead, anyway."

Carly grimaced, then slanted Marca a look reminiscent of their college years when Marca was forever tangling herself in impossible relationships. "It sounds as though your relationship with Richard really is getting serious."

Marca drew a breath, then let it out. "I admit I'm tempted to accept his proposal, Carly. This thing with Ted Matsuda…it made me realize just how perilous life is. If something should happen to me…" She turned to look at her boys, now so healthy and happy, and safe. "I know my mom and dad would take them, but what with Dad's heart being so iffy, and Mom's arthritis—"

"Marce, you know Mitch and I would take the boys and make them our own," Carly chided gently. "But nothing's going to happen to you."

Marca smiled ruefully. "I imagine that's what Mitch thought right before that druggie smashed a crowbar into his spine."

Carly drew a deep breath. "Point taken." She hesitated, then asked softly, "Are you in love with Richard?"

Marca started to nod, but her old nemesis, the honesty drummed into her by her deeply religious parents, refused to let her lie to her best friend or, for that matter, to herself. "No, but I like him a lot and I respect him. He's been a wonderful friend, and after the first few rather intense attempts, he's accepted my reluctance to sleep with him. After six months of steady dating, not too many men would be that understanding…or patient."

"Maybe he's gay."

Marca had considered that. But she'd felt Richard's arousal when he'd kissed her. "No, he's a gentleman."

Carly swirled her glass, making the ice tinkle musically against the Baccarat crystal. ''What about Ian? Do you still love him?

Marca's smile felt stiff. ''Carly, I was with the man a total of seven hours. How could I possibly fall in love with a man I scarcely know?''

In answer, Carly directed a pointed glance toward her husband. As though sensing her gaze, Mitch turned and smiled at her before a shout from one of the boys reclaimed his attention.

''I fell in love with Mitch the moment he smiled at me in that tacky bar in Palm Springs,'' Carly admitted softly. ''I just...knew.''

Marca slid down in her chair and stared at her outstretched toes. On a whim last week she'd bought lavender pearlescent polish instead of her usual conservative damask rose. At the time it had made her feel frivolous and sexy and young.

''Even if I did love him—and I'm not saying I do—he's gone. Vanished. The number he gave me was disconnected with no referral number. His landlady and post office had no forwarding address.'' She drew a long breath. ''No, I was just a one-night stand to Ian MacDougall. It's humiliating to admit, but true nevertheless.''

''That's what I thought about Mitch and me.''

''Fate brought you together again. It was meant to be.''

''The same thing could happen to you.''

Marca shook her head. ''No, fate did enough when the condom leaked and I ended up blessed with those three adorable rascals yonder.''

''True. But—'' Before Carly could complete her thought, the French doors leading from the rest of the mansion opened and Tilly walked in.

Close to sixty now, Tilly was on the short side of average height, with a pleasantly homey face and curly gray hair. A blue-eyed, Irish colleen, she'd come to Oregon as a teenager to marry a boy from the same Irish village, who'd migrated to the States to take a job on a logging crew. When Tilly sailed steerage to join him, she learned that he'd been killed in a barroom brawl.

Stranded in a strange country with no money for return fare to Ireland, she'd started working at Alderson House as a maid and never left.

"Sorry to disturb you, Miss Carly," she said when she reached the poolside table, "but you have a visitor. A fine-looking, brawny sort of a man with the devil's own eyes and the air of a scoundrel about him."

Carly looked mystified. "Did he give his name, Tilly?"

"He did, and very politely, too." A soft smile played over the housekeeper's usually prim mouth. Marca decided that the man with the devil's eyes must also have a bit of the devil's charm as well. "It's a Mr. MacDougall who's come to see you, Miss Carly. Mr. Ian MacDougall."

# Chapter 3

Childish shrieks and giggles blended with the sound of wild splashing and Mitch's deep, infectious laughter as Marca and Carly stared at each other in utter shock. Recovering first, Carly cleared her throat.

"Are you sure he asked for me?"

Tilly looked puzzled. "Now who else would he be asking for at the president's house but you or Mitchell?" She huffed out a breath to punctuate her point. "In this case, he specifically asked for *President* Scanlon."

Carly glanced at her watch, then at the door and finally at the housekeeper again. Five minutes to five on a Sunday afternoon was an odd time for callers. "Did he say what he wanted?"

"No, only that it was important and that he would explain it to you personally—if you would be so kind to see him."

"Did he give you a card?" Marca interjected before she remembered that a man who worked as a maintenance worker in an apartment complex was unlikely to need a business card.

"No card, just his name," Tilly said, her eyes taking on a

twinkle. "With a way about him that would curl a Mother Superior's toes."

"*That* doesn't surprise me a bit," Carly commented dryly before shifting her gaze to Marca. "I assume you don't want Tilly to bring him in here?"

"Dear Lord, no!"

Tilly glanced from one to the other, looking very much as she did when both women were coeds keeping secrets. Finally her gaze settled on Marca and bored in. In the thirty-nine years since she'd started working for Carleton and Felicity Alderson at the president's house, Tilly had seen her adopted family through a fair number of crises. In many ways she'd been more of a mother to Carly than Felicity had ever been, and over the years, both Carly and Marca had come to rely on her practical wisdom and generous heart.

"Are you all right, Miss Marca?" she demanded, her County Clare brogue thickening as it always did when she was mothering one of her own. "You've gone as pale as Marley's ghost."

"Fine." Marca's voice came out thin as a reed. Furious, she cleared her throat—twice. "Fortunately I'm good in crunch situations."

"The best I've ever known," Carly agreed a bit too quickly, Marca knew. She wouldn't fool Tilly.

"Of course, this could all be academic. We don't know for sure it's the same man." Marca shifted her attention to the housekeeper, whose gaze narrowed even more. "Does...does he—Mr. MacDougall—have black hair and a beard?"

"Sure, his hair is as black as an Englishman's soul, but his jaw is clean shaven and hard as a rock, if you don't mind hearing my opinion."

"No, I don't mind," Marca said with a sinking sensation in the pit of her stomach. "And his eyes. They wouldn't happen to be gray?"

"As a storm cloud over the winter sea."

Marca didn't know whether to shout in happiness or dismay. Instead she drew a shaky breath and took a minute to gnaw at the corner of her mouth. It was a habit she had that helped her to organize her thoughts. She considered it a good sign she was only concentrating on the right corner. In times of true crisis, she gnawed at each in turn.

Carly stood up and pulled on her presidential persona. "Tilly, you show the gentleman to the west parlor and, uh, offer him a drink. Tell him I'll be there shortly."

"I'm sure he's looking for you," Carly said in a low voice as the housekeeper disappeared into the den and closed the doors behind her. "He probably figured it was the fastest way to find you."

"I wrote my home number on the back of my business card."

"Well, there's no sense trying to figure it out. I'll just go find out."

"Yes, right. In the meantime, I'll—no, *wait!*" She'd been away from Madison Avenue too long, she realized, as she pressed her palm against her fluttering stomach muscles. The ability to remain calm under stress used to be second nature. "Let *me* go. I'll tell him you're delayed or something. If it's him, the man on the beach, I'd just as soon find that out now. In the meantime, you get the boys out of the pool and dried off. There are diapers and a change of clothes for each of them in my bag. As soon as I know, one way or the other, I'll excuse myself and come back here."

"And if he is the boys' father, then what?" Carly's voice was calm, her expression unruffled. President Scanlon at her unflappable best—in spite of the threads dangling from the edge of her cutoffs and the lack of makeup. But then, it wasn't her life that was being upended.

"I guess it would be pretty tacky of me to welcome him to Bradenton, ask him what he wants and then as a sort of afterthought casually mention that the trusty, 'just in case' condom I had in my purse failed and he is now the father of three identical little MacDougalls."

Carly rolled her eyes. "Tacky *and* certifiable. You don't know the first thing about the father of your sons. If this is the man...if you admit that he's their father, it gives him certain rights. If I were you, I'd be very careful about what I say.'' She glanced toward the pool where Mitch was sitting on the steps, listening attentively to something Letty was telling him. ''In fact, I *was* careful, remember? Unlike you, I could have located Mitch anytime I wanted to, but there was no way I was going to tell the man I'd hated for years that he had a precious daughter he didn't deserve.''

Marca drew a breath. She intended to tell her boys the truth when they were old enough to ask about their father. She just hadn't expected to deal with the issue of telling their father about the boys.

''Okay, how's this? I'll keep the boys occupied and out of sight.''

''But if he's come to see you, he'll want to spend time with you.''

Marca fought down an almost violent hope that that was exactly what he wanted. ''I'll make some excuse. The important thing now is to get the boys out of here, so I can have some breathing room…time to figure out…what to do next.''

Marca slipped her feet into her thongs and tucked in her shirt. ''A closetful of power suits, and I have to take one of the most important meetings in my adult life in my grubbies.''

''Pretend they came with designer labels and obscene prices.''

''Carly, is something wrong?'' Mitch's voice gave Marca a sudden start. She and Carly exchanged looks before turning in unison toward the pool.

The boys' swimming lessons had ended. Letty had taken off on her own, swimming toward the opposite end of the pool like a sleek little tow-headed water baby, with her father's sturdy body and her mother's grace.

Mitch was still sitting on the top step in a patch of sunshine streaming through the wall of windows, with Ryan on one knee and Nan on the other. Looking sleepy-eyed, Nan was using her finger to draw patterns in her daddy's golden chest hair while

Ryan nestled against Mitch's chest, his thumb planted securely in his mouth.

"I'll fill Mitch in and get the boys ready," Carly promised, scuffing her feet into her sandals.

Though Marca would have preferred the protection of the dark glasses, pride had her tossing them onto the table. "Wish me luck."

Carly grinned. "Seems to me you said the same thing to me once, and it worked out beautifully."

"Hold that thought."

The room made Ian uncomfortable, like a walk through a museum when he'd been a kid. Furniture that had curlicues and spindles and shiny upholstery invariably had him checking his boots for mud and reaching into his pocket to pay an entrance fee. Even the walk down the hall had reminded him of the National Gallery in Washington, with its row after row of solemn-faced men who looked as though they'd just come from a particularly bloody hanging. Former presidents of the college, the housekeeper had told him. From the founder of the college to the father of the current president. The Alderson family. A damn dynasty.

According to the feelers he'd put out during a stop at one of the pubs in the nearest town of Bradenton Falls, Caroline Alderson Scanlon had a reputation for being a straight shooter and a savvy administrator. Most folks seemed to think the college was good for the town—and a decent employer. No one had been openly racist, even when he'd salted a few comments of his own in his conversations.

He figured a fast in-and-out on this visit. No sweat. Drop his credentials on the lady president and charm her into extending her full cooperation. Eddie had given him six weeks to come up with something solid. Since he'd driven from Florida, he'd already used up five days of his forty-two.

Wishing he could smoke, he stood at the arched window at the end of the vaulted room and watched a pair of gray squirrels playing tag on the lawn. Was Ms. Kenworthy still here? he wondered. Maybe living in one of those picturesque farm houses dotting the county roads.

He realized he was rubbing his weak wrist, and knotted his hand into a fist. The odds against her remembering him hovered close to astronomical. One night with a beat-up beach bum almost three years ago didn't figure to be on a classy lady's top ten list of memorable events. Even if she did remember him, the chances of her being available—or interested—were damn slim, even by the most optimistic reckoning.

"Ian?"

For the space of time it took him to turn and face the door, he was convinced he was hearing things. But there she was, his angel gypsy, framed in the fancy doorway. His first reaction was a blazing happiness that shook him to the soles of his boots. The second was an instant wariness—and far more in character.

"Marca?"

She walked into the room and offered her hand. "Small world, isn't it?"

"Guess it is." Her handshake was firm, but brief, as though she were eager to reclaim her hand. He couldn't really blame her. "I was expecting to meet Dr. Scanlon. The woman who answered the door acted as though I was in the right place."

"You're in the right place. I'm not—at least not permanently. I just visit now and then. Carly—President Scanlon—and I are old friends. We were once roommates here, in the dungeon."

"Dungeon?"

"'Dungeon' was just our affectionate term for the freshman dorm. Like just about all of the older buildings it had thick ugly granite walls that held in the heat in summer and leeched in the cold in winter. We hated it."

Her smile flashed, teasing a pixie dimple into one corner of the mouth he'd once tasted so leisurely under what had seemed like a million twinkling stars. He drew a slow, settling breath against the quick mental plunge into dangerous waters.

"I read a couple of articles about the Timberwolves. Saw Mitch Scanlon on the tube a couple of times."

He'd been impressed as hell by the miracle Scanlon had pulled off, turning a laughable bunch of rag-tag losers into winners in his first season of coaching. He'd been even more impressed with the man's guts.

Scanlon had been throwing bullets and dazzling fans and sportswriters alike at UCLA at the same time Ian had been slogging through Fresno State, working security at night to pay his way. He'd been human enough to feel more than a few jealous pangs when he'd seen Scanlon's Hollywood grin splashed all over the news. He'd also been human enough to feel a deep empathy a dozen or so years later when Scanlon's blazing NFL career had been ended by irreversible paralysis.

"What brings you to Bradenton?" she asked, careful, it seemed, to keep a shadow's length between them.

"Some business I need to take care of."

"What kind of business?"

He considered telling her the truth, but the years he'd spent living just one mistake away from a slow, painful death had taught him not to trust anyone without testing them first.

"Business with President Scanlon," he said with a smile meant to soften the sting of evasion. The flash of hurt in her dark eyes told him that he'd failed.

"Then of course, I won't keep you any longer."

He couldn't let her go, he realized, jumping in fast to say, "I'm with the Bureau of Alcohol, Tobacco and Firearms, Marca. I'm here on a job. There's a possibility some stolen weapons were used in the recent attacks on your campus here."

"Is that where you went when you left San Diego? To join the ATF?"

"No, I'd been with them for some time. I was on an extended leave when we met. At the time I really was working as a kind of handyman at the place I rented." He still cringed when he thought about the self-pitying sot he'd been in those days.

She blew out air, her eyes clouded. "You must have thought

I was pretty silly, clucking over you like a mother hen because I
was afraid those bozos would track you down and hurt you."

"It wasn't silly. It was sweet. *You* were sweet."

She shook her head. "I was foolish. I realized that, when I was
on the plane going home. I couldn't stop shaking."

A look he read as self-disgust touched her features for an instant, giving her a vulnerability that tore at him. He wanted to
take her in his arms and kiss away all her hurts. Because he also
wanted to fist his hand around the thick tumble of black curls
framing her face and explore that silken throat with his mouth,
he took a mental step back.

"For what it's worth, I know seasoned agents who would have
hesitated to take on hopped-up junkies without a drawn weapon."

That helped some, he noted with relief. At least she'd un-
clenched her jaw. "Trust me, I wouldn't do it again."

He felt a rare urge to laugh and gave in to it. It felt good.
Maybe too good. Maybe too addictive. Like touching her. Ian
shifted, suddenly as uptight as an untested rookie heading into his
first raid.

"You look good, Marca. Happy." The words were out before
he'd had time to test them in his mind. Her lashes fluttered, as
though the words surprised her, as well.

"I am happy," she said, her face softening, as though thinking
of some private pleasure. "Very. I didn't realize it showed."

"It shows. And very nicely."

Because he wanted to read more than simple courtesy into the
smile she offered, he made himself take it at face value.

"You look...different. I'm not sure I would have recognized
you."

He felt a jolt of disappointment until he realized she was looking at his chin. He'd almost forgotten the beard he'd worn during
his drinking days because shaving had taken time away from the
boozing.

"Yeah, well, I cleaned up some when I went back to work."

Ian took a chance and moved closer. Her perfume was subtle,
reminding him of sun-warmed peaches. The skimpy shirt hugged

her breasts, stretching the faded red cotton snug against the hard little nipples, and her shorts were short enough to make a man break out in a sweat, just thinking about that lush bottom almost bared to view. And yet, it wasn't just the idea of making love to her that drew him.

It was more than that. So much more that it scared him a little. A part of him knew he wasn't ready to see her in any context other than as a woman he'd loved one night on the beach. But another part, the part of him that had been dead for so long, wanted to link his hands with hers and ask her to take a walk in the rain. Or to share a bowl of popcorn in front of a crackling fire. Because he wanted to rush ahead, he made himself slow down.

"You, uh, cut your hair. I like it."

The surprise was back in her eyes. He realized he liked the way they tipped up slightly at the ends—as though she was poised on the brink of laughter.

"I think it's shorter than yours actually," she said with another quick laugh.

"Probably." His hand was steady as he reached out to touch the thick cloud of dark hair brushing her jaw. It was as soft as it looked. Cool silk. The urge to hold her—simply hold her—was unexpectedly fierce, stunning him. And with it the nearly overpowering need to bury his face in that dark cloud.

"Are you involved with anyone?" he asked as he dropped his hand.

Her eyes flashed, giving him a glimpse of the fiery lady he'd met in the moonlight. "Is this a casual question?"

"I'm not sure I can do 'casual,' Marca."

"It's been two and a half years since I gave you my phone number. You never used it. Not once."

"Did you want me to?" He'd thought her eyes were black. He saw now that they were really a dark, rich brown rimmed with amber—and suddenly cool.

"Yes, Ian, I did. Very much. But you didn't call, and I stopped waiting."

He slid his hands into his pockets. "I was in a bad place in my life, Marca. I wasn't in any shape to begin a relationship."

"And you are now? Is that what you're telling me?"

"I don't know," he admitted. "I only know I'd like to see you again."

"You mean sleep with me, don't you?"

"I won't deny it. But I want more this time. Friendship, for starters, if that suits you better."

"I'll have to think about that. Things have changed in my life since San Diego. I've changed." She drew a breath, then exhaled slowly. "How long do you expect to be in town?"

"I don't know that, either. I'm on temporary assignment."

She nodded. "My home number hasn't changed. That is, if you still have it."

"I can get it."

"In other words, you tossed the card I gave you."

He heard the low throb of anger she directed at him along with the words, and accepted it because he'd earned it. "I threw it away because I was afraid I'd use it someday," he admitted, because now that he was shaving regularly again, he had to face himself in the mirror every morning. "That would have been a mistake for both of us."

"Why?" There was defiance in the question, and hurt.

"Because you wouldn't have wanted to know the man I was then."

She stood a little taller. "What makes you think I would want to know you now?"

"The way you said my name when you came in. Like it meant something to you." Because he needed to know he hadn't forgotten how to be gentle, he touched the back of his hand to her cheek. Her eyes darkened and turned vulnerable for an instant, before the curtains came down.

"Don't, Ian," she whispered. "I can't be wild and free here the way I was in San Diego."

His gaze searched for the fire in her eyes. Something tore inside his gut when he saw only wariness. "You weren't wild, Marca. You were so beautiful you took my breath."

"But you still let me go, didn't you? And never looked back."

He saw the pain flicker deep in her eyes, as though it was always there, hidden by the fire and laughter. "I looked back," he admitted. "More than I wanted to. Or thought I would."

"Thank you for that, at least." She smiled, pulling inside herself. "It's been nice seeing you again, Ian. I'm sure Dr. Scanlon will be with you shortly. She was just finishing up a small project when you arrived."

She was halfway to the door when he called her name. She paused to look over her shoulder, buttoned up tight again. He'd figured to have a fence or two to scale; it seemed he had a damn brick wall instead.

"Can you recommend a place to stay? Not too expensive, given the government is picking up the tab."

"By the day or by the week?"

He ambled toward her, enjoying the thrum of anticipation warming his insides. "Let's start with a week and see how it goes," he said, stopping just outside of hugging distance.

"A lot of visiting parents stay at Oak Manor out on 52. Nice rooms at decent prices, I'm told—unless the T-wolves are playing at home, of course. Then you'd be lucky to find a place to park, let alone sleep. You passed it when you drove to the campus."

"Yeah. Looked like a nice place at that." Actually he'd marked it as too conspicuous and thought to find something more remote. A day or two wouldn't hurt, however—in case she wanted to reach him. "Guess you'd know of a good place to eat, too."

"Gallagher's on Pine. Ask for Gallagher himself and tell him I sent you. He'll treat you right."

"How about we go together? For dinner tomorrow night?"

Surprise softened the corners of her mouth. He fought off a need to taste. "Are you asking me on a date?"

He'd thought he'd become too cynical to feel that fast clutch of fear when he put his ego on the line with a woman. He realized now that he hadn't been asking the right woman. "Guess I am, yeah."

"You move fast, MacDougall. I'll give you that."

"Only when I see something I want." The fear sharpened. Seeking to blunt it, he backed down enough to give them both room to maneuver. "Look, I know San Diego was an exception to a lot of rules. For me, the timing was lousy. Maybe the timing is lousy for you now. But we won't know that until we test the waters. So how about we start over? Take it slower this time."

Frowning, she considered. "Slower, meaning?"

"Guy and girl stuff. I just asked you on a date, which is your cue to say yes." He tried a smile that felt stiff. "We'll have a nice dinner, exchange personal histories. I'll do my darnedest to impress you, you'll flirt with me. The usual drill."

Her mouth curved, and his hormones gave a hopeful kick. "Call me later. I'll have to check my calendar."

He moved closer until his chest was only inches from the lushly rounded breasts that had once filled his hands. She held her ground. Courage against superior forces. It was one of the things that had drawn him in.

"If you're putting me through hoops to pay me back for not calling you, don't bother," he said, settling just enough silk in his voice to make it count. "I admit I was a jerk. I screwed up. I'll pay for my mistake by being patient, but if you're not interested, say so now." He took a breath and, just to make sure he'd made himself clear, added more softly, "I never learned how to play games for fun. When I play, I play to win, no matter what it takes. And I'm very good at what I do."

She shifted, cocked a hip, planted a small fist on the impudent angle of her small waist. "I'm good, too, Ian." Her eyes heated, daring him. "I can sell anything to anyone, given the right motivation. A little flash, a fast sizzle, a few well-chosen subliminals and I could have you begging to play the game by my rules."

She closed that last inch of distance, went to her tiptoes and linked her arms around his neck. Before he could do more than catch his balance, her mouth was warm and eager on his.

He reacted damn slow for a man who could draw a department-issue 10 mm Smith & Wesson from the small of his back and fire within the span of a wink. Shock made him stupid, he realized, as she slipped free from the arms that he'd only started to close around her.

"Hey, stop a minute," he said, his voice hoarse with the hunger that she'd fueled.

"Sorry, I have people waiting for me." She looked a little stunned, a little smug, and as pink as the pretty glass vase he'd been studying before she'd walked in.

"I owe you one," he called after her as she hightailed it out of the room. And then, to his utter amazement, Ian MacDougall, crack agent and all-around badass, threw back his head and laughed. It felt damn good.

# Chapter 4

As Carly walked purposefully down the mansion's gracefully curving front stairs, she realized she was vaguely nervous. In her experience, unexpected visitors invariably brought change—not all of it good. Though she ran what in essence was a million-dollar business with a decent amount of confidence and efficiency she had an innate wariness of the unforeseen.

On the other hand she was eagerly looking forward to meeting the man who'd been able to get through that thick shell Marca had been moldering behind after her marriage had imploded.

The girl Carly had met at eighteen had been a dreamer and optimist and a free spirit who'd believed in white knights and Prince Charming and happy endings. While others of their generation had turned cynical and strident, Marca had clung to her dreams of true love. A broken marriage and an empty career had finally worn her down, however. Her dreams had hung on for a long time, but they *had* died.

Crossing the foyer, dressed now in tailored slacks and a silk blouse, Carly frowned at the memory of the depressed woman she'd waved off to a conference of college publicists two and a half years ago. When Marca'd returned, however, her personality had been revved to high again and that special glint in her eyes had returned, brighter than ever. One night with the man now waiting for Carly in her mother's parlor had accomplished that.

MacDougall was standing by the fireplace when Carly entered the parlor, his gaze on the cold embers of last night's fire. Deeply tanned, with the look of a man more comfortable outdoors than in, he was dressed in worn black jeans and a burgundy sweatshirt, the sleeves of which had been pushed to the elbows, revealing forearms thick with muscle and dotted by fine black hair.

"Mr. MacDougall, I'm Caroline Scanlon." Her stride was deliberately brisk as she approached, her hand extended and her professional armor firmly in place.

He met her halfway, giving her a fast first impression of stern features, a street fighter's wariness and an immense set of shoulders that rivaled Mitch's for breadth and depth. His handshake was firm without being bruising. His palm was wide, dry and edged with the rough furring of calluses.

"Dr. Scanlon. Thank you for seeing me without an appointment. I appreciate it—and I apologize for intruding on your Sunday at home."

"Welcome to Bradenton, Mr. MacDougall," she said, reclaiming her hand. "And Alderson House."

"Thank you. I'm impressed by both, but I imagine everyone is."

"Not everyone. In fact, I'd venture to say that every single member of the University of Oregon's football team disliked us all intensely by the time they boarded the bus for home yesterday afternoon."

He flashed a grin. "Thirty-five—zip makes for a lot of hard feelings, I suspect."

"You attended the game?" she asked.

"No, but I wish I had. I saw the marquee on the stadium sign when I drove past."

"Ah."

In Carly's admittedly biased view, her husband was the most

attractive man alive. This one was definitely a very close second.
But while Mitch's face was square and his strong features mor
even than not, MacDougall's face was angular, with asymmetrica
features and a nose that had been broken more than once. Framed
with thick lashes, his eyes were the same beautiful gray as hi
sons'—though textured by a cynical wariness.

"I must admit to a certain curiosity about the nature of you
visit, Mr. MacDougall. Before she left, Ms. Kenworthy mentioned
something about you being a government agent."

"Yes, ma'am." His face impassive, he pulled a thin leather
wallet from the back pocket of his button-fly jeans and flipped i
open to reveal a small gold badge and a laminated ID card.

"Department of the Treasury," she read aloud. "Like the
FBI?" she asked, shifting her gaze from the small color photo o
a younger Ian Connors MacDougall to the face of the man him
self.

"Though it pains me to admit it, Dr. Scanlon, ATF is mor
like Treasury's bastard child."

She allowed herself an appreciative smile. "As we learned
when the T-Wolves were the conference goat, lack of respect i
the pits, Mr. MacDougall. Or do I call you Agent?"

"I answer to both," he said, returning the leather case to hi
back pocket.

"Which do you prefer?"

"Ian."

"Ian, then."

Carly smiled a little as she seated herself in her mother's fa
vorite chair in front of the marble fireplace. "Marca mentioned
that you're here because of the attacks on Bradenton personnel?"
she asked when he'd seated himself opposite.

"I am."

"Officially?"

"Before I answer that, I'd like to ask you something. Have you
ever heard of a white supremacist group calling itself the New
Aryan Freedom Brigade?"

Frowning a little, Carly searched her mind. "I believe I have," she mused aloud, trying to gather the bits and pieces of memory. "Something to do with skinheads?"

He nodded. "The Brigade was started in Orange County by a man named Hutch Renfrew, who claims he was born on the day Hitler supposedly stuck his Luger in his mouth and committed suicide in his bunker. Bragged he'd gotten a message from God that Hitler's soul now resided in his body. It was his duty to create the Fourth Reich in order to cleanse the earth of the 'mongrel races.'"

Carly grimaced. "He really believes that? It's not just a gimmick, an excuse to inflate his importance?"

"He not only believes it, Dr. Scanlon. He's able to make the sociopaths he recruits believe it, too. I worked undercover as his second-in-command for almost three years, and there were times when I almost believed him myself."

Carly doubted that anyone could shake this man's core beliefs. "But that's the power of charisma, isn't it? An ability to reach into a person's mind and manipulate thought and even belief."

Something very like admiration crossed his face. "Exactly. Renfrew is a master at mind control. He's also a brilliant motivator. His 'soldiers,' as he calls his pack of hoodlums, are required to swear a blood oath of allegiance to him personally—including the vow to die in order to protect him."

Carly shifted her gaze to a lemony oblong of sunlight stretched out on the faded rug between them. She thought about the articles she'd read, mostly about confused and almost always hostile young men and women looking for someone to blame for the ills of the world—or, more likely, a scapegoat for their own insecurities, unhappiness or failures. Damaged souls, feeding on rage. Angry enough to kill.

"Are you saying you think that the incidents of violence at Bradenton are related to this Brigade?"

"I'm afraid I do, yes." He stood suddenly and took a photograph from his back pocket. "This was taken three years ago when he was arrested for murder. I'd like you to take a good look and tell me if you recognize him."

Carly took the photo and studied it. It was two snapshots side-by-side. A mug shot.

"You said he was arrested. Was he convicted?"

"No, he walked on all three counts."

It could have been anyone, she realized, studying the unsmiling face. A middle-aged man with medium brown hair worn in a buzz cut, a neatly trimmed brown beard, pale blue eyes. Nothing to make him stand out. Nothing to make her blood run cold. Nothing but some inner instinct.

"He doesn't look like a monster," she mused, memorizing the features. "But then neither did Ted Bundy."

"Renfrew worked in Hollywood for a time. He's a master of disguises." He shifted, his expression hooded. "Try to imagine him with different-colored hair, maybe clean shaven or with a mustache."

Carly did her best, but the man still looked like a faintly bemused accountant. "I'm sorry, Ian. He doesn't look like anyone I know," she said, handing him back the photo. "Are you positive he's in the area?"

After returning the photo to his pocket, he resumed his seat. "Nothing's predictable about Renfrew. I admit it's only an educated guess when I say he's here. But my gut tells me he's behind the trouble you've been having."

"I didn't realize people in your line of work relied on hunches," she said, smiling a little.

"Some don't," he admitted, smiling back, but briefly. "In this case he, or rather one of his goons, left the Brigade calling card."

Carly leaned forward in her chair, her throat tight. "Which is?"

"A swastika carved on the victim. The attack on the Ethiopian student two weeks ago."

"There's been another one," she murmured, chilled to the bone. "Two nights ago, the dean of our Asian studies department was attacked by a group of men in ski masks while he was out jogging a few blocks from his home. Dr. Matsuda is Japanese-American. His wife is a fifth generation Virginian, like my own mother. His attackers kept railing on about—well, men of Matsuda's ancestry 'taking their women.'" She paused to clear the sudden thickness from her throat.

"His fourteen-year-old daughter found him when her mother got worried and sent Penny out to look for her dad," she explained when she had herself under control again. "Luckily, some people who witnessed the attack at a distance had already called for help. The doctor said he would have bled to death if the paramedics hadn't gotten to him so quickly."

MacDougall uttered a ripe curse, then immediately apologized. "How is he now?"

"The last report I have on his condition is about four hours old, but it was positive. Barring complications from the two surgeries he had to undergo, he should make a full recovery."

"And the student from Ethiopia? Keilasie?"

Carly was impressed. The man had indeed done his homework. "Jarmid was very lucky. The blow to his kneecap only cracked the bone instead of shattering it. His leg is still in a cast and will be for several months. He's back in Addis Ababa now. His father insisted he come home immediately, and Jarmid had no choice but to obey." She sighed and shook her head. "He promised to come back and testify if there's a trial, but according to the sheriff's detective on the case, he really can't testify to much more than vague impressions."

"If I'm right about Renfrew, the vandalism and violence are only the beginning."

Carly felt a sudden swell of anger. "There must be something we can do to keep that from happening!"

His mouth relaxed, and she sensed that she'd pleased him. "With your cooperation, we might be able to take the bastard down."

Hutch Renfrew sighted down the barrel of his M-16 rifle at the graceful little doe grazing in the distant clearing. He had the perfect shot, yet he made himself wait, allowing the blood lust to build inside until it was a hot, raging beast.

He would go for the heart. Only a barbarian went in for a head kill.

Beauty in all things was sacred. Like a perfect rose. A bloodline without the taint of the mongrel races. A child's pure heart. A mother's sweetness. Power.

His blood was hot now. Pulsing.

He closed one eye, sharpened his focus, concentrated. Letting out his breath in an even flow, just as he'd been taught as an eager, gung-ho recruit twenty-five years earlier, he squeezed the trigger, letting off a single shot. Exulting at the power of the recoil, Hutch let out a shout of release, his cry echoing into the clean mountain air. The doe fell instantly, the kill clean and merciful. Perfection.

After taking a moment to enjoy the heady afterglow of his triumph, he shifted his weapon to safety and began walking down the sun-dappled slope toward the spot where his kill lay, curled gracefully into a patch of emerald grass.

Like the alpha males of other predatory species, he preferred to hunt alone. It was a time for reflection, for planning—and on occasion, for cleansing himself of the poison of a rare failure. He'd hunted endlessly in the bittersweet days following his acquittal, testing his stalking skills against deer and elk and, on two memorable occasions, bear.

Each time he killed, he thought of MacDougall and his deceit. His triumph at defeating MacDougall again in the courts, which all right-thinking men knew to be corrupt, had been tempered by the fact that his mortal enemy had escaped the execution his treachery had warranted.

It had taken him months of killing, months of watching the blood of his prey spreading onto the soil of his isolated Idaho retreat—and later, onto the deep snow—before he'd realized the truth that had been there all along.

Execution was too merciful a punishment for the man he'd known as Gage Masters. No, it had been far better to let the traitor live out his days with the memory of his dying daughters and their dead mother torturing him with every breath of life he took.

It was the perfect revenge.

Hutch had only one regret—that he hadn't been there in person to watch MacDougall screaming out his anguish as they'd loaded what was left of the twin girls into the ambulance. But he'd made the two men who'd been his eyes and ears repeat the story so many times it was imprinted on his brain.

MacDougall had lost it after the trial. He'd sold his house with the furnishings included, moved to a seedy rooming house at the beach and dived headfirst into a bottle. The last report Hutch had received had described a broken man who'd become just one more drunken bum living from bottle to bottle.

Hutch smiled as he knelt next to the doe. Like this dead carcass, MacDougall was finished. Unlike Hutch, he'd failed.

The Brigade was stronger than ever.

Soon he would step up the recruiting already quietly underway in the town of Bradenton Falls and on the Bradenton College campus. According to the demographics of the area he'd studied while training his elite corps in Idaho, this part of Oregon was ideal for his purposes.

He'd made a mistake in concentrating his first campaign in a highly populated area where the media was privy to his every move. Bradenton Falls had only one newspaper and no local TV. The population was largely rural—plain, hard-working folks who minded their own business and resented government interference of any kind. Decent, God-fearing *white* folks, for the most part.

He'd already tested the waters and found them perfect. The four attacks he'd already orchestrated had gone off without a hitch. With enough force to send a warning, yes, but no killing, he'd ordered. Not yet. Not until their power base was more solid and their forces up to greater strength.

No, the attacks had been simply a scouting foray to see what kind of local response he could expect. The result had been more than gratifying—an insipid, badly written article on an inside page of the newspaper after each raid, a halfhearted attempt by a lard-ass sheriff's department detective to find witnesses and gather evidence, a collective shrug from the community.

Soon Hutch Renfrew would be too powerful to stop. Very soon.

The boys had been fed, the dishes were stowed in the dish-washer, and the last load of laundry folded and put away. After a flurry of nonstop activity and noise generated by three rambunctious toddlers, the house was finally quiet.

Still wound up, Marca poured herself a glass of wine, grabbed the portable phone from the cradle, and wandered out to the back deck of the converted barn she called home. The sunset was nearly spent, with only the faintest tinge of orange hovering like mist over the distant peaks of the Cascades. September was turning out to be a glorious month, with bright Indian summer days and clear, starlit nights with just a hint of the cooler air to come.

Of all the seasons, she loved those few golden weeks between summer's end and fall's official beginning, when the weather was wildly unpredictable, and the air was thick with the heady perfume of summer's last lingering roses and the first wisps of burning leaves.

Feeling her forty-three years and then some, she settled wearily into the soft cushions of the old-fashioned glider and waited for the tension to seep from her tired muscles.

Upstairs, in the part of the barn that had once been a loft, the babies who were her life were fast asleep, each with his own tattered blanket nearby.

Ryan had been a little fussy, and though his temperature was normal, he had always been the first to catch whatever bug was going around. With nearly twenty thousand students coming and going from all parts of the world, Bradenton had its share of exotic bugs as well as the mundane. She would check his temperature again before she went to bed, she decided, as she took a sip of wine.

The sun was down now, and the air was still. Soon the stars would appear, winking on one by one until the sky was crowded with twinkling pinpoints of light.

"I wish I may, I wish I might," she murmured, resting her

head against the cushion, her gaze searching the gathering dark for her special star. She'd stopped wishing for Ian long ago.

It was Murphy's Law, of course. As soon as she stopped longing for him to walk through her door, he appeared.

So he was the boys' biological father. Big deal, she thought, lifting her head for another sip. He had no business showing up without notice after nearly three years of silence, looking so virile and sexy and tempting.

She took another sip, rubbing the glass against her lips as she swallowed. His mouth had been soft and yielding under hers. Familiar. And terribly hungry, as though he hadn't kissed a woman in a very long time. Damn him, she thought, bolting down the last of her wine before rising quickly. A nice warm bubble bath was what she needed. And then a good long snooze.

She'd just finished locking the sliding door when the phone rang. After answering warily, she heard Carly's voice on the other end. "Did I interrupt anything?"

"Just a semi-critical bout of self-pity, but it'll keep," she said, making her way through the long, narrow living room to the front door. As a general rule, her nanny, Kimbra Ruenda, didn't return until late on her Sundays off. Since Kimbra had her own key, Marca always locked up before she went to bed.

"Well, aren't you going to ask me what we talked about?"

"Who?"

"Sean Connery, of course. Or didn't you see his helicopter landing when you left this afternoon?"

"Ah, that *who*. I have so many ex-lovers dropping by, it's difficult to keep track." Suddenly worn out, she wandered over to the staircase and plopped down on the steps.

"Well, you might not be shook up, but I am. Big-time."

The sudden shift in Carly's tone from teasing to serious had Marca gripping the phone a little tighter. "What's wrong? What did he say?"

"That we might have more of a problem than we thought."

Two minutes later Marca was on her feet and pacing as Carly finally finished recounting her conversation with Ian.

"The New Aryan Freedom Brigade," Marca mused aloud. "It sounds obscenely familiar, somehow."

"He showed me a picture of this Renfrew. I swear, Marce, the man looked like a wimpy numbers cruncher."

"I assume you didn't recognize him?"

"No. I don't know if that's positive or negative, actually. MacDougall wants access to the personnel files of all of our employees, which if you will recall, have photos attached. Some of the more recent hirees also have fingerprints, but unfortunately, that's only a small percentage."

"Are you sure you have the legal right to open personnel files? Maybe you'd better check with legal counsel."

"I already have. After MacDougall left, I called Uncle Thaddeus at his weekend place in Maryland. He said that as far as he knows, we could refuse, which means MacDougall would have to get a court order. But Uncle Thad advised me to cooperate— if MacDougall's credentials are bona fide. He's going to check with someone at ATF and promised to get back to me by noon tomorrow."

Marca had only met Carly's formidable and influential godfather once, when he'd come to Letty's christening four years ago. Thaddeus Pendleton and Carleton Alderson had been roommates at Bradenton, and the former attorney general and ambassador to Great Britain was still very active in alumni affairs. In fact, he'd recently been elected to the board of trustees.

"I thought the ambassador was with the State Department."

"He is, but I figured one government agency was as good as another."

"Or as bad," Marca muttered as she sank into the nearest chair. "I don't think I've ever heard of this Renfrew person, but from what you've just told me, he sounds like a twisted sociopath." She shuddered. "Imagine thinking you're the reincarnation of a monster like Hitler."

Carly's sigh was heavy. "Ian said that he's as convincing as an evangelist and just as charismatic."

"Ian, is it?"

The sudden silence on the other end was telling. "That's what he asked me to call him. It felt right, somehow. There's just something very straightforward and appealing about him. As Mitch says, no BS."

"That's certainly true enough. A man who doesn't make promises doesn't break them." Eyes narrowed, she stared at the discarded sneaker on the rug. It had blue laces, which meant it belonged to Trevor. "Did he...say anything about me?"

Carly chuckled. "Try to pump me for information, you mean?"

"All right, yes. Did he?"

"No, but then he came to see me on official business, and he doesn't seem to be the type to mix the professional and the personal." On the other end of the wire Carly cleared her throat. "Have you decided yet whether or not to tell him about the boys?"

She sighed. Trust her always-practical friend to ask the question she'd worked hard to avoid even thinking about since she'd returned home.

"I keep waffling. One minute I'm absolutely certain he has a right to know his children—if that's his choice—and then, minutes later, I'm absolutely terrified that having an absentee father or an indifferent father or a father that only sends cards at Christmas, or whatever, will screw them up royally." She sighed. "I realize now why you were so adamant in your decision not to tell Tracy anything at all about her father. Or inform Mitch that the few hours you'd spent together had produced consequences. It's so much easier that way."

Carly sighed. "Tangled webs are the pits."

"I'll give you a heartfelt amen to that," Marca said, getting to her feet. "And on that note I'll say good-night. I have some serious thinking to do before tomorrow, and I might as well get it over with."

"Good luck."

"Thanks. And, Carly, let me know what Thaddeus has to say, okay?"

"Absolutely."

After she hung up, Marca turned out the lights and went upstairs to check on her sons—and Ian's.

# Chapter 5

The campus campanile was chiming eight on the following, rain-soaked Monday morning when Marca's ultraefficient assistant, Winston, buzzed her with a call from Richard Hartson.

As she punched the blinking light on her console, her gaze fell on the bright roses in a milk glass vase that held court at one corner of her desk. Already one of the blossoms was shedding petals like drops of blood.

"Good morning, Richard," she said, propping the phone against her shoulder while she scooped petals into her palm and deposited them in the wastebasket.

"The same to you, beautiful lady. I was afraid I was calling too early." She heard the affection in his voice and visualized his easygoing smile and steady brown eyes. A pleasant man offering a pleasant life.

"Actually I've been in since seven." She shifted the phone to her other ear and sat back. Because of her crowded schedule she would have to consider this conversation her morning break.

"Ah, a dedicated woman. Very commendable."

"Not so dedicated. Desperate. You haven't seen my desk."

His chuckle was predictable, but pleasant. "That can be easily remedied. I was calling to suggest meeting for lunch today at Gallagher's, but I could just as easily stop by campus to pick you up."

"Today is not a good day for lunch, Richard." Leaning forward again, she flipped through her calendar, then frowned at a sudden idea. "Look, I owe you a meal after that lovely breakfast yesterday morning. Why don't I fix us dinner at my place on Friday night? I make a mean lasagna."

"You're on! I'll bring wine. Six-thirty? Seven?"

"Make it seven-thirty. Getting the boys bedded down for the night takes a major chunk of time, even with Kimbra's help."

There was a pause. "I wouldn't mind having the boys join us. After all, I'm hoping to become their daddy."

At the mention of her sons, Marca automatically focused her attention on the color photo of them that sat behind a stack of course catalogs.

Until yesterday afternoon she'd abandoned all hope of ever seeing Ian again. But now that she had, how did she feel about another man raising his sons?

"That's really sweet of you, Richard," she said, temporarily shelving the question with the other more critical one she'd spent half the night trying to answer. "But the chance to carry on an adult conversation without having to wipe up spills or referee spats between sentences is too appealing to pass up."

His easy laughter rang out, yet she found herself frowning, without really knowing why. "I assume that means the elusive Kimbra won't be joining us, either?"

"I'd forgotten you two haven't met yet. And no, she has night classes on Monday, Wednesday and Friday."

"In that case, I'll look forward to spending the evening with you...alone."

Marca was mildly surprised that the sexually charged timbre of his voice didn't arouse even the faintest excitement. "I'll see you Friday at seven-thirty."

She hung up, her thoughts already turning to work. Foremost

on her priority list was the request from one of the sports networks for permission to do a feature on the Timberwolves' winning streak which was now within six games of tying the conference record. It was exactly the kind of national publicity they needed.

The only obstacle was Mitch. He hated the cameras and microphones. No matter what the focus of the story, it invariably included a sidebar about him and his handicap, complete with before and after pictures.

She was considering the best way to approach him when the door to the outer office burst open and Winston hurried inside. A part-time student, talented graphic artist, all-American wrestling champ, and full-time friend, Winston Trenton Charters III had worked for her for nine months, during which time he'd made himself indispensable—especially as a fill-in baby-sitter.

The boys adored him, but then in many ways Winston, for all his great work ethic, had the instincts of a mischievous toddler. At present he was between lovers, which tended to give him an overly dramatic view of life.

"Pinch me, boss lady," he demanded in the fog-horn voice that rumbled from his man-mountain chest. "I think I'm hyperventilating."

A firm believer in positive thinking, he tended to dress in bright colors on gloomy days. Today he was wearing his favorite Hawaiian shirt, the one with pink pineapples on a field of electric yellow. Marca decided it made him look like a large catamaran under full sail.

"Don't tell me!" Marca said, holding up both hands. "You've just encountered the man of your dreams."

His bulldog features took on a dreamy look. "You know that I've never gone for the dark and dangerous type. Much too hard on an artist's finely tuned nervous system, but with this one, I could make an exception."

"Ah, a bad boy!"

"The baddest! Mean to the bone. I get shivers."

"And where, exactly, did you encounter this paragon?"

"In the cramped cubicle otherwise known as the outer office."

His massive shoulders heaved in a sigh. "Alas, he's here to see you. MacDougall's his name."

"Oh." Marca bit her lip and drummed her nails on a clear patch of blotter, thinking furiously.

"Marce, is something wrong? Should I haul out the trusty 'she's in conference' ploy and send the gorgeous hunk on his way?"

She filled her lungs, then emptied them slowly. *Think, Marcella!* "Carly is right," she muttered. "Tangled webs are the pits."

Winston's eyebrows climbed toward his thatch of flaxen curls. "Do I sense a minidrama unfolding here?"

"Just don't say anything to him about my personal life, all right?"

She saw the exact moment the light dawned—right before his gaze shifted to the three miniature faces in the photo. "Well, bless my soul."

"Not one word, Winston, or I swear I'll burn your Gay Power sweatshirt."

His gaze shifted to hers, and he offered a sly grin. "I have spares."

"Not autographed by Elton John you don't!"

He snorted, but his gaze was warm with genuine concern. "Obviously he doesn't know."

"No, and don't ask me if I'm going to tell him. I'm waiting to hear from Carly about...something, and then I'll make my decision."

"In the meantime, want I should show him in?"

"Go ahead. No, wait!"

He froze in the act of turning and watched as she jerked open the bottom drawer. Her conscience gave a niggling kick as she tucked the photo inside and closed it away.

"Ready now?" Winston asked, his expression a mixture of empathy and amusement.

"No, but send him in, anyway."

Needing a buffer, she stayed behind the desk. Beneath its cluttered top, her second-best suede pumps were pressed hard against the floor, and her spine was as straight as a die.

The unflappable Ms. Kenworthy at her steeliest.

All it took was the click of the door opening to have butterfly wings battering at the wall of her stomach. One sight of that long, rangy body, and her mouth went dry. So much for steel, she thought as he closed the door behind him. More like melted solder.

He was wearing jeans again, the cowboy kind worn slick in the seat and ragged at the boot-cut bottoms. In spite of the morning damp, he was bare-chested under a soft wool V-neck sweater the color of a cloudless summer sky. The sleeves had been pushed nearly to his elbows, his wide forearms stretching the ribbing thin against the hard-packed muscle. He'd pulled that sexy shoulder-length hair back into a little queue secured with what looked like a broken shoelace, and a small gold stud winked at her from his left earlobe.

It would take some doing, she decided, but she intended to rise above this need she felt to fling herself into his arms every time he came within catching distance.

"Have you always had a phobia against making appointments, or are you trying out a new behavior here at Bradenton?" she asked in her best senior executive tone, the one she almost always paired with a decent imitation of Felicity Alderson's Southern matron stare.

"Actually it was tougher getting in to see you than finagling a pass to a Fleetwood Mac concert," he said as he approached the desk. One large fist was wrapped around a twig of scarlet oak leaves. The bright color seemed to fill the room with whispers of crisp wind and the warm tang of cider. The man carrying them added hints of tobacco and shaving soap.

Pulling back from the tug on her senses, she picked up her pen and twirled it. "I'll admit to a definite uneasiness as to your reasons for bringing a tree branch into my office."

His mouth quirked. "Guess it's a little strange at that, but I saw them and I remembered you said you liked autumn leaves."

He laid the clutch of leaves atop one of the piles. ''I thought they might take some of the gray out of the day.''

He'd remembered an offhand remark, made over wine in a noisy bar? She was surprised and moved. ''They're beautiful.''

''Yeah? So you like them?''

''Very much.'' Even more than the roses, she realized. Anyone with a phone and a credit card could order roses, but selecting the perfect sprig of leaves took thought and care—and imagination.

His smile developed slowly and ended up a little crooked, with a hint of shyness around the eyes. The man was flat-out adorable when he smiled, which, from the lack of crinkle lines around his eyes wasn't all that often.

''I thought maybe those big fluffy things you always see around this time of year, but the florist shop doesn't open until nine.''

''You wanted to bring me flowers?''

Looking acutely uncomfortable, he dipped his fingers into back pockets. ''I'm a little rusty in this fence-mending business. I thought flowers might help you overlook the rough edges when they crop up.''

She felt a little bubble of delight forming in her chest and reminded herself to be cautious this time around. ''Couldn't hurt.''

He reached out a hand to touch one of the roses. ''Looks like I wasn't the only one looking to impress a pretty lady.''

Smiling a little, she picked up the twig and sniffed one of the leaves. It was still a little damp and smelled like rain. ''I've always liked oak leaves best.''

Ian saw a little light come into her eyes and figured he'd made it over the first hurdle. It wasn't much, considering all she'd given him the first time they'd met, but it was better than the frost he'd expected. And, yeah, okay, deserved.

''Did Dr. Scanlon tell you I'm going to be hanging around here for a while?'' He picked up a hunk of granite from her desk and ran his finger over the rough surface.

''She told me about a white supremacist named Hutch Renfrew

and that you think he plans to recruit students into a group called the New Aryan Freedom Brigade.''

"I think it's a strong bet, yeah. Young people make the best zealots, especially the ones who like to play with guns and hurt people."

"I hate the very idea of skinheads and neo-Nazis and that ilk." She sighed. "When I was a student here we had our share of radical organizations. One or two even advocated some fairly outrageous actions against the government, but we weren't sociopaths—or lunatics."

"Probably weren't carrying an M-16 and a skinning knife, either."

She paled. "Dear God, no. Although I did carry a fairly wicked metal hair pick in my Afro period."

He could see it, he realized. A young and passionate Marca Kenworthy marching a picket line, that tidy little body in a miniskirt and a tube top. It was enough to make a man forget his name and a hefty amount of his personal history. Scowling a little, he returned the rock to the desk before taking out the picture of Renfrew he carried everywhere like a damn talisman.

"This is Hutchinson Renfrew three years ago," he said, placing it in front of her. "Look like anyone you know?"

Marca took her time. Carly was right. The man in the photograph looked harmless. Even a little weak, especially around those nearly colorless eyes. And yet, she felt a crawling sensation just under her skin as she looked into the man's blank gaze.

"As far as I know, I've never seen him before."

Disappointed, but too disciplined to let it show, Ian returned the mug shot to his pocket. "It was worth a shot. Though us G-men types would rather fry than admit it, most cases are solved by civilians dropping a quarter or remembering a face."

"Why don't you show it to Winston on the way out? I don't know how he does it, but he seems to know everyone on campus, especially the younger members of the faculty. He—"

The intercom buzzed, interrupting her. She excused herself politely before picking up the phone. "Yes, Winston?"

While she dealt with a call from an ex-jock turned sportscaster, Ian seized on the opportunity to satisfy his curiosity by prowling her office. Though not large, it was in the power corner of the big old building, with high ceilings and tall, narrow windows. The paintings, mostly bright, sexy-looking slashes of color and light looked like originals. On one of the shelves sat a small jade statue of a lion-faced dog that he suspected was worth more than his yearly salary.

"If Renfrew is here, how do you plan to stop him?" she asked after hanging up. Back to business, he thought, and wondered how she would react if he stepped past his need to test each step before he took it and simply yanked her out of her chair and into his arms.

"Don't know yet," he said, turning to look at her. She appeared almost prim in the neat pink suit, with subtle flashes of gold in her ears and at her slender neck, and her hair swept back into some kind of twisted knot. How many women were there in that neat little body? he wondered. Each time he'd seen her, she'd been different. It made him uneasy—and fascinated the hell out of him. It was dangerous, this way she had of sneaking under his guard to crowd his thoughts and mess up his sleep.

"Nice painting," he said when he realized she was watching him. "What's it called?"

"*Still Life with Nude.*"

He narrowed his gaze. "Guess the pink squiggle in the middle is the nude, huh?"

She laughed. "To tell you the truth, I don't know. The artist was trying to raise money for a year in Paris, and I had an empty spot on my wall."

"Sounds like you need somebody to protect you from that soft heart of yours."

"Sorry to break it to you, MacDougall, but this is almost the twenty-first century. Ladies in distress carry their own lances these days."

It was a warning, delivered with a smile. It rankled anyway.

"Hell, here I was hoping to slay a dragon or two to impress you."
He shoved his hands in his pockets and prowled again.

"Why doesn't this Renfrew just come out in the open and make
speeches like some of the other zealots?" she asked after a moment.

The lady was definitely tenacious. But then, so was he.

"I don't know for sure. Maybe he'd decided that keeping a
low profile is more effective. Like a rattler waiting under a rock."

"Any idea where this particular rock might be?"

"That's what I'm hoping to find out." He stopped in front of
a framed diploma. It was a master's degree in advertising from
NYU. Brains as well as beauty, he thought. He figured his
chances of impressing the lady just took a sudden nosedive. Not
that they were all that high to begin with, he reminded himself.

He heard her huff out air and knew that if he turned, she'd be
scowling at him. Perversely he kept his back to her as he wandered over to the window. The campus streets were slick with
puddles, and a pall of gray fog hung over the peaks to the east.
Students crossing the quadrangle carried umbrellas or wore slick-
ers. Ian didn't own either.

"Find out how?" she said after a moment's silence.

"Hang out around campus, keep my eyes and ears open.
Sooner or later I'll hear something interesting."

"How long do you think it'll take?"

"Don't know that, either." Because he liked watching her eyes
when she was mulling something over, he turned to look at her.
"Why? Are you trying to get rid of me already?"

Her eyes flashed a testy impatience that had him wanting to
drop a quick kiss on the tip of her nose. "I don't even *know*
you."

"Would you like to?"

That succulent little mouth pursed a little. "Yes."

They looked at each other over the clutter of piled papers,
unopened mail and her empty coffee mug. Marca thought he had
beautiful eyes, but too sad. And a starkly compelling face.

This was an indomitable man, she thought. And a solitary one.

It scared her a little to realize how much she wanted to walk around the desk and lay her head against the strong heart she knew beat there.

"We'll start with dinner tonight," he said. Ordered. "Give me your address. I'll pick you up at seven."

"Sorry, I'm busy." It wasn't a lie. Evenings were *always* busy at her house. And mornings and afternoons. The only quiet came when the triplets were sleeping.

"Name a time, then."

Pushy. Definitely pushy. Trevor was his daddy's son, no doubt about it, she thought as she leaned forward to flip through her calendar. It was jammed. Not a spare moment for a solid week.

"Tomorrow. For lunch." She made a mental note to call the editor of the alumni magazine and reschedule their regular Tuesday lunch date. "You can pick me up here at noon."

Ian felt a fast rush of satisfaction. "Yes, ma'am."

Though she laughed and got to her feet, her gypsy eyes remained troubled. "I'm glad you stopped by. And thanks again for the autumn leaves. They're lovely."

"No problem. I figured that big old tree by the bell tower wouldn't miss 'em."

Politely she walked with him to the door, her long rosy-pink skirt flaring a little around the prettiest ankles he'd ever seen. The boxy jacket was a little too loose for his taste, though, hiding her figure the way it did. But he figured that was the point—one of those executive-suite power plays designed to keep a man from thinking about the woman across the table as a sex object. Since he'd rather be force-fed grand opera than dress in a suit and try to talk contracts around the ever-tightening knot of a silk tie, he was having trouble thinking about anything else *but* sex.

At the door she turned to him and held out her hand. As he took it in his, his throat went so tight he nearly reached up to adjust the neckline of his sweater. *Damn.* He could smell her skin, that warm scent of peaches and sun. His need to hold her spiked again. Fighting it, he lifted her hand to his mouth and kissed it.

"I'll see you tomorrow," he said before releasing her.

He left before he could change his mind and take her to the floor. As it was, he needed to run a dozen circuits of the football practice field before he had himself under control again.

Carly called around ten. She'd heard from Thaddeus Pendleton.

"Hang on a minute, Carly," Marca said, smiling apologetically at the student intern seated across from her. "Would you mind, Sal? This is personal."

"Of course not, Ms. Kenworthy," the girl said, jumping up. "I'll just go pester Winston for a few minutes."

Marca waited until Sally Wong closed the door behind her before demanding tersely, "Well?"

"Ian is most definitely an ATF agent. But if you want the particulars you'll have to come up here to get them."

"Give me twenty minutes. I'm just finishing up here."

"Okay. And Marce, bring pastry."

Marca laughed. Carly was passionate about the cinnamon buns baked by the semiretired couple who ran the coffee cart in the lobby of the administration building.

"You're on. Twenty minutes, with food."

With another quick smile, she hit the speed dial to order the pastry.

The tower office that had seemed so austere and intimidating in Carleton Alderson's day was now bright and cozy. When Carly had taken over after her father's sudden death from a stroke, she'd had the rich wood paneling removed and the walls textured in white, exchanged the drab brown carpeting for slate blue and removed the heavy gold draperies that blocked the light, replacing them with custom-made wooden blinds that were almost always raised to let in the breathtaking view of the campus and the mountains beyond.

Photos of Mitch and the children were everywhere. There was even one of Marca herself at nineteen, striking an impossible athletic pose in her cheerleader's costume. Both she and Carly had made the junior varsity their freshman year. Carly had had to quit when she'd become pregnant. Marca had cheered for the T-wolves all four years, enjoying every frenzied, throat-wrecking moment.

"Ian's originally from California, went to Fresno State on a track scholarship where he majored in police science, earning respectable grades, and was recruited by both ATF and FBI before he graduated. According to Uncle Thad's source, he chose ATF because he didn't own a tie and refused to buy one. He's a crack marksman, well respected by his peers, though considered a difficult man to know, and a definite loner, with, and I quote, 'maverick tendencies.'" She glanced at Marca over her reading glasses. "To sum up, and to quote Uncle Thad one more time, 'MacDougall's a tough SOB who gets the job done any way he can and worries about the consequences later.'"

Marca pinched off another bite of Carly's half-eaten cinnamon bun and popped it into her mouth. "Is that all Thaddeus said?" she asked when she'd swallowed.

"No. He ran down a list of commendations, glossed over a couple of reprimands for untoward recklessness, and then went on to expand a little on Ian's years undercover. *Deep cover,* Uncle Thad said it's called."

"Sounds kinky," Marca said flippantly.

Rolling her eyes in feigned exasperation, Carly paused for breath and to consult the notes scribbled in distinctive green ink on a legal pad. Glancing up, she caught Marca's eye. "Marce, he was actually a *member* of the Brigade. For three years. Apparently he made a very convincing fascist. Even shaved his head."

Marca lifted her cup to her mouth, then returned it to the desk without drinking. "Ian was a...a skinhead?"

"It was an extremely dangerous duty, so they wouldn't order him to do it. It had to be his choice. Uncle Thad made that very clear."

Marca thought about Ted Matsuda's ruined face and went cold inside. Ian had huge hands and a powerful body. "Surely he didn't hurt anyone? I mean, the government wouldn't condone cold-blooded violence by one of its agents, would it?"

Carly's gaze became troubled. "I asked Uncle Thad the same question. He told me not to be naive."

"I...see." Marce drew air between her parted teeth, then exhaled slowly. "I suppose that kind of thing is common in the world Ian lives in."

"And necessary," Carly said softly.

"Yes. Certainly."

Marca bit her lip. The idea that Ian might actually have used those huge, hard fists on someone whose only crime was to be born to a certain set of parents was utterly frightening. And nauseating. Dedication was one thing, violence was something else altogether. Yet there was a part of Marca that accepted that these atrocities would go on and on unless someone did the mean and nasty work required to stop them.

"There was something else," Carly said as she neatly folded her notes, then tore them in two before dropping them into her wastebasket. "About his...personal life."

Marca felt a chill. "I knew it. He's married."

"No, divorced." She hesitated, then sighed. "His ex-wife and twin daughters were killed when a bomb exploded under Ian's Camaro. The girls were only six."

"Oh, my God." Marca pressed her hand to her lips, her throat suddenly filling with bile.

"According to Uncle Thad, there was enough evidence to arrest Renfrew, but not enough to convict him."

Marca swallowed down most of the sickness. The pain in her stomach was worse than the searing burn of the ulcer she'd had in her New York days. "When...?"

"About three and a half years ago.

Not all that long before they'd met. He'd been grieving, she realized numbly. The flashes of something bleak and helpless in his eyes—that had been grief. Marca sat frozen, her eyes stinging.

*Oh, Ian,* she thought. I wish I'd known. But what could she have done?

"How can he bear it?" she wondered aloud, thinking about her little boys. Every day the love she felt for them grew richer, with nuances and facets that shone and sparkled inside her. Sometimes, when she was lying in the twilight world between sleep and consciousness, she was sure she'd felt one of them kick in her womb. She knew she would die to protect them. She would certainly kill to keep them safe. But to lose them?

"Think what it would mean to him to find out he has three sons!" she murmured, picturing that austere face lighting up. "Not that they could replace his daughters, but still, it's like a wonderful gift. I can't wait to tell him."

"A gift he could lose," Carly pointed out quietly. "If Renfrew could plant one bomb, he could plant another."

Marca froze, her mind sifting through horrible, unthinkable images. "Oh, God, you're right. If Ian's instinct is correct and that man Renfrew *is* somewhere nearby, how can I possibly take the risk of his coming after Ian again? And maybe...killing my boys this time?"

Carly's green eyes were eloquent with understanding—and sympathy. "I don't know, Marce. I wish I did. I just know that when I say my prayers tonight I'm going to include one for Ian—and you."

# Chapter 6

It was still drizzling when Ian went for a run on Tuesday morning. Though it was a good half hour after sunup, the few cars he encountered along the road required headlights to cut through the deep overcast.

The air smelled of rain and damp foliage, reminding him a little of the Everglades and the week he'd spent chasing down a couple of mean, old Cuban boys running arms into the country. His skin itched at the memory of the mosquitoes. His face had been swollen for days.

Instead of saw grass and palmettos, this part of the country ran to pines and blackberry brambles, which had lined every road he'd driven so far. He blew out air and shuddered a little at the thought of chasing a suspect through those twisting canes. Better to scratch a few bug bites than end up shredded by thorns, he decided as he eased over onto the gravel shoulder of the road to let a pickup with a bad muffler chug past.

Once the cream-colored Ford had gone by him, Ian cut back onto the asphalt, resumed his speed and focused his thoughts on planning his day. The job interview with the head of Bradenton's maintenance department, Michael J. McNabb, was set for eight. Since the interview had been arranged by madam president herself, it was pretty much a given he'd get the job. As a cover, it was about as good as it was going to get in this godforsaken place.

A professor he wasn't. Hell, he couldn't even fake it. To try to get through a fifty-minute session talking to a bunch of bored students would be torture for him.

No, manual labor was definitely preferable. Something to burn away the hot-wired tension that had thrummed in him since he'd crossed the state line. Besides, nobody ever paid attention to the guy with a rake or a broom in his hand. Just went on talking like he was a part of the landscape or a stick of furniture.

A guy could learn a lot in a short time while puttering around, pretending to do his job. Being in the right place at the right time. Listening. Watching. Waiting.

From the beginning Ian had been a natural at that particular monitoring tactic. A kid who had felt like an outsider from the age of six, and who knew he was a burden his uncle had accepted only on sufferance, he had quickly learned how to blend into the woodwork. A human chameleon, Stebbins had called him once, when the two of them had been sharing a long, boring stakeout.

Waiting for the right time to make his move had come harder for Ian. He'd banged his head against a lot of mistakes and frustration before he'd learned that patience and perfect timing was everything.

That applied not only to his work, but to coaxing a certain, skittish lady into his bed. He'd already begun the coaxing. Today at lunch he'd do a little more.

As for the job he'd come to do, it was on track, too. Yesterday afternoon he'd started combing the files of the male employees, both staff and faculty, working in a dusty cubbyhole in the basement of the administration office. So far he'd gotten nothing but a headache from the clattering of the steam in the old pipes.

He figured to start blending into the campus "woodwork" tomorrow, maybe the day after. According to Dr. Scanlon, a position for a combination garden assistant and general handyman had been open for two weeks. The fall cleanup was already underway, so the head of landscape maintenance was screaming for help, and the department of building maintenance was shorthanded as well.

As Ian jogged around a curve, he saw that an ancient oak growing at the edge of the road had shed a goodly number of leaves on the asphalt below its overhanging branches. A smile flitted across his mouth as he thought about the soft sheen of pleasure in Marca's eyes when he'd given her that stupid bunch of dead leaves yesterday. Damn, but it had been a sweet moment.

Since then he'd felt different. More alive. Even sort of happy.

It scared him a little that he might be wading into trouble, the dangerous, emotional kind that he'd sworn to avoid. His instinct told him to cut and run, but every time he made up his mind to keep his distance, he remembered the peace that had come over him when he'd been with her that night on the beach. He'd be okay if he kept it sexual, he told himself, making the turn into the motel driveway.

He cut back on the pace for his cooldown and made six loops of the circular entrance drive, two at a slow jog, the remaining four at a walk. Hands at the hips, shaking the kinks from his legs, he inhaled deeply, *whooshing* on his exhale, the sound reminding him of a surfacing whale.

He definitely could feel the difference in elevation. His legs felt heavier, and his lungs burned from cooler air. But it was a good burn—and a familiar one. Except for the relatively brief period of time when he'd holed up in the cracker-box apartment in Ocean Beach, trying to drown his grief in a bottle and letting his body go to hell, he couldn't remember a time when he hadn't run. Away from trouble, at first. And then, later, because it gave him a rare high he found addictive.

He felt free when he was running. Even as a kid, it had been his means of escape. Away from the demands of a mean-spirited old man who'd always resented his younger brother's success and being saddled with his kid.

Still, Ian owed his uncle for one thing at least. It had been the strength in his runner's legs and the endurance he'd built up bucking hay on his uncle's ranch that had earned him the track scholarship that had helped pay for four of his six years at Fresno State.

His specialty had been the decathlon. He'd placed best in the state three years running, a record of wins still unequaled in the state of California. He'd done well in the strength events, especially the javelin throw, but it had been in the final event, the fifteen-hundred-meter run, that he'd truly excelled.

The motel parking lot was all but empty as he jogged along the row of spaces. A woman in a red jogging suit was playing with a miniature white poodle in the fenced area reserved for pets. A man with the look of a salesman was loading a minivan at the far end of the long, two-story building. Ian's room was on the ground floor, one of the few reserved for pets. By some odd quirk of human logic it was also a nonsmoking room. He'd had to choose; take his smokes outside or leave the damn dog in the Jeep.

The ungrateful mutt was waiting for him when he unlocked the door, its absurdly long tongue lolling, and that pathetic excuse for a tail wagging like a tattered flag.

"You still here?" he groused as the mutt sniffed eagerly at the pocket of his running shorts. "Yeah, yeah, I know. You love me for myself alone, right?"

Mutt gave an exuberant "woof," looking for all the world like a collection of mismatched dog parts packed into a bad canine suit that sagged, bagged and generally elicited laughs from startled passersby.

"Here, you mangy beggar," he grumbled as he tossed the dog the treat he always carried in his pocket in case he met a too-aggressive watchdog on one of his runs. "Don't get used to it, 'cause you and me are gonna part company one day."

Dumb ass that he was, Mutt glanced up with adoration in his eyes. Hell, didn't he know when he wasn't wanted?

Stripping off as he crossed the room, Ian paused long enough to flip on the TV. Mutt was addicted to the morning mind candy. The cooking demonstrations were his favorites.

"Shows what kind of intelligence you have," he muttered as he dropped his soggy tank top into the corner. Him, he went for the ladies in their shiny body suits.

"Hey, I almost forgot to mention it," he said when Mutt padded over to sit in front of the set. "I got me a date with our beautiful friend today. You remember, the lady who saved our miserable hides?"

The bedsprings creaked under his weight as he sat down to take off his shoes and sodden socks. "Gonna charm her out of her reservations about this good old boy."

Mutt woofed, and his tail gave a few happy thumps. Grinning a little, Ian draped a wet sock over the dog's head. Mutt yipped indignantly, and shook himself free before turning to rest his nose on Ian's thigh. Automatically Ian reached out to scratch the spot behind the dog's ragged ear before hitting the shower.

For the first time since she'd been waddling through her last months of pregnancy, Marca was late getting to the office. It was Ian's fault. She'd woken up sobbing from a nightmare, with her mind filled with horrible images prompted by the revelations about his past.

When she should have been showering, she'd been pacing instead. By the time the boys were up and Kimbra was singing over the oatmeal, Marca had gone through an entire pot of French roast coffee. By the time she'd torn through her closet to find the "good luck" blazer she'd retired last year, and snagged two pairs of panty hose by wiggling into them too fast, she'd been two hours behind her usually rigid schedule. Determined to catch up, she'd hit the door to her office with her creative engines already racing, issuing orders as Winston grabbed up his book and scrambled after her to take notes.

She'd been hanging up the phone after taking a call from Scotty Bendix at CableSports network, finalizing arrangements for Saturday's nationally televised game—and smugly congratulating herself for packing four hours of work into two—when her fingers snagged her earring and sent it flying.

Now, as the campanile chimed twelve, she found herself scrambling around on her hands and knees under the big kneehole desk, trying to find the small gold hoop that had belonged to her grandmother. As her fingers combed the rug, dust billowed from the nap, assaulting her nose. Before she could stop herself, she let out a violent sneeze and cracked her head on the underside of the desk.

"*Hell's bells,*" she shouted, then froze when she realized that the door had just opened. Two large, impeccably polished cordovan loafers were suddenly visible in the ten inches of open space between the front of the desk and the floor. Above the shoes, perfectly creased soft wool slacks the color of a dove's wing broke perfectly over the insteps.

Winston invariably wore desert boots, and, of the male acquaintances who might be expected to appear in her office unannounced, Mitch Scanlon was the only one who routinely wore loafers and his were attached to steel braces.

"Having a problem under there, Marca?" Ian's voice had the deep timbre of a man trying very hard not to laugh. "Or are you hiding from someone?"

Her breath huffed out in a little rush of embarrassment flavored with jittery anticipation. "If you must know, I'm looking for a lost earring."

"Having any luck?"

"Not much."

Cheeks flaming, she combed frantic fingers through the plush pile. Relief raced through her when she touched metal, only to fade when she came up with a mangled paperclip, one of those she often twisted into knots when she was engrossed in a conversation.

"Want some help?" he asked, his tone much too innocent. "I'm told I'm pretty good at finding lost things."

She thought about that hard-muscled body folded in next to

hers, thigh to thigh, hip to hip and sucked in. "No thanks. I can manage."

"Uh-huh." He moved, then bent. An instant later he extended his hand palm up under the edge of the desk. "Is this it?"

"Yes, thank you," she said primly, fumbling a little as she removed the small gold loop from his hand. As she did she let her gaze linger on the pale and puckered skin that ran like a manacle around his wide wrist. When she'd caught sight of those scars in San Diego, she'd been hesitant to ask a perfect stranger what kind of wound had caused so much trauma to his flesh, but she'd wondered, just as she wondered now.

Had his wrists been damaged as well as scarred? Was that why he always pushed up his sleeves? And why, she recalled now, he carried a pocket watch?

"Bad day?" he asked with a perfectly straight face as she backed out from under the desk and stood.

"More like hectic," she said as she affixed the hoop to her earlobe. The nerves were back, tingling along the edge of her usually unflappable poise like the hum of an electric charge.

Over the past two and a half years, it had taken Marca considerable effort and a great many hours of internal dialogue to convince herself that the almost violent attraction she'd felt for this man had simply been a symptomatic reaction. That it had been a syndrome of some kind, precipitated by her violent confrontation with those dog-killing gang members on the beach. Sort of like the intense physical attraction a man and woman could feel for each other after close brushes with death—only for her there'd been a hefty measure of gratitude thrown in because Ian had come to her rescue. A perfectly normal and explainable reaction to the fear and the adrenaline surge combined with a little leftover adolescent hero worship, she'd told herself. Just a human quirk, nothing more—and probably such a common one, that clinical psychologists had a name for it, though she'd never troubled herself to look it up.

Well...so much for that theory.

Unless destroying two pairs of panty hose qualified as a traumatic experience, she couldn't blame her reaction to Ian this morning on human nature. Moist palms, a racing heart, a sensation in the pit of her stomach that made her feel as if she had breakfasted on live eels. No two ways around it. This was pure, unadulterated lust. The man had only to level those enigmatic gray eyes her way and her hormones started singing. He was big and slightly rough at the edges, a man who'd never be really tamed—exactly the kind of man she'd always avoided. A lone wolf with something wild and volatile lurking just below the surface.

"I haven't got time to drive into town so I made reservations at the 1889 Room for twelve-fifteen," she blurted out when she realized his expression had turned quizzical. "That's a restaurant on the top floor of the student union, by the way. Named for the year of our founding, in case you haven't guessed. The food's decent enough, and I thought you might enjoy seeing the old photos on the wall."

"Are you always this bossy with the men you date, sugar?" he drawled, reaching out to adjust the collar of her favorite silk shirt.

"Sugar?" she repeated. Because she wanted to lean into his touch, she made herself step back. "I didn't realize you grew up in the South?"

"I didn't." He shoved his hand into the pocket of his slacks. "I tend to pick up the local accent wherever I go. Guess I just haven't been here long enough to exchange Florida vowels for your Oregon twang."

"We don't twang," she said, far too aware of the flutters in her stomach.

"Don't get me wrong, sugar," he said, his voice low and intimate. "I like that crisp way you have of snapping out words. Makes me feel as though I should brace back and salute."

She couldn't quite prevent the laugh that escaped. "That I'd love to see."

Smiling a little, he pulled a watch from his pocket. Nickel-plated and thicker than most she'd seen, it had none of the trappings of a gentleman's timepiece. It had been made for railroad conductors, he'd told her in San Diego, and was extremely accurate.

"Are you ready to leave, or should I amuse myself for a few minutes while you clear the decks?" he asked, his gaze lingering for an instant on the spray of leaves she'd stuck in a crystal bud vase she'd brought from home this morning.

"Give me five minutes to proof this press release so that Winston can get it in shape for distribution."

"No problem."

Ian pocketed his watch again, then glanced around for a chair. The nearest one was presently occupied by a child's rag doll. A little girl with china blue eyes and yellow hair, dressed in a pink-and-white checked dress with a kind of apron thing over it. He'd seen one very like it before. Two in fact. Tucked under a Christmas tree. For a split second he thought he was going to be sick before he beat back the pain. Still, his hand shook a little as he carefully propped it against a stack of books on the desk before settling his butt in the chair.

"Friend of yours, is she?" he asked when she glanced up.

"No, a present for Nan Scanlon. She turns two in three months." She opened a folder and picked up her pen which she waved like a baton at the doll. "In case you don't realize treasure when you see it, *this* is a Darling Clementine, which is the latest rage among the toddler set. The stores here are out of them, so Winston bought this one in Portland when he went up to visit his folks over the weekend."

"Nice of him." Careful to keep his gaze away from the stupid doll, he shoved down in the chair and stretched out his legs.

"Oh, Win will do anything for Nan. She's our resident charmer. By the time she was a year old she had just about everyone on staff in love with her. Her daddy is already talking about convent school. He also adores her."

"Yeah, well, some fathers are like that." His voice came out flat and cold. A dead giveaway to anyone who knew him well that he was hurting badly—and no one had ever known him that well.

She made a little sound, and he braced himself, his gaze sweeping the room. Satisfied that the place was secure, he returned his attention to her face. Her eyes were bright with unshed tears.

"I'm sorry, Ian," she apologized softly. "I should have realized."

He felt a quick roll of panic before he slammed it down. He started to reach for his cigarettes, then remembered the No Smoking signs he'd seen damn near everywhere in the building.

"Realized what?" he asked, catching the quick, nervous clenching of her fingers around the pen.

"That the doll might remind you of your daughters." She hesitated, then grabbed the doll and stuffed it into one of the bottom drawers. "I can be incredibly thoughtless sometimes. It's one of my worst failings."

He iced his mind. She'd surprised him, and that was dangerous. Before things went any further, he'd damn well better find out what else she knew. "Who told you?" he asked, careful to shade his voice toward nonchalant.

She looked a little flustered. "Carly. Dr. Scanlon. She needed to be sure you were really who you said you were before she opened personnel records to you, so she checked you out with a friend who works in Washington."

He'd pegged the lady president as one savvy, tough lady. He was glad to see he hadn't lost his touch. He was less sanguine about her running straight to Marca with the info she'd collected.

"This friend, does he work at Treasury?"

She shook her head. "If you want to know his name, I'm sure Carly will tell you. I just don't feel it's my place." She almost pulled off a smile. He gave her points for trying. "Even college types have their sources."

"Whoever he is, he's got juice. Otherwise, no way could he access my service record."

Outside, the bell tower he'd seen in the quadrangle below bonged out the four notes signifying the quarter hour. Twelve-fifteen. Ian shifted and tried to ignore the craving for a cigarette. "So this 'source' told your friend and she told you."

"Yes. She knew I'd be interested."

He let his curiosity show. "Because we once slept together?"

"Yes." She dropped her gaze. "He told her about your undercover work. And that it cost you your family. I'm so terribly sorry."

"It happens," he said, getting to his feet so fast she started. "You about ready?"


"It wasn't Lewis's infidelity that bothered me so much," Marca said with an edgy grin. "He and I had pretty much fizzled out by then, anyway, but Darlene had been a whiz at blue-skying slogans. I would have kept her on, but when she told me she was pregnant with Lewis's baby—and then asked for a raise in order to buy a bigger condo—it was just a little over the top even for me." She lifted her napkin to her lips. "I heard later that she found him in bed with the au pair."

"Life in the nineties," Ian replied, taking a sip of coffee from the cup he'd asked the waiter to keep filled. For the caffeine buzz, he'd told Marca, to replace the nicotine since the restaurant didn't allow smoking.

They were halfway through the blackberry cheesecake, and it hit her suddenly: as she'd done in San Diego, she'd been doing the lion's share of the talking. No matter what subject she introduced, he'd led her back to herself. Deftly, subtly, Ian had gradually shifted the conversation from a discussion of the college and its history to a recitation of her own life. Before she'd realized what was happening he'd charmed her into telling him of her growing-up years in Henderson and the fierce determination she'd had then to escape from a future as a housewife, office assistant or fruit packer which, in those days, were just about the only options available to a female without a college education.

From there, he'd teased and bullied and cajoled her into recounting her adventures in the Big Apple.

The 1889 Room wasn't large, but the restaurant was a perfect little jewel of Victorian opulence. With its mellow cherry wood paneling, deep burgundy upholstery, authentic antiques and two stained-glass windows, it was a classy place, one that had, since its opening night, hosted its share of intimate candlelit dinners and high-powered lunches. It was Marca's favorite place to take visiting dignitaries and generous benefactors.

Ian seemed suitably impressed. He also looked perfectly at ease as he'd seated her. Marca hadn't missed the curious glances sent their way by the other diners, mostly faculty members or upper-echelon staff. The social director, Georgiana Boski, had darn near taken a bite of her wineglass as they'd walked past.

Marca had to admit the man did look superb. Mouth-wateringly handsome, in fact. Not even the bulky knit of the Irish fisherman's sweater could soften the all-but-lethal impact of the hard-packed muscle and sinew beneath. It was rather like the iron fist in the velvet glove, she thought.

"Do you miss the city?" he asked.

"Not really." She put down her fork and pushed aside her dessert plate. "How about you? Do you miss San Diego?"

"No." He forked the last of his cheesecake into his mouth and swallowed. "You gonna eat that?" he asked, eyeing the half-eaten slice she'd pushed aside.

"Be my guest," she said, pushing it across the snowy damask.

He exchanged one plate for the other. "Tell me about this high roller who sent you the long-stemmed jobs. Is it serious?"

She leaned back, her hands lightly gripping the arms of the Queen Anne chair. "Ian, am I under suspicion of something?"

He narrowed his gaze as he swallowed. "Not that I know of, why? Do you have a guilty conscience?"

Because that hit a little too close to the mark, she lifted her water glass and took a sip to settle herself. "We've been here nearly an hour and you've spent most of the time asking me questions about myself."

He leveled his gaze directly on hers, and she felt the gentle slam of leashed power. "Most women take it as a compliment when a man's interested enough to ask."

"Interested because you want to get me into bed?"

"And because you intrigue me." One side of his mouth slanted. "It's been a long time since I've been inclined to let anyone call the shots for me."

"Anyone, meaning female, you mean."

"Anyone, meaning *male* or female." Frowning a little he pushed his sleeves higher before shoving aside the plate in order to rest his forearms on the table. "Mostly I work alone because I don't want the responsibility that comes with close relationships that develop between partners. But I also work alone because I've never been one to take to the kind of restrictions and limits that are imposed by even a temporary partnership, sexual or otherwise."

"Is that a warning?"

"Nope. Another compliment. I'm willing to make an exception with you." His grin flashed, tumbling a few of her hastily erected defenses. "In other words, sugar, I'm willing to let you have your way with me."

A fresh flurry of nerves assaulted the pit of her stomach. "Does that mean I can get out the whips and chains?"

His eyes went flat and hard for the span of a breath before they turned lazy. "If that's what turns you on, although I thought we'd try the cuddling and stroking approach first."

Marca drew a slow breath, then let a smile bloom. "Are you always this pushy with your dates—sugar?"

He frowned, then burst out laughing. She found herself grinning, absurdly pleased that she'd put a devil's sparkle in those eyes, if only for a few beats.

"I think I'm going to enjoy getting to know you, Marcella Kenworthy," he drawled as the waiter approached with the coffeepot. This time Marca accepted a cup.

"I know you haven't had much time yet, but have you managed to find out anything about Renfrew?" she asked after a sip.

He leaned back and angled his body so that he could stretch his legs. His face changed, hardened. It was a subtle thing. A fractional tightening of his facial muscles, a narrowing of his gaze, yet she sensed the burn of deep emotion beneath the steely control.

"He's here, I feel it."

"Where?"

He shook his head. His big hand was curled around his coffee cup, which seemed almost tiny in comparison. "Someplace isolated. A place where he could train his recruits." He glanced toward the Cascade mountains beyond their window table. "Up there, maybe."

Marca followed his gaze with hers. "I know someone who lives on Daily's Mountain. I could ask him if he's noticed any strangers in the area."

Though his mouth curved a little, she felt a sudden spine-tingling tension. "Someone?"

She felt heat climb her neck. "A friend. Richard Hartson. He's a very pleasant man. A true gentleman. I think you'd like him."

His expression as he glanced around the cozy room disputed that. "Depends on how many tweedy jackets with elbow patches he owns," he said laconically.

A quick look around had her grinning. One in every three men in the restaurant was garbed in tweed—with leather patches on the sleeves. By way of contrast Ian seemed larger and far more masculine in his casual attire.

"So far I've only seen Richard wear tweed once," she admitted, struggling against an urge to smile. "A very nice Harris weave."

"Figures."

"He's a gunsmith and runs a mail-order business dealing with antique weapons. I'll introduce you if you'd like."

"I don't like." He sighed. "But I'll talk to him. Renfrew might have brought a weapon in for repair, although that's a long shot. Still, your friend might have heard the sound of gunfire. If he knows his stuff, he might even be able to give me some idea of the type of weapon."

"Just from the sound?"

He slanted her a look. "It's possible for someone who's familiar with firearms."

"Like you?"

"What do you think?"

"I think there are a lot of things about you I don't want to know," she said with perfect truth before taking another sip of the restaurant's special blend. "Is it true that you were Renfrew's second-in-command?"

His face hardened into taut lines. "Believe me, Marca, that's one of the things you don't want to know."

"Was it bad?" She had to know just how much blood he had on the hands that very conceivably would hold her sons in the very near future.

"Bad enough." He shifted until he could pull his watch from his pocket. "Much as I hate to give up your company, sugar, I have an appointment at two with the sheriff's detective who's investigating this latest attack on Professor Matsuda."

Marca signaled the waiter for the check, then reached for her purse. "I can't think of anyone less deserving of that kind of attack than Ted Matsuda. He's just about the nicest, gentlest soul I know."

"That's the way it works with bullies, Marca," he said tersely as he returned his watch to his pocket. "They make it a point never to pick on anyone who can fight back."

"Bastards," she muttered.

"Yeah."

The waiter arrived with the check, which he started to put at Marca's elbow. "I'll get it," Ian said.

"Next time," Marca told him, reaching for her purse.

"This is my party, son," Ian drawled, stopping the young man cold.

"Yes, sir," he said, backing away.

"Is this on the government?" she asked as he pulled out his wallet and dropped several bills atop the check.

"No way, sugar. This is strictly personal." He rose to help her with her chair. Marca felt the curious looks of her colleagues as she led the way to the anteroom where she'd hung her raincoat. She could almost hear the gossip mill revving up.

"Are you free at four?" he asked, taking the coat from her hands and holding it for her to slip into.

"Why?" she asked, tipping a glance at him as she pushed her arms into the sleeves.

"Matsuda doesn't know me," he said, gliding his palms over the shoulders of her coat before adjusting her collar. "I need to talk to him, and I figured having you there would reassure him, encourage him to talk to me." Instead of removing his hands, he settled them to her shoulders again, holding her immobile just inches in front of his body.

"I can't imagine why he would hold back," she said, her voice hitching as he leaned closer. Though she knew it was impossible, she felt as though the heat of his body was penetrating her clothing to warm the bare skin beneath.

"People do strange things after a violent attack," he said, his voice low and intimate next to her ear. "Afraid to talk about what happened sometimes."

"I'll have to check my calendar."

"I'll count on it." He lifted a hand to gently tug her hair from beneath the coat. "You smell irresistible."

Before she could reply, he slid his mouth over the sensitive skin beneath her ear, then touched his tongue to the pulse he'd turned frantic. She gasped, then jerked free, her skin burning where his lips had been.

"MacDougall, did anyone ever tell you to practice a little restraint?"

"Too many times to count. I generally ignore it."

"Take my advice, don't make this one of those times." Too impatient to wait for the elevator, she stalked toward the door to the stairs.

"Guess that's one thing your informant forgot to mention," he said, laughter in his voice as his big hand reached the knob an instant before hers.

"What's that?" she demanded as she preceded him into the stairwell.

"I hate taking advice."

## Chapter 7

Ian hated hospitals. In his experience—and it was considerable, given the fact he'd been shot three times in the line of duty—the damn places were only one notch above some medieval torture chamber. His memories of the three "sentences" he'd served in places very much like Bradenton Falls General Hospital were vivid and uniformly rotten—long hours of unrelieved tedium interspersed with periods of intense discomfort and, on one or two memorable occasions, teeth-gritting humiliation.

Even worse, though, had been the times when he'd stood at the bedside of victims, his own feelings buttoned up tight and his gut in a knot.

So far the lunch with Marca had been the bright spot in the leaden day, he decided as he and Marca crossed the small hospital lobby, heading toward the bank of elevators. After leaving her office, with her promise to rearrange her schedule so that she could accompany him into Bradenton Falls still sweet on his mind, he'd driven to the sheriff's office in the county seat of Glenville. As he'd suspected, he'd found a wary friendliness and a laid-back operation that nevertheless appeared to run smoothly enough—at least for the kind of small-town trouble they mostly handled.

On the sunny side of forty, Detective John Brandt was short, stocky and balding, with twinkling blue eyes and an infectious laugh. Brandt had pictures of a pretty ginger-haired wife and three kids plastered all over his crowded cubicle.

When they'd finally gotten down to business, his conversation with the easy-going detective hadn't yielded much in the way of clues, but Brandt *had* been able to tell him a lot about the area, and most specifically, the seedier dives where skinheads and bikers tended to congregate on a rum-soaked Saturday night.

He'd been late leaving the county seat, which was twenty miles on the other side of the campus from Bradenton Falls, and consequently had been twenty minutes late picking Marca up at her office.

The door to 221 was open, and they entered quietly, just in case the professor was sleeping. The room was small and as gloomy as the day outside. The two chairs for visitors were empty.

The man in the bed was lying motionless, his head turned toward the window. An IV was attached to one arm, and a portable stand equipped with a variety of electronic monitors stood nearby, as though ready in case he took a turn for the worse—or perhaps had recently been disconnected and were waiting to be removed.

Ian sized up the man as a little below average height and weight, with graying black hair and fine-boned build—no match for the kind of bruisers Renfrew preferred.

At the sound of Marca's low, gentle greeting, the professor turned to look at them standing by his bed. The instant he caught sight of Ian standing there, fear tore across his battered features. The hand that wasn't bandaged groped toward the call button looped around the bed's aluminum railing. Only Marca's murmur of reassurance stopped him.

"It's okay, Ted. He's a friend."

Matsuda's face was a mass of bruises and cuts, and so puffy the features were grossly distorted. One eye was swollen nearly shut, and a wide piece of adhesive held the bridge of his nose in place.

"'Lo, Marca," he mumbled, then winced and closed his eyes for a long moment during which his rasping breathing seemed to fill the room.

"Don't talk if it hurts you, Ted," she whispered, sending a pleading glance Ian's way. There were tears in her eyes and pity—and the same flame of outrage he'd seen in her when she'd been kicking and spitting at the bullies on the beach.

"Sir, if this is a bad time, we'll come back later," he said as he moved closer to the side of the bed.

Matsuda took a deep breath and cleared his throat. "Who...?"

"Ian MacDougall, sir," he said, holding his ID within easy sight. "I'd like to ask you a few questions if you're up to it."

Matsuda's bloodshot gaze focused intently on the photo on the laminated card before lifting to study Ian himself. Studying the educator in turn, Ian saw strength and courage and quiet determination in the man's thin—and terribly battered—face.

"You know...identity of those...animals?" Matsuda said, with what was clearly painful effort.

Ian returned the case to his pocket before admitting the truth. "No, sir, only a strong suspicion. I was hoping you could help slip some pieces into place."

"Don't...remember much. Told sheriff."

"Yes, sir. I've seen the report and your statement, but if it wouldn't tax you too much, I'd like to show you a picture and ask you a few questions of my own."

The man attempted a smile, earning Ian's admiration. "Fire away."

"It bothers you, doesn't it?"

Marca watched Ian take a moment to shift his attention from the fog-shrouded road to her question. Even then he spared her only a quick glance.

"What 'it' are you talking about, sugar?" The drawl was lazy, the voice flavored with a wicked seductiveness she knew was designed to melt female resistance, but his gaze was shuttered, his thoughts and certainly his feelings carefully locked away.

She shifted in the close confines of the Jeep's bucket seat in order to better see his face. "Seeing someone suffering," she amplified. "It bothered you."

"I've seen worse," he admitted, moving one of his big shoulders. "In my business you get used to it, or you find another line of work."

"Of course. That's why you promised Ted to talk to the sheriff about assigning someone to watch over his house."

"Standard procedure, something the deputy who caught the case should have already figured out. The bastards might go after the daughter, since she's of so-called 'mixed blood.'"

"Who isn't?" Marca muttered.

"Me for one. Got MacDougall on one side, Connors on the other—and a few English types thrown in."

"No wonder Renfrew took to you."

The look he gave her was glittering steel. "It was a part I played, Marca. Don't ever think it wasn't." The words came low and fast and lethal, with a fierce intensity that momentarily stunned her into silence.

"It must have been terrible for you."

His lashes flickered, but his gaze remained fixed on the road. In the sudden silence the wipers thudded in a dispirited rhythm and the rain pounded the Jeep's top.

"Your friend, the professor, he'll make a good witness if I can shake loose a few more details."

"You're a very good, uh, interrogator, I guess you'd call it. In a matter of twenty minutes you took him from being absolutely convinced he'd told the sheriff everything he remembered to helping him put together a fairly detailed picture of the ringleader."

He braked for a slow-moving pickup, then checked the mirror and sped up to pass. "Everything but his face."

"Yes, but the rest was good." She thought about the details Ian had drawn from Ted with patient probing and intuitive listening. A large, burly young man easily as tall as Ian or a bit taller, with a barrel chest and a hand that was missing the tip of the little finger. A man who moved like an athlete.

"I assume you're going to check with the athletic department for someone who answers that description?" she asked after a moment's reflection.

"First thing tomorrow." Calm again, his gaze lingered long enough to edge her toward uneasiness. "Scanlon's the athletic director, right?"

"Yes, since Pete Gianfracco retired to marry Carly's mom."

He grunted, then flipped the blinker for a left turn. Startled, Marca peered through the windshield to get her bearings. When she saw the distinctive sign for the Oak Manor Motel, she sucked in hard.

"The college is two miles ahead," she said, sitting straighter.

"Yeah, I know. I have something to take care of first."

She felt a flare of panic. "Can't it wait? I have to get home."

He downshifted, checked the mirror and swung the Cherokee into a neat left before accelerating up the slight incline toward the motel parking lot.

"Heavy date?" he asked, tossing her a hooded look. He looked tired, she realized. And a little lonely.

"A meeting, actually. With some very important people."

"What time do you have to be there?"

"Six."

Kimbra was officially off duty then—unless Marca had something special scheduled in which case they juggled their schedules. Though Kimbra was almost always flexible, Marca was careful not to take advantage of her young friend.

He pulled into a spot near the end of the two-story, white-clapboard structure. The rain was coming down in a steady sheet, puddling the paved lot and dripping from the eaves.

On occasion a guest of the college had been booked in here, when the official guest suite in the mansion was filled. Marca had frequently been the official hostess and chauffeur. The best room was on the second floor at the south end. The motel called it a suite since it had a small sitting area at one end equipped with a couch, table and two chairs, and a minibar.

Ian's room appeared to be on the opposite end, close to the ice machine and the lobby. He parked in front of number 2.

"Ten minutes, okay?" He made it sound like a question. She suspected it wasn't. Still, she glanced at her watch. It was nearly five-fifteen. She had a few minutes.

"Okay, but no longer."

She waited while he circled the Jeep and opened the passenger door, then let him help her down from the high-slung frame. "Thanks," she said, withdrawing her hand from his.

"All part of the service, ma'am," he said as he shut the door.

She heard the dog's excited yipping the moment Ian slipped the key into the lock, and a smile bloomed in her mind.

"You kept him?"

His jaw set itself in belligerent lines. "Couldn't find anyone foolish enough to take the good-for-nothing beast."

The quick stormy glare he shot her dared her to challenge him at her peril. Too diplomatic to give in to the laugh bubbling in her throat she merely pursed her lips and nodded.

"Better let me go in first," he muttered, withdrawing the key before turning the knob. "Damn mongrel's got lousy manners."

He opened the door slowly, keeping his body between the parking lot and the interior. Half-hidden behind his bulk, Marca had a fast impression of four scrambling paws, glossy brown fur and a lolling tongue before Ian braced for the assault.

Though a little gruff, his deep laughter was almost as infectious as his sons'—and utterly beguiling. Watching him trying to fend off the adoring canine's sloppy kisses had her heart doing a sweet, slow roll in her chest.

The man with the lethal eyes and vicious, dirty job was a stranger, one she wasn't yet certain she dared let into her life. But the man now wrestling with a furry heap of canine adoration— *he* was the man she'd never been able to forget. The sweet, compassionate Ian MacDougall who'd paced the waiting room of the animal emergency hospital with her in the dead of night, chain-smoking and swearing under his breath over a dog he'd never seen before. The virile, wildly attractive man who'd made love to her as though his salvation depended on pleasing her.

"Behave yourself, you stupid mutt. Can't you see there's a lady present?" he grumbled on another boyish laugh that curled like a smile inside her.

The dog barked wildly, its ragged tail beating the air. "I can't believe how good he looks," she said, laughing as Ian took a tongue assault squarely on his averted cheek.

It was true. As large as a border collie, which it only vaguely resembled, the animal was clearly of indeterminable breed and not even remotely pretty, or even cute, with its outsized head, oddly tufted ears and sagging skin. But the mottled coat shone with good health and a recent brushing, and his eyes were bright.

"Say hello to the lady who saved your worthless hide, you ungrateful mutt," Ian ordered, grabbing the dog's collar, which jangled with the tags of inoculations and licensing—and permanent ownership.

"Hello, baby," Marca crooned, stepping around Ian to present the back of her hand for a sniff. She got a sloppy lick and eager "woof" instead.

"Yeah, I know, she's something special," Ian said, grinning at her as she dropped her purse to the floor and knelt beside it to nuzzle the animal's head. The thick fur smelled of baby shampoo, and she thought of her babies. She'd been considering a pet for them. A kitten, she'd been thinking.

Too rapidly to curtail, an image of the three of them wrestling with their dad and his dog formed in her mind, bringing with it a bone-deep longing, one she warned herself to banish instantly, before it took hold and clouded her judgment.

"What did you name him?" she asked, turning to look at him again.

"I didn't."

"Why not?"

He shrugged. "I figure it wasn't right since I don't intend to keep him."

"Don't you have to call him something when you want him to come to you?"

"Mostly he just does what he pleases. Same as me. Sometimes we end up in the same place."

"C'mon, Ian, you have to call him something," she insisted, narrowly dodging a wet doggie kiss on the lips. It landed on her ear instead, and she giggled.

He leaned a shoulder against the doorjamb and watched her struggling to keep the dog from knocking her to the floor in his eagerness to lick her face. "Guess he might answer to 'Mutt' if pressed."

"Then he does have a name."

"Not to me."

Frowning a little, he stepped across the threshold and lit a cigarette, inhaling deeply, the pleasure of the first taste smoothing some of the lines in his face.

"Hold still, Mutt, and let me look at you," she ordered, holding the dog's face between her hands. One eyelid drooped, and the eye itself was unfocused, and one ear was ruffled where it had been shredded. But the knife slash across the muzzle had healed, leaving only a thin, neat line of pale skin.

"I just knew you'd be a handsome fellow under all that blood and grime," she murmured, rubbing her chin against his soft head. "Such a brave boy you were. Trying to protect me."

Sudden hot—and totally unexpected—tears welled in her eyes as she remembered the desperately wounded animal's valiant attempts to tear into one of the men who'd shoved her onto the sand. The poor thing had been gashed and bleeding, with the bone of one leg protruding through the skin, and, yet, he'd still tried to defend her.

"Oh, hell," she muttered, quickly swiping a hand across her face. It didn't help.

One instant Ian was leaning against one of the posts holding up the overhang. The next he'd thrown away his cigarette and was pulling her into his arms. She went instinctively, her arms going around his wide waist in order to meld them closer. Using her nose, she burrowed her way beneath the rain-spotted jacket to find a warm, dry spot for her cheek to rest against his shoulder.

A quiet word from Ian had Mutt padding over to one corner where several sweatshirts had been arranged in what was obviously intended to be a bed. Tail dragging, the dejected dog turned around twice, then settled himself comfortably, his muzzle on his front paws and a worried look on his funny face.

She closed her eyes and hugged Ian tighter, trying to scrub away her tears against his soft sweater. She didn't realize her shoulders were shaking until she felt a hand rubbing her back.

"Cut it out, honey, okay?" he pleaded, his voice verging on the panic even the strongest of men seemed to feel when faced with a crying female. "I'm sorry I blew it, but I figured it would please you to see the ugly mutt again."

"I'm just so glad you *kept* him," she said fiercely, her fingers digging into the wool at the small of his back.

He cleared his throat. "Yeah, well, like I said, it's only temporary."

She smiled against his chest, and the knot in her throat eased. His body was solid and steady, his arms holding her close, yet not crushing her as she knew they could. The mingled scents of the cigarette he'd just smoked and the wind that had ruffled his hair clung to him, reminding her of the night they'd given and taken comfort in each other's arms.

She lifted her head and, looking up at him, tried a smile. It felt a little watery, but his eyes crinkled. "I must have been suffering from some kind of delayed reaction," she told him with a little nod for punctuation. "I'm over it now."

"Happens that way sometimes." His tone was gruff, his face taut. Darkly compelling in its stark beauty. A strong face for a strong man, seasoned by a life on the edge and anything but perfect: the bridge of his nose was a good quarter inch off center, and there was a small half-moon scar etched into his right temple at the spot where the thick black eyebrow ended. His eyes were by far his best feature, sometimes silver, sometimes charcoal, and rimmed with a double row of lashes. When he smiled at her, his eyes crinkled into new lines at the corners, and it was as though they shared something very intimate. Very special and rare. She couldn't define it, nor did she fully understand it.

A wave of longing ran through her, as strong as a shudder but infinitely sweeter. The need she felt for him was elemental and primitive. Instinctual. Her breathing quickened, and her face suddenly felt hot and itchy.

It was time to leave. Now. But when she tried to pull away, his arms tightened.

"Ian, I...uh, I think—"

"Don't think," he whispered fiercely, an instant before his mouth sought hers in a gentle, testing kiss that sent heat spiraling to her womb. She melted, the years of her heart's longing for him overcoming the reticence forced on her by her head. It felt so right to be in his arms, she realized, as she returned his kiss with an eagerness that all but overwhelmed her.

His mouth was ardent, his eagerness matching her own. He lifted a hand and threaded his fingers through her hair until he could cup the back of her head. His body shifted until his thighs bracketed hers.

She felt his arousal only partially contained by the soft material of his trousers, and the memory of his hard, hot flesh sliding between her legs and entering her slow inch by slow inch, had her breath catching.

As though he were privy to her thoughts—or perhaps lost in his own memories of that special moment—he groaned against her mouth. Fingers splayed, he pressed his hand against the curve of her spine, urging her more tightly against him.

Out of air, she pulled away, her face hot and her heart racing. His expression was intense, his eyes hungry as he looked down at her. And yet, it wasn't simply the desire of one body for another that sizzled between them. That she could have resisted. Had resisted many times with other men. But the desire to love and cherish was far more powerful—and much more difficult to resist.

"Stay," he urged. His voice rasped with the same need and

urgency she felt pounding in her veins. It was the same with the heat she felt pouring from him. A fire in the soul, a phrase she'd read once and never really understood until now.

She wanted him desperately. Now. Forever. At the moment it didn't seem to matter.

"I can't," she murmured, lifting her hand to that stark, lonely face where the shadows of desperate sacrifices still lingered. "I have obligations."

His mouth gentled, seducing her. "Yeah, I forgot." His voice was thick, his eyes glittering and needy. The same mix of desperate emotions she'd felt in him before.

"I can come back. Later, when my...meeting is finished." Even as she said the words, she realized she was quite possibly making a serious mistake, yet it didn't seem to matter.

He covered her hand with his, trapping her palm against his cheek. Beneath her fingers she felt the stretch and play of hard muscle as he smiled. The emotion in his eyes threatened her knees.

"Give me your address. I'll wait for you at your place."

She drew a shaky breath. "No, I have a foreign student living with me. I'll come here."

"What time?" he pressed, his gaze intensely focused.

"Eight-thirty. Nine at the latest."

He brought her hand to his mouth and touched the pulse point with the tip of his tongue. She moaned a little, her resolve weakening.

"Stay the night, then," he urged, his breath warm on her skin.

"I want to, but I can't." Still a little dazed at the decision she seemed to have made, she went to her toes and kissed him. As they drew apart, a shudder ran through him, and he dropped his forehead to hers.

"Damn, but I want you, lady," he said, drawing a deep, steadying breath before raising his head again. "More than I should, I suspect."

"And I want you. But for now I think you'd better take me back to the campus before I lose what's left of my reason."

His sigh was ragged—and heartfelt. ''I like knowing I can rattle the very elegant Ms. Kenworthy, considering how rattled I've been since I looked up to see you standing in the doorway of Dr. Scanlon's parlor, looking like every man's secret dream, in that skimpy little shirt and butt-hugging shorts.''

Before she could reply, he let out a tortured groan and dragged her against him for a very long, very thorough, very satisfying kiss. Marca was still tingling ten minutes later when he dropped her off in front of the administration building.

# Chapter 8

The nursery was by far Marca's favorite room in the house she'd taken apart and put together bit by bit over a period of five years. Tucked under the eaves, with a peaked ceiling and a large window, where an opening had once allowed the hay to be hoisted into the loft, it was warm and cozy, with its sunny yellow paint and the clean scents of soap and baby powder lingering in the air. Originally intended to be a library, the oblong room had floor-to-ceiling shelves built into one wall. Toys and books filled them now. In the years to come the boys would fill them with their own clutter. Treasures and keepsakes and stereo equipment. Perhaps sports trophies or academic awards, or almost certainly, photos of girlfriends.

Marca smiled a little at the thought of her boys falling in love. Someday. In fifteen years or so.

"Make the choo-choo sound, Mama," Trevor ordered, bouncing up and down on his bed. Now that Sean had had his story, his night-night glass of water and his game of kiss-and-tickle, it was Trevor's turn.

It was a nightly ritual she'd devised to make each child feel special and unique—just as she dressed each differently. Each got to choose his own story from the books filling the bright yellow shelves. One story per child, read while she sat on his bed and cuddled him close.

"Choo-choo, Mama, pease."

"Okay, just for you, munchkin."

She cleared her throat, and Trevor snuggled his wiggly, pajama-clad body a little closer, his face alight and his eyes as bright as silvery stars. All three boys were due for a haircut, and thick black curls flopped over his forehead. Like Ian's when the wind had whipped at them in the hospital parking lot.

Warm anticipation as heady as mulled wine filled her at the thought of being with him later. The decision was made, she realized. How could she not share his sons with him, once she'd shared her body? Once he'd shared his with her?

She suspected it wouldn't be easy working through the dynamics of a relationship with a man as restless and driven as Ian. A man with scars on his heart as cruel as the ones on his wrists. But together they could make it work.

A smile curved her lips as she anticipated the joy he would feel when he realized he had three adorable, healthy sons waiting to shower him with love. A family. A home.

Tonight, when she was lying in his arms, she would tell him about the three miracles they had created together.

Tears pricked her eyes as her gaze shifted to the window. Though the miniblinds were shut and the striped draperies closed against the night's chill, she sent a wish to the star she knew twinkled above the thick overcast.

*Help me love enough to heal him.*

"Mama!" Trevor's impatient little voice had her laughing out loud.

"Sorry, darling, Mama was just dreaming a wonderful dream," she murmured, before planting a kiss on those glossy curls.

In the next bed Sean was already snuggled into his pillow, his tattered blanket bunched against his cheek. His eyes were closed and his lashes made little dark crescents on his tanned cheeks.

Ryan was lying on his side, his face a little pale, and Marca frowned.

His forehead had been cool when she'd checked after his bath, and he'd eaten well. Still... After deciding to take his temperature following his story time, she exchanged her frown for a bright smile.

"Ready?" she asked Trevor.

He bobbed his head, his gaze already going to the picture in the book opened on her raised knees.

"'I think I can, I think I can,'" she chugged before imitating the sound of the plucky little engine. Trevor furrowed his brow and chugged right along with her. At almost the same moment, they made whistle sounds, and he dissolved into giggles.

*"Mama?"* Ryan's wavering voice cut through the mirth. One look at his ashen little face had her putting the book aside and hurrying to his side.

"Sweetie, are you sick?" she asked gently, pressing her palm to his forehead. The heat she felt there had her heart in her throat.

"Oh, baby," she whispered, just as he made a gagging sound. She reached for him, but it was too late. He'd already thrown up all over the bed—and her.


The rain had stopped, and only the rhythmic creaking of the rocking chair's eighty-year-old runners broke the silence in Marca's dimly lit bedroom. Nestled in her arms with his cheek against her breast, Ryan had finally settled into a restless doze. Marca herself was wide awake, the fear that had gripped her earlier still tumbling in her head. It was less now, but alive nonetheless.

Down the hall Sean and Trevor were also fast asleep, unaffected so far by the infection that had settled in their brother's left ear. Kimbra, bless her heart, had taken care of the soiled sheets and remade the bed. In the thorough way she had, she'd even sprayed the room with a disinfectant air fresher that still teased Marca's nose when she inhaled too deeply.

Dressed now in her robe, Marca had managed to strip off her

ruined blouse between frantic phone calls to first the pediatrician's service and then to the doctor herself. Ry had simply picked up a bug, Dr. Spears had soothed. Something that was making the rounds in the area. It was scary, yes, but not serious, something Marca had been hard-pressed to believe at first, given the fact that Ryan had been screaming in pain in his nanny's arms at the time.

After soothing Marca's fears, the doctor had promised to phone in a prescription for an antibiotic, issued calm, detailed orders for his immediate care, which Marca had made the woman repeat, and then prescribed a glass of medicinal wine for Marca herself.

Marca had sent Kimbra into town for the medicine, then followed every instruction to the letter—with the exception of the wine. In her presently wired state, she was afraid the alcohol would completely muddle what was left of her brain.

As she rocked her baby in her arms as she'd done so often in the past two years, she let her eyes drift closed. Now that the crisis seemed past, her head ached abysmally, and exhaustion seemed layered into her very marrow. But Meg Spears's instructions to bathe Ryan in tepid water had brought the fever down from its terrifying high of 103 to a far-less-terrifying half degree above normal, and some of the color had returned to Ryan's cheeks.

The antibiotic Kimbra had brought back from the hospital's emergency pharmacy was already pumping through his system, and the baby aspirin had helped to ease some of the pain in his ear. But he was still hurting, which meant she was hurting, too.

"Is he sleeping?" Kimbra whispered from the doorway. A native of South Africa, Kimbra Ruenda was as small as an average twelve-year-old, with the beautiful dusky skin color and exotic features of her Bushman ancestors and the fine-boned grace of a dancer.

"Yes, finally," Marca whispered back. "Poor little guy, he wore himself out crying."

"Why don't you let me take him for a while?"

Marca shook her head. "You have a research paper to finish."

"It is nearly done," the pretty young woman murmured as she

entered. Marca saw the steaming mug in her hand then, and smiled her gratitude. "I thought you could use some tea," Kimbra added, carefully setting the mug onto the small table by the chair. "It's chamomile, for the nerves."

"You're a sweetheart, thank you."

Marca smoothed a hand over Ryan's silky curls and sent a fast little prayer of gratitude to the god of harried mothers for sending her Kimbra.

Desperately in need of good doctors, the people in Kimbra's rural township had raised the money to send her to the States, where she hoped to enter medical school after completing her undergraduate work in physiology at Bradenton. As part of its ongoing program to help disadvantaged foreign students, Bradenton had offered her a full scholarship, and Marca had offered her a home in exchange for help with the boys.

In the eighteen months since Kimbra had been part of her extended family, Marca had come to think of her as a younger sister instead of an employee. She'd also become fond of Kimbra's fiancé, Dennis Swenson, a husky blue-eyed, flaxen-haired Nebraska farm boy who'd come to Bradenton to play football for his childhood hero, Mitch Scanlon.

"Poor Dennis. He came over to see you and ended up helping you clean up a mess. Please tell him for me that I owe him a steak dinner as a thank-you for all his help."

Kimbra's smile was soft and dewy. "He is used to such messes from his brothers and sisters."

Marca drew in a weary breath. "He's a treasure."

Adoration shone in her sloe eyes as she nodded. "Before he left, he said to tell you he's sure Ry will be fine. Little boys are tough."

"Before he left? Already?"

"Yes. He didn't want to, but he's very careful to honor the coach's curfew."

Curfew? Surely it wasn't close to eleven. A quick glance at the clock had reality returning with a rush. "Oh no, Ian!"

How could she have forgotten?

"Marca, is something wrong?"

"I hope not." Careful to keep from jarring Ry awake, she eased herself straighter and shot a beseeching look Kimbra's way. "Honey, do me a big favor and bring me the phone and the phone book—and hurry."

Renfrew stood under the red, white and black flag emblazoned with the swastika and clenched fist of the New Aryan Freedom Brigade and watched the three burly recruits accepting the congratulations of their fellow Brigade members.

His blood still ran hot from the soul-stirring speeches each had made, pledging their bodies, hearts and minds to the battle for racial supremacy. To a man, they were all superb examples of genetic purity and breeding. Renfrew was supremely proud to be their leader.

One, the strapping nineteen-year-old son of exemplary upper-middle-class parents of German descent had already won the right to display the badge of a warrior in the cause. Tonight, before he left, Renfrew himself would tattoo a cobweb in the young man's left armpit, marking him as a man who'd shed the blood of an inferior. Had he killed the yellow bastard Matsuda, the web would have been etched under the right arm.

That would come soon enough, Hutch knew. By winter's end this cell of the Brigade would be up to full strength.

"Krauss has the look of a leader," he said when his second-in-command appeared at his elbow, a glass of celebratory cider in his hand.

At seventy-two, Jackson Smith was old enough to be Renfrew's father, but the years had been kind to the native Oregonian, and most of his fellow professors considered him a decade younger.

"With training and experience, I think he'll be as skilled at assassination as Jack, Jr.," Jackson declared with a quiet pride.

"I agree. Peterson has possibilities, as well, although he's somewhat shorter than the ideal soldier."

"Perhaps, though his performance on the football field has shown him to be a fierce competitor."

Renfrew chuckled. "He certainly proved it last Saturday, didn't he? Bloodying the nose of that *African* quarterback."

The thought that the descendent of slaves was actually shouting out orders to white men, even on a football field, had bile rising to his throat. Soon, though, all that would change.

Jackson nodded, his expression suddenly pinched with distaste. His hatred of his racial inferiors had been born almost fifty years ago in the frozen squalor of a North Korean prisoner-of-war camp, and his dedication to the NAFB was absolute. In spite of their differences in age and education, Renfrew counted the professor as a friend as well as comrade.

"Peterson has already proven his devotion to our cause by uncovering another case of interracial fornication." Smith's gaze glittered with a sudden anger that Renfrew shared. "A fellow player by the name of Dennis Swenson and a black woman from South Africa."

Perhaps it was time to escalate the intensity of their efforts, Renfrew mused as he cast a thoughtful eye over the crowd of muscular young animals ready and eager to follow his every command.

"Give Peterson my compliments and tell him to take care of this situation as he sees fit. Of course, you will remind him to leave no clues and make sure no one dies. The time is not yet right. But soon, Smith. Very soon."

The motel parking lot, well lit and pockmarked with puddles, was nearly full when Ian returned from running off his disappointment. Most of the license tags were out of state, something to be expected in a college town. Nevertheless, habit had him skimming the makes and models, memorizing them in his head. One, a cherry red Civic had a Just Married sign tucked in the back window.

Ian had been outside on latrine duty with Mutt when the newlyweds had arrived a little after eight. A cute couple in their mid-twenties looking smugly happy and embarrassingly eager to rip each other's clothes off.

At the time Ian had been looking forward to doing a little clothes ripping himself and had returned their greetings as they'd unlocked the door next to his. The chubby, laughing bride with flowers in her pale hair and stars in her eyes had flashed him a sweet smile when he'd wished them happiness.

"Forever and ever," she'd said, casting an adoring gaze at her brand-new husband whose chest expanded visibly at her obvious reverence.

Now, as Ian passed their door, he felt a heavy weight settling over his tired shoulders. Disillusionment was a bitch, he thought as he slipped the key from the pocket of his running shorts and inserted it in the lock.

The message light on the phone was blinking when he walked in. It infuriated him that he'd looked even before he'd crossed the threshold. It infuriated him more to realize he wanted her to have an excuse he could accept without sacrificing too much of the self-respect he'd worked so hard to reclaim.

Mutt greeted him at the door, tail wagging and tongue lolling as usual. After devouring his treat, the mangy beast walked to the door and whined, looking back over his shoulder expectantly.

"In a minute."

Tossing the pathetic beggar another treat, Ian walked to the phone and called the desk. He let it ring for a full minute, the strident buzzing hammering in his head. There was no answer. A quick check of the watch he'd left on the dresser told the tale. It was half past midnight. The switchboard closed down at eleven and didn't open again until six.

Absently winding the heavy old Hamilton that had never failed him since he'd bought it from one of his uncle's cowpunchers, he fought the urge to pick the lock on the office door.

The security system was a joke, and the manager had the look of a closet boozer about him. By now, Ian figured, the guy was well on his way to his nightly buzz. Even if the manager was stone sober with the hearing of an owl, Ian knew he could be in and out without detection.

He was tempted, he admitted as he finished with the watch and glanced again at the blinking red light. He'd bent the law before—yeah, okay, broken the hell out of it on occasion—but with one shaming exception, always when a life was at stake. In this case it was just his ego that was taking a beating.

Much as he hated loose ends, it wouldn't kill him to wait until tomorrow. Besides, bad news was always easier to take in the daylight.

"Right, you stupid cur?"

Mutt poked his muzzle into his hand, then turned and trotted toward the door. At the threshold, he paused and looked back to give an impatient yip.

Needing a smoke, anyway, Ian let him out and waited for Mutt to race toward the fenced area reserved for pets as he'd been accustomed to doing since their arrival. Instead, Mutt went straight to the passenger's side of the Jeep and, letting out an exuberant "woof," jumped up to peer inside.

Ian blew out smoke and scowled at the disloyal beast. "Forget it, slick. The lady didn't show."

Mutt dropped to all fours and padded over to the post where Ian had propped his tired body. *Do something,* his expression seemed to say.

"Hey, I tried," Ian muttered.

Mutt cocked one shaggy ear, a reproachful look in the one, sighted eye.

"Don't look at me like that. Begging's your thing, not mine."

With a dejected yip, Mutt gave Ian a token lick on the back of his hand before padding inside.

Ian walked to the edge of the overhang and looked up. The last of the clouds were drifting toward the east, leaving wisps of silvery smoke behind.

Which star was hers? he wondered, scanning the twinkling pin-pricks that seemed indistinguishable, even in the clarity of the rain-washed air.

*That one? See, Ian, the one with the golden halo? Just below Orion's Belt. That's my very own wishing star, and now, it's yours, too.*

After he'd put her in the rental and watched her drive away that night, he'd stared up at that stupid star, trying to think of a wish. A reason to get through one more empty night. Something to hang a future on. Something—someone—to believe in. He'd come up empty. So empty he didn't have the heart to try again. Just as he didn't have the heart to feel more for a woman than affection. Even that, it seemed, was risky.

Ian finished his cigarette and tossed it into the cement urn filled with sand provided for that purpose before heading inside. Damn, but he was whipped.

Marca tugged the lapels of her robe more tightly against her throat as she left the nursery and headed downstairs. The crisis had passed. Ryan was sleeping peacefully, his skin blessedly cool and all traces of pain smoothed from his face.

Thank heavens for medical science and the resilience of youth, she thought, yawning her way across the living room.

It was still early, not quite dawn. It was so quiet she could hear the sound of her moccasins scuffing against the wide pine planks salvaged from the barn's horse stalls as she entered the kitchen and switched on the light.

The sudden glare seared her retinas, making her flinch. She'd slept poorly, scarcely at all, in fact, and her head was muzzy. After she'd left the message for Ian, she'd paced for what seemed like hours, then tried to sleep. But when she hadn't been padding down the hall to check on Ryan and his brothers, she'd been tossing and turning on sheets that felt hot and sticky against her skin.

Ian would understand, she'd told herself a few dozen times, with varying degrees of certainty. Once she explained...except that she couldn't really. Not without lying. And a lie, even a little fib was just one more way of hurting him.

God knew, he'd suffered enough.

Her breath hitched as she thought about the agony he must have endured when he'd buried his children. More than her mind could take in, she thought as she pried the lid from the two-pound can of Hawaiian blend. More, she suspected, than most parents could endure without veering into despair—or madness.

He'd survived. Through grit and sheer will, she suspected. And courage.

Yes, she had to tell him about the boys, she told herself as she spooned grounds into the filter.

Now that the decision was firm and irrevocable, the question was when...and where?

Not here, certainly, unless she had Kimbra hustle the boys over to Carly's. Or on an outing. No, not with Ryan just recovering. And definitely not someplace public, which pretty much precluded a restaurant or a bar. She grimaced at the thought.

She was really beginning to hate that tangled-web concept, she decided as she set the coffeemaker to brewing. The aroma that filled the silent kitchen made her mouth water and her stomach roil.

She would suggest a rain check, she decided as she impatiently watched the stream of dark brew drizzling into the pot. And go to his room. Tonight. She would take pictures of his sons to show him—and their baby books. When he was ready, she would invite him home to meet them in person.

Shoving her hands into her pockets, she walked to the window overlooking her vegetable garden and gazed up at the sky. As always the sight of her star brought a smile to her lips and a calm to her mind.

"He needs a home," she murmured, "even though he may not realize it yet. An anchor and a haven. And people who love him and need his love in return. Trevor and Sean and Ryan, and their mother." She inhaled a shaky breath. "His family—if he'll have us."

# Chapter 9

High heels clattering furiously against the wood, Marca flew down the stairs and all but ran toward the kitchen. A tune from Paul Simon's "Graceland" album blared from the small boom box on the counter, something with an infectious beat. Kimbra's favorite start-the-day-off-right music. Marca, herself, preferred country, the more twanging guitars and wailing fiddles the better.

Kimbra, dressed in jeans and a Bradenton sweatshirt, with a bright turquoise scarf covering her tightly braided hair, had Sean in her arms, practicing some complicated steps and dips that had him giggling helplessly.

Trevor and Ryan were still seated at the small table near the window where they ate when it was only the three of them. Between bursts of song, Kimbra was wheedling Sean into eating the oatmeal in his bowl instead of using it to fingerpaint figures on the plastic tabletop.

As was the household custom, Marca had gotten the boys up and freshly diapered, while Kimbra showered. Then, in a process resembling a Marx Brothers movie, she and Kimbra managed to get all three settled into their chairs and fed.

While the boys ate, Marca showered and got ready for work. Then she and Kimbra coordinated their schedules for the day. This morning, however, before letting any of her imps out of bed, she'd checked temperatures. All were normal—including Ryan's.

"Kimbra, did I hear the phone ringing?" she asked as she sailed into the roomful of noise.

Kimbra glanced toward the wall phone, then shifted her gaze to the cordless receiver in Marca's left hand. Her confusion apparent, the girl shook her head. "Is there something wrong with that one?"

"Apparently not," Marca said, a trifle curt as she put her briefcase on the floor next to the kitchen's center island. Just in case, however, she pressed the button to check the dial tone and heard a monotonous hum.

"I don't suppose you checked the machine when you came down?" she asked as she exchanged the phone for a towel to wipe away the smear of banana between Ryan's fingers.

Kimbra turned down the volume. "No, but then I'm not expecting a call." She drew back to give Sean a grin. "How about you, handsome boy? Are you expecting some pretty lady-bird to ring you up?"

Sean giggled and shook his head. Kimbra gave him a smacking kiss before setting him on his feet. Marca grinned when she realized he was wearing mismatched slippers again. One tiger face, one puppy dog with floppy ears and a protruding pink tongue.

Her breath stuttered a little as she pictured Mutt waking Ian with a swipe of his slurpy tongue across a hard, unshaven jaw. In the fantasies she'd woven in an endless chain, she'd seen him lying on his stomach, his big arms outstretched, his warrior's face relaxed. At peace for a few hours. Peace she'd given him, along with her body—and her love.

If things had gone as planned, she might have been snuggled against that magnificently male body for most of the night. The feeling of loss all but knocked her over, before she made herself take a mental step back.

As they had been since the moment she'd first held them, her sons were her top priority. Giving them a happy, secure, beloved childhood was paramount—which meant that mommy couldn't let herself become a basket case. Routine was vitally important for children, especially when the house was fairly bulging with rambunctious, mischief-making little boys.

"Sean, sweetie, the tiger goes with the tiger," she said in her patient-mommy voice. "The doggie with the doggie, which belongs to Trev, remember?"

Sean shook his head. "Nope," he said cheerfully before racing off toward the family room and his morning session with Big Bird and the rest of the gang.

"'Sesame Street' time!" Ryan shouted in an echo of his mother's oft-repeated words. He threw down his spoon and jumped up, looking anything but sick as he raced after his brother, still wearing his Pooh Bear bib—and a pair of slippers identical to Sean's.

Bemused, Marca noticed that Trevor's restless little feet were encased in Ryan's bunny slippers. "We need some order in this chaos," she muttered as she picked up the abandoned cereal bowls.

"Trev go, too, Mama?"

Marca shook her head. "Not until you finish your oatmeal, darling."

Trevor's cherub face turned devilish as he poked a finger in the gooey mix of milk and oats. "It's icky."

"It's also good for you, sweetheart. It'll make you grow up big and strong." Like your daddy, she added silently, glancing at the phone that sat there like a lump of hard blue plastic and mysterious electronic gizmos, taunting her.

"What time does Ry see the doctor?" Kimbra asked, opening the daily planner Marca had given her on her second day as a member of the Kenworthy household.

"Two-thirty," Marca replied, retrieving a matching diary from her case. Since today was Tuesday and Kimbra didn't have any classes, she didn't anticipate any major problems. "I can handle that if you can pick up Sean and Trev from day care and take

them to their play date at Alderson House at three. I'll pick them
up on my way home.''

''Right.'' Kimbra jotted a note. ''Dennis and I can handle the
marketing and—''

The phone rang, startling them both. Marca's hand shot out
nearly knocking the portable from the counter before she managed
to grab it up. It rang again before she steadied herself to answer

''Hello?''

''Good morning, my dear. You sound very bright and cheery.''
It was Richard.

''I'm not sure about the bright part,'' she said with a laugh she
hoped wouldn't betray her disappointment. ''How are you, Richard?''

''Hopeful.'' He chuckled. ''I understand there's an old-
fashioned carnival coming to town this weekend. A Bradentor
Falls tradition, according to the morning disk jockey. To raise
money for the fire department.''

''Actually for the firefighters' Christmas fund. They distribute
food baskets and toys to the needy.'' Marca rested her spine
against the counter and watched Trevor creating an oatmeal mas-
terpiece, his little face scrunched up and his tongue clamped between his baby teeth.

''Well, it suddenly struck me that I haven't been to a carnival
since I was a kid,'' Richard continued, his voice soothing and
warm. ''What do you say we bundle up those scamps of yours
and make a day of it? Popcorn, cotton candy, the rides—do it
all?''

Marca poked at a toy truck with the toe of her shoe, trying to
find the words to let him down easily. Last week she would have
jumped at the chance. But now she realized she'd only been thinking about Richard as a place holder. Someone to fill the empty
space in her life and the lives of her children where Ian belonged.
Guilt ran through her as she realized how unfair—and selfish—
she'd been. Richard didn't deserve to be treated so shabbily.

''That's a lovely idea, Richard, and I appreciate your thinking of us. But I can't accept." She drew a quick breath. "In fact, I was going to call you today to—"

"If you're trying to break our date for Friday, I'm afraid I simply can't allow that." His words were clearly spoken in jest, yet a chill ran through her.

"No, I wouldn't do that. I owe you, remember?" She cleared her throat. "But I think you should know that a man I was once...involved with has come back into my life. I'm not sure what will happen. Maybe nothing at all, but seeing him again has made me realize that I'm not emotionally free to begin a relationship with you—or anyone else for that matter."

"Is he the boys' father?"

"I told you once that I'm not going to discuss the boys' father, and you promised never to push me."

"Of course, my dear, and I meant it. Forgive me for asking."

She cleared her throat. "I didn't mean to mislead you, Richard. And I treasure our friendship, but for now, that's all I can offer you. I'm sorry."

His chuckle was resigned. "Don't apologize, my dear," he said, his voice normal again. "It isn't necessary—and besides, I don't intend to give up."

"That's really very sweet of you—"

"Not at all, Marca. It's simply fact. I'm a man who knows what he wants—and what he deserves—and will never rest until he gets it." His voice had suddenly taken on an unfamiliar edge of arrogance she wasn't sure she liked. "You and I are meant to be together, but I realize you need some time to accustom yourself to the idea. For that reason I'll respect your wishes and back off. For now, anyway."

She closed her eyes and rubbed at the worst of the ache in her temple. "Yes, well, thanks again for the invitation to the carnival and for being so...understanding." She glanced at the clock and winced. "I have to run now, Richard. I have a staff meeting at nine, and the agenda is still lurking in my computer half finished."

"Then I won't keep you." She heard his smile, but this time

the warm feeling it usually generated in her was missing. In fact, she felt slightly chilled she realized with a mild surprise as they exchanged goodbyes and hung up.

"I'm sorry, Ms. Kenworthy. Mr. MacDougall still hasn't returned, but I'll be sure to add this message to the other two you've left this morning."

Marca felt something crunch in her jaw and consciously relaxed her facial muscles. "I appreciate it," she said in her sweetest voice, before very carefully returning the phone to the cradle.

At least he hadn't checked out, she thought as she picked up her ham on rye and took an enormous bite. Normally she had a salad sent up from the lunch cart, but stress made her ravenous.

So what if she packed on a few more pounds? she thought, chewing with extra vigor. The heck with trying to look chic. The heck with wanting Ian to find her attractive. The heck with *him*, she decided as she took another bite. Mustard squirted onto the press release she'd been reading, and she winced. She was wiping it up when some sixth sense warned her that she was no longer alone. Swiftly she glanced up to find Ian standing in the doorway, watching her with enigmatic eyes.

He seemed so immensely male. So fierce, even though his dark, angular face was a study in calm. A man of power and spirit and complexity. And, she was almost sure of it, great sensitivity and compassion.

Having spent most of the night picturing him in jeans and a sweatshirt—or sometimes in nothing at all—she was a little startled to see him in the beige shirt and dark brown windbreaker of the campus maintenance crew. He wore the traditional baseball cap most of the grounds crew favored.

"Should I toss my hat in first, or have you taken the edge off your hunger?" he asked when her gaze found his.

"I think it's safe," she managed after swallowing. "I see you've started work."

"Seven-thirty this morning." He cast a glance downward. "Had a little trouble finding trousers long enough." The brown twill trousers that looked mundane and even a little ugly on the other guys of the crew molded his thighs to snug perfection. And definitely counter to the theory of invisibility. What woman with blood in her veins could walk past a man with a body like Ian's and fail to notice? Or react?

Reacting far too much for her peace of mind, she put down her sandwich and wiped her mouth. "I guess it's too soon to ask if you've found out anything useful."

"Well, I did find out one thing for sure," he said as he settled into the chair opposite and stretched out his legs.

"What's that?"

"I hate raking leaves."

She laughed. "Maybe you should ask for a change in assignment."

"Yeah, maybe."

He glanced around, then took off his hat and dropped it on top of a stack of file folders. It looked as though he'd had some of the shagginess trimmed from his hair, she realized as he ran his fingers through the front to take out the flatness. The back, she was happy to note, was still long enough to tie back in a sexy little tail. As though to celebrate, her hormones did a dance. In spite of the emotional turmoil and stress his return had brought, she was still wildly attracted to him.

"Something come up last night or did you change your mind?" His voice had the slightly bored tone of a man discussing the weather.

Marca bristled—until she noticed the way his mouth had flattened at one corner. "Something came up," she said with an apologetic smile. "A domestic crisis I couldn't leave."

"I thought you lived alone."

"No, I have roommates." Another knot in the tangle, she thought with an inner sigh.

"Male or female?"

She was beginning to feel like a suspect undergoing questioning. "Both," she admitted with a tight smile. If it weren't for the fact that she was due at a meeting of the senior staff in exactly forty-five minutes, she would turn the picture around on her desk and let him draw his own conclusions. It had taken Winston a flat five seconds. She was bang-on certain it would take Ian far less.

"Guess this crisis kept you from picking up a phone, too."

"Well yes, temporarily. But as soon as I had things handled, I called the motel. The man on the desk said you'd gone out running."

He lifted one eyebrow. "Seemed like a good idea."

He didn't seem angry. Simply detached. She narrowed her gaze and sat straighter. "I wanted to be with you. I'd intended to be there when I said I would."

Though his expression was mild, even lazy, his eyes were suddenly chilled steel. She braced herself for his anger. Instead, he simply nodded. "Okay."

"You're not angry?"

He shifted. "Not now, though I'll admit to having some damned heated thoughts about you around 2:00 a.m."

"Why 2:00 a.m.?"

He shifted, then grinned a little. "That's when I woke up and realized the couple in the next room were having a heck of a lot more fun than I was."

Her mind filled in the details, and she wanted to whimper. "I can see why that might be rather annoying."

His mouth quirked. "I figure I'll let you make it up to me tonight."

Marca resisted the urge to squirm in her chair. "I'll certainly do my very best."

"As I recall, your *best* had me walking crooked for a week."

He sounded a little awestruck, and she wanted to hug him. It scared her to realize just how smitten she was with a man she scarcely knew. A man who was about to find out he was a father.

Now, she decided. *Right* now, before things got out of hand.

At the thought of what she was about to say, all that she was risking, her hands went ice-cold and clammy, and her heart took off like a triphammer.

The coward in her wanted to spend a little longer worrying over the words. But the deep core of common sense that had saved her more than once told her that the time was right.

"Ian, about my roommates—"

She was interrupted by the sound of Kimbra's voice calling her name. The urgent note in the nanny's voice had her breath catching.

"In here, Kimbra," she called back before offering Ian an apologetic smile. "Here's one of those roommates now."

"Yeah?" A look of lazy interest crossed his face as he turned his attention toward the door.

"I'm sorry to interrupt," Kimbra said as she hurried in with Ryan tucked securely against her side, "but Ry threw up in the car on the way to day care." Oblivious to the big man who'd gone deathly pale as he slowly rose from his chair, Kimbra smiled down at the little boy who was sucking his thumb and looking miserable. "Poor little darling wants his mommy."

# Chapter 10

For an instant Marca couldn't move. The air in the room seemed electric. She didn't know what to do, what to say. This wasn't the way she'd planned to tell him. Her tangled web was about to strangle her.

"Mama," Ryan cried piteously, holding out his chubby arms. "Ry *sick!*"

"I know, sweetheart," she said, hurrying around the desk to lift her son from the nanny's arms into her own. His warm body snuggled into a familiar position, one arm around her neck, the other on her breast. His hair smelled like baby shampoo and chocolate chip cookies, and his cheek was warm against her neck. She took a deep breath and felt emotion quiver like a bowstring.

"Meet Ryan James," she said softly to Ian. "He came down with an ear infection last night. I thought we had it knocked for a loop. Apparently I was wrong."

Ian swallowed, his gaze riveted on his son. His jaw was set, his face ashen, breathing uneven.

"Yes." Marca cleared her throat. They needed a diversion. A

drain for the emotions she felt whipping between them. "Kimbra Ruenda, this is Ian MacDougall."

Making a visible effort to regain his composure, he shifted his gaze and nodded. "Ms. Ruenda." His voice was deep and not quite steady.

"Kimbra, please," she murmured in her lilting South African accent. Marca admired her poise. Her own was pretty much shredded.

First things first, she reminded herself. "Kimbra, would you do me a favor and phone Dr. Spears's office? See if I can bring Ry in now instead of at two-thirty?"

Understanding and profound empathy flashed in Kimbra's dark eyes as she nodded. "Of course. I'll just use Winston's phone, shall I?"

"Yes, good idea."

Kimbra dropped a kiss on Ryan's plump arm where it lay across Marca's shoulder, gave Ian a bemused look, then fled, closing the door behind her.

Silence settled between them, broken only by the sound of Ryan's deep breathing. Sometime during the brief conversation she'd had with Kimbra, Ian had drawn into himself, becoming aloof and distant.

"He's mine, isn't he?" he said finally, his voice quiet but distinctly rough.

Smiling a little, she rubbed Ryan's back—to reassure herself as much as her child, she realized. She wasn't sure what she'd expected exactly, but she knew now she'd been hoping for even a small slice of the joy she'd felt when she'd seen Ryan and his brothers for the first time. "Yes, he's your son, Ian. The protection we used failed."

He lifted a hand to touch the scuffed toe of Ryan's sneaker, his fingers very gently skimming the leather briefly before he pulled back.

"He...looks like the girls. Maybe a little bigger."

"I had intended to tell you last night when I returned to your room. By the time Kimbra and I got his fever down and I felt comfortable leaving him, it was almost eleven.''

"And I was out running."

She nodded. "When I discovered I was pregnant, I did my best to locate you. I thought you had a right to know." She took a breath. "To have the option of being there at my delivery and being a part of his life after he was born."

He closed his eyes for a moment, then drew in air. "It went okay, though. Delivery? Your pregnancy? No problems or... anything?"

"Yes, fine."

In fact, she'd been deathly ill during the last trimester. And the strain the babies had put on her uterus had led to an early delivery—and ultimately, a hysterectomy.

"If you need money—"

"I don't. The college has an excellent health plan and I make a good salary." It was a man thing, she realized, his concentrating on the practical. Down-to-earth details he could handle more easily than the emotions she sensed churning inside him. The shock had been clear. And then disbelief.

She'd felt the same sequence of emotions when her pregnancy had been confirmed. The joy had come next—along with a terror that she would mess it up. But it wasn't joy she saw in Ian's eyes. Or excitement. It was deep unhappiness that settled into those world-weary eyes. She bled a little more inside.

"Is he a good boy?" His gaze skimmed Ry's little body before sliding away.

"As good as any male two-year-old, which, according to the books, is merely a matter of semantics." She pressed a kiss onto the top of the baby's head, and Ian glanced away, his jaw hard again.

"Marca—"

The intercom buzzed.

"That must be Kimbra," she murmured, shifting Ryan to a more comfortable position as she offered Ian a hopeful smile. "Would you like to take him while I talk with her?"

PLAY...
“ROLL A DOUBLE!”
EEL OFF LABEL
ND PLACE INSIDE
GET 2 BOOKS
AND A
ABULOUS MYSTERY BONUS GIFT
ABSOLUTELY FREE!
SEE INSIDE...
(U-SIL-IM-11/98) 245 SDL CJQT

# NO RISK, NO OBLIGATION TO BUY...NOW OR EVER!

# GUARANTEED

## PLAY "ROLL A DOUBLE" AND YOU GET FREE GIFTS! HERE'S HOW TO PLAY:

1. Peel off label from front cover. Place it in space provided at right. With a coin, carefully scratch off the silver dice. Then check the claim chart to see what we have for you – TWO FREE BOOKS and a mystery gift – ALL YOURS! ALL FREE!

2. Send back this card and you'll receive brand-new Silhouette Intimate Moments® novels. These books have a cover price of $4.25 each, but they are yours to keep absolutely free.

3. There's no catch. You're under no obligation to buy anything. We charge nothing – ZERO – for your first shipment. And you don't have to make any minimum number of purchases – not even one!

4. The fact is, thousands of readers enjoy receiving books by mail from the Silhouette Reader Service™. They like the convenience of home delivery...they like getting the best new novels BEFORE they're available in stores...and they love our discount prices!

5. We hope that after receiving your free books you'll want to remain a subscriber. But the choice is yours – to continue or cancel any time at all! So why not take us up on our invitation, with no risk of any kind. You'll be glad you did!

## THIS MYSTERY BONUS GIFT COULD BE YOURS <u>FREE</u> WHEN YOU PLAY "ROLL A DOUBLE"

# "ROLL A DOUBLE!"

Place label here

SCRATCH HERE

**SEE CLAIM CHART BELOW**

245 SDL CJQT
(U-SIL-IM-11/98)

**YES!** I have placed my label from the front cover into the space provided above and scratched off the silver dice. Please send me all the gifts for which I qualify. I understand that I am under no obligation to purchase any books, as explained on the back and on the opposite page.

Name
_____
(PLEASE PRINT)

Address _____ Apt.# _____

City _____ State _____ Zip _____

## CLAIM CHART

**2 FREE BOOKS PLUS MYSTERY BONUS GIFT**

**2 FREE BOOKS**

**1 FREE BOOK**

CLAIM NO.37-829

All orders subject to approval. Offer limited to one per household.

# The Silhouette Reader Service™ — Here's how it works:

Accepting free books places you under no obligation to buy anything. You may keep the books and gift and return the shipping statement marked "cancel." If you do not cancel, about a month later we'll send you 6 additional novels and bill you just $3.57 each, plus 25¢ delivery per book and applicable sales tax, if any.* That's the complete price — and compared to cover prices of $4.25 each — quite a bargain! You may cancel at any time, but if you choose to continue, every month we'll send you 6 more books, which you may either purchase at the discount price...or return to us and cancel your subscription.

*Terms and prices subject to change without notice. Sales tax applicable in N.Y.

If offer card is missing write to: Silhouette Reader Service, 3010 Walden Ave., P.O. Box 1867, Buffalo NY 14240-1867

## BUSINESS REPLY MAIL
FIRST-CLASS MAIL    PERMIT NO. 717    BUFFALO, NY

POSTAGE WILL BE PAID BY ADDRESSEE

SILHOUETTE READER SERVICE
3010 WALDEN AVE
PO BOX 1867
BUFFALO NY 14240-9952

NO POSTAGE
NECESSARY
IF MAILED
IN THE
UNITED STATES

"No, he needs his mom," he said gruffly before snatching up the phone. "Yeah?"

He listened intently to what the person on the other end was saying, his gaze on Marca's half-eaten lunch, his big rough-gentle hand idly toying with one of the oak leaves in the vase.

"Yeah, okay, I'll tell her." There was a pause, and then Ian thanked Kimbra politely and hung up.

"What did she say?" Marca asked quietly.

"The doctor was on her way to lunch, but she'll wait for you. She—" He broke off, his gaze riveted on the photograph of the triplets. The color that had begun to return to his face disappeared.

"Oh, God," he said, his voice dull and almost pleading. "Triplets?"

Marca smiled. "I'm afraid so. A ready-made gang." And family. The family Ian seemed to be rejecting more with each breath he took.

"What are the names of the other two?" His voice was detached now. Cool. Controlled.

"Trevor Allen and Sean Mitchell." Her smile felt stiff. She supposed it looked the same. This wasn't going the way she'd always imagined. "Ry here is the eldest. He's also the one who catches every germ first and then passes it on to his brothers."

He nodded, then wrenched his gaze away from the grinning faces of his sons and onto the watch he pulled from his pocket. "The doctor's waiting. We'd better go."

It would be all right, she told herself. Later, when the shock settled, he would be eager to know his sons. How could he not want them? Three rambunctious, curious-as-kittens, bright-eyed little boys who tore into life, their eagerness to love and be loved filling every day. Every hour.

Since the boys had blessed her life, she'd never felt so glad to be alive. So grateful for every day. The world was different when seen at a child's level, through a child's wide-eyed innocence. Simpler in some ways, but far more complex in others.

Like love.

"My purse is in the bottom drawer," she said, deciding to

leave her briefcase here. "And I'll have to leave a note for Winston to call Carly and tell her I might not make the staff meeting."

Without a word he scrawled a note on her yellow pad, writing she realized, with his left hand. A southpaw like his sons. Finished, he tore off the page and grabbed her purse from the drawer.

"Where's your car?" he asked, putting on his baseball cap and pulling it low. "I'll drive you."

The trip into Bradenton Falls usually took Marca ten minutes in good weather. Though the day was again overcast, with an intermittent drizzle, Ian kept the speedometer well under the limit and drove her minivan as though the road were sheeted in ice.

He hadn't said much. In the parking lot outside the administration building he'd asked for her keys. Politely, remotely, he'd helped her settle Ryan in one of the three child's seats in the back of the minivan. He'd helped her into her own seat and made sure she buckled her seat belt before climbing into the driver's seat. His legs were too long, so he'd adjusted the seat. Conscientiously he'd also adjusted the mirrors. What he hadn't done was look at her. Or smile. Or pull her into his arms to tell her that they would work it out.

"What are you going to tell the head gardener when he asks you why the leaves aren't raked?" she asked, when she couldn't stand the heavy silence one more instant.

A ghost of a smile flitted over his mouth as he shot her a fast look. "Depends on how he asks."

"He might fire you."

"I'll talk him out of it."

She heard the steely note in his voice and pitied the hapless soul who got in his way. "I could always talk to Mike McNabb if you'd like. The head of maintenance? He looks like a grizzly on the outside, but he's really a sweet soul on the inside. Like you."

This time his gaze was startled. "I look like a grizzly?" He sounded a little offended, and she laughed a little.

"No, you're a *sweet soul*."

His expression turned grim. "Don't count on it."

"No one who wasn't could possibly have fathered such sweet children."

His hands tightened on the wheel. A car whizzed past. The tires hummed on the pavement. "Marca, you don't even know me."

"I think I do."

He shifted. "We spent a few hours together, had a conversation over drinks. Slept together. That's all." His voice was even and a little impatient. "I threw away the card you gave me."

"Yes, well, I admit that's a bit hard to take, but I understand why. You were still grieving."

His jaw flexed. "I was a drunken bum. I can't believe you even let me touch you."

"You were a little seedy, yes. But a gentleman."

He snorted. "You must have been in shock."

"Don't laugh, okay, but I knew the moment I saw you running toward me over the beach, with your teeth bared and a wild look in your eyes that you'd come to my rescue before. In another lifetime. Maybe in dozens. And I knew we'd been lovers—and friends."

"Soul mates, right?" His tone wasn't precisely sarcastic. More like ironic.

"Okay, I admit that's trendy right now, but that doesn't mean it's not a valid concept."

His sigh was heavy and a little sad. "Maybe for you."

"Guess that means I should cancel the order for the cake and the flowers, huh?"

His head turned with a snap, and she held up a hand. "It's a joke, Ian. I do that when I'm under stress." Or terribly afraid.

"Hell," he muttered returning his attention to the road.

The silence beat heavily, like the rain that had pounded the roof last night. She drew a breath and spread her hands on her thighs to keep from clenching them. From the corner of her eye she saw him check the rearview mirror again, something he'd done frequently during the drive.

Leaning forward, she turned around to smile at Ryan who was sucking his thumb and kicking his feet. The color had returned to his face, and his eyes were alert and shining.

"I think this is a false alarm," she said, shifting her gaze to Ian. "Maybe it was something he ate."

His glance went to the mirror again. "Is he taking medication for the ear infection? Antibiotics?"

"Yes. A lovely pink liquid, one half dropper every four hours. Why?"

"He...it might be a reaction to the drug." He drew a breath. "Lucila used to throw up whenever she took antibiotics."

Marca felt her stomach muscles contract. "Lucila was your daughter?"

He nodded, then cleared his throat. "Gracia never had a problem, although they were identical. Or supposed to be."

"I know what you mean," Marca said quickly, leaning forward as far as the seat belt allowed. She wanted to touch him. To tell him that she understood how hard he was trying. "Trev and Sean were nearly impossible to tell apart for the first six months, but Ry was always just a little bigger. None of the books I read have an explanation. And their personalities are different, too." She laughed a little. "Sean is easy-going and a little lazy. Trev is a maverick and more than a little bullheaded. Carly claims he gets that from me, but I'm sure that has to come from you. Now Ry—"

"Where do I go when we hit town?" he interrupted, his knuckles white.

Marca sat back and told herself to give him time. "The Medical Arts Building is just behind the hospital. Turn left at the first light."

The rest of the trip was completed in silence.

"Doctor had a *kitty*," Ry said with a toothy grin as he tugged at the ear of the Beddie-Bye Bunny Marca's mother had given him last Easter. All the boys got one, of course. It was one of Marca's hard and fast rules. No favoritism allowed. To make each one unique, Gladys Kenworthy had made each rabbit a different-colored coat. Ryan's was bright green.

"Did you like the doctor's kitty?" she asked as she finished with the diaper and pulled down his shirt. Ian had been right. Meg Spears had changed the medication that had made Ry sick, with an admonition to watch him carefully. Other than that, he was on the mend. And extremely curious about the big man who watched him in silence.

Other than exhibiting relief that his son was in no danger, he'd continued to be brooding and remote on the trip back to Marca's house. And though he'd come upstairs with her to the nursery, he'd done little more than wander around the bright room, occasionally touching one of the toys or pulling out one of the books and glancing through it before carefully returning it to its place on the shelf.

"Ry have kitty, okay?" Ryan was tenacious when he got a notion into his head. Meg's new little calico had renewed his interest in having a pet.

"One of these days, sweetie," she promised, sitting him up on the edge of the changing table. "When it's summertime again and you can play outside with the kitties."

"I want a kitty now!" Ryan drew his black eyebrows together in one of his thunderous little frowns, and his eyes got very dark. It was nap time, Ryan's least favorite occupation, which tended to make him cranky.

"Uh-oh," she murmured in a dramatic tone. "Here comes my little storm cloud again." She bent down to nuzzle his neck, and he giggled.

"No tickle, Mama!" he protested, grabbing a fistful of her hair.

"Oh, please, Sir Ryan," she pleaded, slipping easily into Ry's favorite nap time game. "Just one little tickle."

"No tickle," he repeated more loudly, his eyes shining with anticipation.

"Okay, just a nuzzle-nuzzle," she declared before nuzzling the other side of his short little neck.

He giggled and kicked and thoroughly destroyed Marca's

hairdo before she called a halt. "Time to settle down now, sweetie," she said as she lifted him to her hip. "Say night-night to...to Ian, okay?"

Instantly Ryan turned his curious gaze toward the window where Ian now stood gazing out over the fenced play yard, his big hands in the back pockets of his brown work pants.

"Night-night, Ian," Ryan singsonged.

Shoulders braced, Ian turned to give the boy a smile. "Have a good one," he said, his voice gruff.

"'Kay." Ryan's obviously puzzled gaze lingered on his father for a moment longer before shifting to Marca. "Is Ian staying here now like Kimby?"

Of all the boys, Ry had the most logical mind and consequently the greatest need to keep his world ordered and under control. To Ry, Ian was a variable he didn't recognize. A new adult in his small world who didn't yet have a proper place.

"Ian is a friend of Mama's," she said as she settled him on the bed and covered him with the small quilt folded at the foot. It smelled like baby powder and little boy sweat.

"Like Richard?"

"Yes, sweetie, like Richard."

"I like Richard," Ryan declared, looking past her toward the window. "He has cookies."

"You'll like Ian, too," she said before kissing his cheek. Ryan looked dubious, and Marca wondered if Ian noticed. Would he even care?

"Sleep tight," she said, smoothing the covers. "Mama and Ian will be downstairs."

Ryan nodded and turned on his side, his eyes already closing. Marca got to her feet just as Ryan opened his eyes again. "Where's blankie?"

Marca glanced around. So, she noticed, did Ian. "This it?" he asked, holding up Trevor's blue and yellow quilt.

"No, there, on the rocking horse. Ry likes to have blankie with him when he rides the range."

Ian's mouth quirked as he retrieved the scrap of faded yellow cotton from the horse's saddle. "I have a rag like this to wash my Jeep," he said with a faint smile as he handed it to Ryan.

"It was new when the boys were born, but when Ry was teething, he liked to chew on the edges. Sort of like a puppy gnawing at a sock."

She grinned down at her son who was busy arranging his blanket under his cheek. She'd patched it repeatedly, snipping away the ragged edges a little more each time until the whole thing was handkerchief size.

"Mommy," Ry murmured in a plaintive, sleepy voice, "don't forget my nebber-nebber."

"I certainly won't." Marca leaned down and pressed a kiss to her son's forehead, his chin and then to both cheeks—a sentimental leftover from her early college days, a legacy of love taught to her by Carly's Irish nanny. A blessing kiss, the affectionate Irishwoman had always explained as she'd collared Carly and Marca to kiss them before they left the house, guaranteed to ward off evil and the mischievous little people, a summons to all the angels in heaven to guard the recipient from harm.

As her lips pressed the last of the blessing kiss to Ryan's left cheek, Marca said softly, "Off you go, now, little guy, to never-never land. Sweet dreams."

"Yup," Ry agreed drowsily, "off to nebber-nebber with Pete and Pan."

As she straightened, Marca gave Ian a conspiratorial smile. "We went to see Peter Pan. The boys were, of course, captivated."

Ian's gray eyes searched hers, his expression slightly bemused. "Where did you learn that?" he asked in a gruff whisper.

"What?"

He dipped his chin toward Ryan. "That...the, um, blessing kiss. It's an—I thought it was something only the Irish do."

Marca had momentarily forgotten his Irish ancestry. Her smile deepened. "Compliments of Tilly. You met her, I think?"

He glanced at Ryan again. "Ah, I remember. A brogue as thick as molasses." He smiled slightly. "My dad—that's how he always kissed me. He died when I was so young, I'd almost forgotten. Until I saw—'' He blinked and hauled in a shaky breath. ''I guess you never really forget those things—the special things your parents leave with you.''

A lump came into Marca's throat. Unwittingly she'd handed down to her sons a MacDougall family tradition. ''Would you like to leave Ry with a memory of his own?'' she asked softly.

Pain washed over his Ian's hard features as he shook his head. ''I'll be outside having a smoke when you're done.''

He walked out quickly, looking like a man desperate to escape.

Ian lit another cigarette and blew out smoke. It was his third since he'd stepped outside twenty minutes ago. The clouds were gathering again over the mountains to the east.

*My little storm cloud.*

He took an impatient drag, then let the smoke dribble out.

Marca had gotten pregnant. A baby. No, three babies.

He'd screwed up. It scalded his butt to admit it, but it didn't surprise him. No matter how carefully a guy planned, life had a way of throwing the unexpected body slam at his gut. This one had him reeling.

His angel gypsy had given him three identical little boys— except each was different and unique. Each his own man someday.

Sons.

He wrapped his mind around the thought, letting the idea settle. Could he be a dad again? Do it right this time?

The doors to the deck slid open, and Marca walked out, carrying two mugs. ''I thought you might like some coffee with your cigarette,'' she said, handing him a mug before turning to slide the doors closed.

''Thanks,'' he said, taking a last drag before flipping the butt onto the thick wet grass.

''You realize that smoking does terrible things to your body, don't you?''

''So they say.''

She took a sip of coffee, then turned to lean against the railing. She'd changed out of the tailored slacks and shirt she'd been wearing, into jeans and a faded sweatshirt emblazoned with Greek symbols. He recognized the sorority. It was the one at Fresno State that pledged the valedictorians and the honor students.

"Are you all right?"

He heard the concern in her voice and felt the knife twist in his belly. The reassuring words were already on the way to his tongue when he realized he couldn't lie to Marca. Not when she'd given him the greatest gift a man could receive.

"I don't know," he admitted, staring down at his old work boots. "Maybe when I meet Ry's brothers, it'll sink in that I'm a dad again. But—" He broke off to take a sip. The coffee was black and strong enough to kick-start a dead mule. Exactly the way he liked it. He took another sip and welcomed the bitter aftertaste. Anything was better than the sting of guilt.

"You hate the idea of a ready-made family, don't you?"

"I hate the idea that I didn't protect you." He lifted his head and made himself meet her gaze. "I'm sorry, Marca. You told me you didn't want children, and now, because of me, you have three."

"First of all, the responsibility for contraception was mine, which I thought I'd handled. As for you giving me the children..." She paused and her smile was like a blaze of unexpected sunshine in the midst of a sodden day. "I'm *thrilled* to be a mother," she continued with a fervor that dared him to disagree. "Because of you I have the three most intelligent, most adorable, most wonderful little guys in the world. And as for that nonsense I kept spouting about not wanting to be a mom, that was pure grade-A baloney."

"It sounded pretty convincing to me."

"That's because I'd said it so often I almost believed it. But deep down, a part of me longed desperately to be a mother. When I was married, Lewis didn't want children, and I respected his wishes. After the divorce, I thought about adopting, but it didn't seem fair somehow, for a single woman to deprive a child of the chance for a more-traditional home.'' Her grin flashed again. ''I realize that idea isn't politically correct, but hey, neither am I in a lot of ways.''

''You could have gotten married again,'' he suggested a little curtly.

''Yes, if I'd met the right man.'' She straightened and picked up her mug. ''After Lewis the Lech, I'm more than a little cautious about taking that aisle walk again.''

Ian knew the feeling. After his divorce, he'd sworn never to risk hurting another woman the way he'd hurt Amalia. ''What about Richard of the cookies and the roses?''

Her lips curved. ''He's asked me. He's talked about adopting the boys if we were to marry.''

A fierce anger swept through him. Over his dead body he thought, then brought himself up short. ''He sounds like one of the good guys.''

''He is.''

''Are you going to accept his proposal?''

''No.''

''I guess you expect a proposal from me now?''

She made an impatient sound. ''No, Ian, I don't. I told you about Richard because you asked. I'm not playing a game of emotional cat and mouse.''

''I know. That's what scares me.''

He propped a foot against the bottom rail and rested his mug on his thigh. She had a good-size yard. A half acre at least. She'd carved out a decent garden in one corner and a play area in another. The swing set looked new.

''I promised Luce and Gracie I'd build them a playhouse. I never seemed to find the time, though.'' The words had come from nowhere, surprising him. But then, Marca had a way of dragging things out of him that were better off buried. Maybe because she listened with more than her ears.

''You were busy,'' she murmured. ''I'm sure they understood.''

He rubbed his thumb over the handle of the mug and watched

a flock of noisy Canada geese flying over, heading south in a ragged, lopsided V formation. They were prey to nature and man both, but their lives seemed so much more certain and orderly than his own.

"I was a lousy father, Marca—and a worse husband." The admission came out low and gruff and with only a fraction of the anger seething inside him. "I made promises and then broke them. Missed birthdays when they were babies, left Amy alone too much. I told myself that what I was doing was for them, that as long as they had their mom and a nice place to live..." He drew a sharp sigh that felt barbed. "I thought I had plenty of time to catch up."

"Ian, you can't blame yourself for someone else's madness."

He shot her an impatient look. "I chose to go undercover. Amalia begged me not to, but hey, she was just my wife. One small little piece of my life. Someone I'd promised to love and cherish and *protect*. My work, now that was what was really important."

He clenched his fingers into a fist on the rail and fought against the emotions surging for expression. "She was too young, just a kid from the sticks who thought I hung the moon. All she ever wanted was a family. A houseful of kids. Thing was she also wanted a man around to help her raise 'em, and when I went undercover—" His voice broke, and he closed his eyes. He'd tried to love Amy. It just hadn't happened. "She found someone else. A nice steady appliance repairman. I don't blame her. I made her life hell."

"Ian, don't torture yourself like this," she pleaded, curving her hand over his. Her fingers were warm and surprisingly strong as they pressed his. "Your work *is* important. People are getting maimed and killed, and you have the means and the guts and the determination to stop it. If you don't fight the monsters, who will?"

"Someone better than me. The bastard walked."

"But you tried." She withdrew her hand. He wished she hadn't.

"We had Renfrew dead to rights. The jury would listen to the man with the badge, the prosecutor kept telling me. Only they didn't!"

He put down his mug and reached for his cigarettes, then remembered he'd smoked the last one. So he paced to the other side of the small deck and stared at the fog-shrouded hillside. After a moment of silence he heard the quiet thudding of Marca's sneakers against the weathered planks as she came to stand next to him.

"That doesn't mean the next jury won't convict," she said with quiet faith, gazing up at him. "Or the next one after that if necessary!"

"It was my fault! I blew it. Something I said, maybe. Or the way I said it."

"Not necessarily. Juries are unpredictable. All you have to do is read the paper or watch the news. You're one of the good guys, too, Ian. I believe that with all of my heart."

What the hell, he thought. If Marca thought him a hero, he might as well let her see just how really great he was.

"I was supposed to take the girls trick-or-treating. Amalia—Amy—and I had been divorced for a couple of months by then. Amy kept the house, and she and I had arranged that I'd come to the house for dinner first." His throat threatened to close, and he dragged in air. "The night before Halloween I got a call from a snitch that the Brigade was going to burn a storefront church that had just opened in East L.A. Four of us staked the place out. We waited until dawn, but the Brigade never showed. We cruised around a little, hunted down the snitch who claimed something had gone wrong. The hit was going to happen that night instead. Halloween night. It was almost noon when I got back to my place. I was wiped out, in a rotten mood."

He glanced her way and caught the quick flash of sympathy in her eyes. "You canceled the trick-or-treating, didn't you?"

Admitting his sin to himself had been easy compared to admitting it to her. But she needed to know. And maybe he needed to tell her. "Yeah, only I called it a compromise when I suggested

Amy bring the kids to my place before she took them around the neighborhood so that I could see their costumes. I had this bungalow a few miles from the house. Five minutes drive, tops. Since I was paying all the bills so she could continue to be a stay-at-home mom after the divorce, I figured Amy could spare the time. And the girls would understand.''

"Did they?'' she asked softly, her tension all but palpable.

"No. Luce cried. She cried a lot, always had. She...she was the one who wanted to be held when we read stories, and the one who needed extra good-night hugs.''

"Sean is like that. I call him my snuggle-baby.''

The need for a cigarette spiked again. More insistent this time. A vicious tension gripped his muscles, prodding him to run until he dropped. Instead, he flexed some of the worst of it from his shoulders and told himself that fresh air was better than smoke.

"Amy had been having trouble with the battery in her Prelude for a couple of weeks, and when she went to leave, the battery was dead. I remember tossing her the keys to my Camaro with an offhand promise to buy her a new battery and then return the Prelude to her the next day.'' He had to stop. The words were bursting pictures inside his head. Bloody, accusing images that tore at him.

"Renfrew had put the bomb in your car,'' she finished for him.

He shifted, flexed his knees a little. "I doubt he did it himself. Bastards like him delegate. But, yeah, sometime between noon when I got home and 6:23 when Amy turned the key, someone had rigged an explosive device.''

He drew a breath. The wind was picking up, and the air smelled like wet leaves. It felt colder, too. A damp, penetrating cold unlike any he'd felt in the San Joaquin Valley—even in winter when the temperature took a rare dip into the thirties.

"It's funny, but in that split second before it blew, I saw it happening. I yelled at Amy, but it was too late.''

"Where...were you when it happened?''

"Standing on the curb, next to a dumpster. It took most of the shrapnel. I got knocked down, had a few cuts and bruises.'' He glanced up at the unrelieved gray, then slowly turned to look at her. "Now you know what kind of father I was."

"It sounds to me as if you were a devoted father, one who did his best, which is all anyone can ask."

"Yeah, tell that to my girls. And their mom."

"We all get busy, Ian. And sometimes, when life makes too many demands on us, we have to disappoint the little people in our lives whom we love the most. It can't always be helped, because, like it or not, having food on the table and getting the electric bill paid *is* more important than trick-or-treating."

He shook his head. "I was a lousy father, I'm telling you. Don't assign your own wonderful qualities as a mother to me. The suit doesn't fit."

Marca could see that trying to convince him was useless. "All right. Assume you *were* a lousy father, then. *Was* and *will be* can be two different things."

He drew a breath. "I don't know if I can handle parenthood again, Marca. I'd like to promise you I'll try, but I don't make promises anymore."

"I guess this is where I'm supposed to tell you to leave and never darken our door with your imperfect presence again, right?"

"You'd be justified."

She gave an indelicate little snort. "Sorry, just can't do it. Whether you like it or not, you're the boys' biological father. Whether or not you want to be their *daddy* is a decision only you can make."

"If I decided I wanted to be part of their lives, then what?"

"Then you will be."

It couldn't be that easy. "Even if I go back to Florida when this mess is cleaned up?"

She nodded. "I admit it'll take some ingenious juggling, but it's workable."

Her cheeks were turning pink in the cool air, and her hair was still mussed from Ryan's fingers. One of her earrings was missing again, and he caught himself smiling. Very carefully, he lifted a hand and trailed his fingertips along the curve of her jaw. She shivered a little, her eyes growing intense.

"I want to make love to you, Marca," he admitted a little too roughly. "Now. This minute."

Her smile promised absolution to a dying man, and he felt some of the tension seep out of him. "I want that, too," she murmured, nuzzling his hand with her cheek. "There's just one thing you need to know first."

"What's that?" he asked, bracing himself.

"Ry takes very short naps."

## Chapter 11

By the time Marca slipped into her bedroom, leaving the door ajar, Ian had already removed his boots and socks and was tugging off his shirt. Underneath was a dark blue T-shirt, the faded cotton pulled delightfully snug against the powerful muscles of his chest.

"What about your nanny? Ms. Ruenda?" He hung his shirt over the end of the footboard. "When's she due back?"

"She had an appointment with her advisor and errands to run, and then she's to pick up Sean and Trev at the mansion. She won't be back until after four."

His gaze went to the clock on the night table. It was a little past two.

"Nice room," he said, glancing around. "Nice bed."

He didn't sound nervous, but Marca sensed that he was. It was there in the tense lines around his mouth and the stiff line of his shoulders as he came toward her. Performance anxiety? she wondered. And then nearly giggled. Still, it buoyed her spirits to think that a man as virile—and as skilled at lovemaking as she knew him to be—was worried about satisfying her.

"I planned to woo you." He drew back the nubby woven spread, then tested the mattress with the quick, practiced movement of a man accustomed to a succession of motel rooms. "Take you out for a wildly expensive dinner to impress you with my generosity and gentlemanly manners." His mouth quirked. "Just in case you had trouble recognizing my good qualities, though, I figured I'd ply you with some of that white wine you like."

"Dancing would be a nice touch," she suggested before neatly stowing her sneakers side by side beneath the dust ruffle she'd crocheted one long, boring winter.

"Not with me it wouldn't," he said as he slipped his callused palm beneath her chin and nudged her head back. "I'm about as graceful as an ox on the dance floor."

"Scratch dancing, then."

His gaze caressed her face an instant before he bent to brush his mouth over hers. His lips were warm and firm, clinging for a sweet gentle moment before he lifted his head.

"I've been going crazy wanting you," he said, his voice hoarse as he curled his hands over her arms and drew her to her feet. "I know it's selfish as hell, but I can't stay away."

"I'm glad," she said, slipping her arms around his neck. He moaned as her breasts flattened against his chest. His mouth found hers, this time in a long, drugging kiss that vibrated nerves she didn't know she had.

"Feel good?" he asked when the kiss ended.

"Very good," she managed, her voice distinctly breathless.

"More?" His gaze was dark, his face taut. His arousal was a hard, rigid bulge against her belly.

"Definitely more."

Her eager fingers raked the elastic tie from his ponytail, releasing the thick silk of his hair. It was longer than she expected and as black as a moonless midnight, almost to his shoulders and smelled of some minty shampoo. To please herself, she sifted the strands between her fingers. Even as she told herself to let him set the pace, her fingers were curled into his hair to draw his head closer.

She found his mouth and concentrated on the wild pleasure pouring through her as he kissed her back. Heat bloomed in the cleft between her breasts and spread. Needing air, she drew back. His breath hissed out, and his body throbbed. She felt an answering response between her legs.

"Feel good?" she echoed.

"Very." His voice was hoarse, his eyes half closed. "Keep it up and foreplay is going to be the shortest on record."

She laughed and drew back far enough to gain access to his belt. "In that case I think I'd better get you naked first."

He jerked a little as she worked the buckle, her fingers dipping between his waistband and his belly. He gave a choked cry and reached between them to grab the hem of her sweatshirt. It was up and over her head before she had time to do more than gasp and raise her arms.

He started to reach for her bra, only to have her press her hands against his chest. "Uh-uh. Fair is fair." Eagerly, her hands shaking a little, she jerked his T-shirt up. "Bend down," she ordered, curving one hand over his shoulder to tug.

"Bully," he teased, as he bent forward. The shirt came free, and as he straightened, she inhaled in pleasure at the sight of his bare chest. His skin was the color of dark honey, textured with a haphazard pattern of smooth perfection and rough scar tissue stretched over densely packed muscle and hard sinew.

"You're beautiful, MacDougall." She splayed her hands against the triangle of crisp dark hair that whorled around his nipples. "I love touching you." Absorbed, enthralled, she worked her hands lower and watched his eyes glaze.

"Sweetheart, you're killing me," he muttered, his fingers framing her face. His mouth covered hers, his tongue already teasing. She parted her lips willingly, and he feasted. When he was finished exploring her mouth, he concentrated on mapping the line of each of her cheekbones with feathering strokes of his mouth. After he'd satisfied his curiosity, he concentrated on exploring her throat. Beneath his seeking mouth her skin burned and her blood heated.

"More," she whispered hoarsely when he lifted his head.

"Your turn to get naked," he said, his chest rising and falling in ragged breaths as he rid her of her bra. Her breasts spilled out, larger now, the nipples darkened by the flood of hormones during her pregnancy.

"I thought I remembered." His breath hissed in, and his gaze turned reverent. "You were perfect before," he murmured, tenderly cupping her breasts in both hands, kneading and reshaping until her skin was warm and acutely sensitive, and her mind was beginning to splinter. "Now you're breathtaking."

His gaze stayed on hers as he massaged her nipples into hard aching nubs. Desire bunched and throbbed inside her, and she pressed into his touch, begging for relief from the building pressure.

"At night when I was alone, I've imagined touching you like this," he said, caressing the nipples that had nursed his babies. "When I wanted to rip open the seal on the bottle of my old friend, Glenfiddich, I pictured your smile, instead. When I couldn't sleep, I imagined you whispering my name." His expression turned haunted. "Say my name, Marca. Please."

"Ian," she whispered. "My dear, dear Ian."

"My beautiful Marca. My angel gypsy."

"Only yours." Desperate, she fumbled with his zipper, her fingers brushing rigid flesh as she drew it down. He groaned and jerked back. Frowning a little, her vision blurred, she pushed his pants down his thighs and he kicked them off.

Her breath caught in her throat when he suddenly scooped her into his arms. He kissed her hard, then put her down on the bed. With a deft motion of his wrist, he had her waistband open and her zipper down.

"Raise up so I can get you out of these," he ordered in a thick voice.

So eager she was nearly breathless, she curled her fingers into the blanket and lifted her hips. With a low growl of impatience, he jerked her jeans free and tossed them on the floor.

"Hurry," she begged, watching him with half-closed eyes as

he slid the dark blue briefs down his legs. She sucked in when she saw how ready he was.

"Damn, I forgot," he muttered, his voice rough with frustration. "My wallet's locked in my truck. I can't protect you—unless you have something?"

"No need. I had a hysterectomy."

"Oh, sweetheart. I don't want to hurt you."

"I'm hurting now," she whispered, opening her arms. "I need you to make the hurt go away."

Ian understood hurt. And a hunger so powerful he was shaking as he settled next to her on the bed. His body strained for release. An instinct older than time prodded him to drive into her, branding himself on her until she wanted no other man.

Because he wanted her so desperately, he forced his mind back to reason and his hand to gentleness as he stroked her breasts, her waist, the sweetly rounded belly where she'd once carried three babies. He wished he could have seen her then.

"Hurry, Ian," she begged, her voice trembling. "It's been so long."

For him, too. Months and months of wanting and not having. Of longing and loneliness.

Fire burned in him as he cupped the soft mound at the apex of her thighs. Burrowing his fingers into the downy fleece, he squeezed gently, then rubbed, then squeezed until she gasped and bucked. He tested her with his fingers and found her wet. For him.

His breath rushed in and out of his body. His reason was shredding, his need building. He needed to be inside her, to become a part of her so that he wasn't alone anymore.

Her eager hands were urging him closer, her urgent, impatient gasps fueling his need. Impulse pulled hard against his control, and he let it go as he nudged her thighs apart with his knee.

"Yes," she urged, nearly sobbing now in her frustration and desperation. "Hurry, Ian, hurry. I'm so close, already, so close. I want you...hard inside me."

It was all he needed, more than he'd dreamed. Still, mindful of the ordeal she'd been through to deliver his children, he entered her slowly, carefully, his body straining with the effort to hold his urge in check when all that was alive inside him screamed for one quick, shuddering thrust.

Her body accepted him, sheathing him in warm, wet silk.

"So...damned...sweet," he murmured between drugging kisses.

"Yes, oh, yes, *Ian!*"

He took a moment to luxuriate in the feeling of exultation and completeness before the writhing of her body and the hot pulsing pressure in his own drove him to move.

He thrust into her again and again, drawing out the pleasure, each breath torn from him as he struggled to wait, to let her lead him over the edge into blessed release. Her fingers clawed at his shoulders, matching him movement for movement. He concentrated on each long stroke. The sweet friction. The heat. She cried out, whimpered, demanded until he was sweat-soaked from the exertion of holding back and the muscles of his thighs were quivering.

"Let...it...go, sweetheart. Fly...for me."

Her body quickened around his, and a low keening sound escaped her throat. Close to breaking, he felt the hot rush of her orgasm enveloping him.

With a harsh, exultant groan he gave one last thrust, exploding into her. He'd never felt so powerful—or so humble. For this one shining moment, he'd been perfect for her.

Ian's head was pillowed on her chest, and his breathing was slow and even. He was asleep, and more vulnerable than she had ever seen him.

His thick, black hair was damp where it clung to his wide forehead, and the musk of their lovemaking hung heavy in the air. He was still heavy inside her, and his considerable weight pressed her against the mattress, making it difficult to fill her lungs to capacity. One of her legs was threatening to cramp.

All in all, she felt divinely relaxed. Sated and a little smug.

It wasn't just sexual release they'd given to each other, even though she suspected he would tell himself it was. Though much of his personality was still a mystery yet to be revealed, she was gradually coming to know him better. With each snippet of information she drew forth, each small piece of his past, a picture was forming of a sensitive, compassionate, deeply wounded man who held himself to impossible standards, then punished himself for his failure to measure up.

Though she felt certain he would deny it to the last of his days and with the last of his breath, Ian was a man of unalterable conviction and integrity. A man who wanted to carve away some of the ugliness of life and create a safe haven for those who wished to love one another in peace. His life had been filled with ugliness and brutality so that others would have the freedom to revel in beauty.

Carefully, so as not to wake him, she moved her head sideways on the pillow until she could see more of his face. The lines bracketing his wide, firm mouth were eased by the healing sleep, but still cut deep. Too deep to fade completely. There were scars, too—a faint crescent over the bridge of his nose, a rosette of puckered skin on the curve of his shoulder, a straight slice along the line of his jaw.

His was a face made strong and beautiful by the choices he'd made, the ideals he embraced. The battles he'd fought. Character was stamped into every line, honor folded into every crease. He was decent when he could so easily have become corrupted and venal. A good man who suffered the agonies of the damned because he hadn't been perfect. A man tormented and driven by sins of omission.

As though privy to her thoughts, he frowned and mumbled incoherently, as though his dreams troubled him. "I love you," she whispered as she pressed her lips to the deeply gouged lines over the bridge of his imperfect nose.

His eyes flew open, and for an instant shock shimmered there before a lazy smile bloomed. "Hey, sexy lady," he murmured, his voice husky.

"Hey, yourself, gorgeous man," she whispered, brushing back

he tousled hair. His cheeks reddened, and she laughed. "You ire, you know."

"Yeah, well, you think that worthless dog you saved is gor-;eous, too."

"He is!" A thought occurred to her and she frowned. "Speak-ng of Mutt, who takes care of him when you're not there?"

"The manager's wife. She's a sucker for butt-ugly animals, ;ame as you."

"Bite your tongue, buster," she teased, tracing his mouth with ier fingertip. He gave her a little nip, his gaze sated and drowsy is it met hers.

"Are you okay?"

"Oh, yeah," she murmured.

"Not sore?"

She suspected she would be. No one had made love to her since the night on the beach. "No, just blissfully relaxed."

For the first time in years she felt deliciously female and glo-riously sexy. Loving him, wanting him, she kissed his stubborn aw. The cruel tension around his eyes eased, and there was a 'aint glow waiting to be fanned into happiness in the back of his lark eyes.

"How about you?" she asked.

He smiled a little as he nuzzled her shoulder with his chin. '"Wishing I were ten years younger so I could make love to you all over again instead of think about it."

She widened her eyes and pouted. "You mean you can't?"

His low rumble of laughter warmed her to the quick. "Believe me, sweetheart, the spirit is willing, but this beat-up forty-six-year-old body needs rest before it can rise to the occasion again."

Groaning dramatically at the lousy pun, she raised her head and directed a pointed look at the clock. "How *much* time, pre-cisely?"

"More than we have at the moment, Ms. Sass." He rolled to his side, ending the intimate bond between them, and she sighed.

"I'm feeling lonely already."

He took her hand and kissed it. "Don't. Because unless my

hearing is playing tricks on me, Ryan James is wide awake and heading this way."

"Uh-oh," Marca said, sitting up a split second before she heard Ryan calling for her.

"Coming, darling," she called back quickly.

Ian laughed as she scrambled out of bed and raced to the closet for her robe. On the way to the door, she picked up his shirt and tossed it in his direction.

"You can have the shower first. Don't use all the hot water or I'll be forced to beat you rather severely."

He laughed again. "I'd like to see you try, short stuff."

The look she tossed him was part temptress, part exasperated mom. "Don't push me, buster. I'm tougher than I look."

His eyes were suddenly sober. "I hope so," he said very quietly as she hurried out. "I already have enough sins on my soul."

Ian stood in the shower and let the warm water cascade over his shoulders and chest. Steam cocooned him in the small tile-lined chamber, filling his lungs with fragrant moist air scented with the soap she used. The same scent that filled him when he'd nuzzled her neck.

Damn, but he felt good, he thought, as he arched his head away from the droplets splashing off his chest. Something was different inside him. Something different from the after-sex energy that normally filled him.

Always before, when the sex had been good, he'd been ready for action. Something physical and demanding. Work if he was on a case, a game of racquetball with a buddy, a dizzying race on his Harley over the dirt tracks in the hills. To his surprise, none of those things tugged at him now. Instead he found himself wondering if she'd let him stay the night.

And if she did—

Suddenly the bathroom door flew open, and he heard Marca calling his name. He shut off the water with one hand and opened the shower door with the other. She had the boy tucked against her hip, and her face was stark white. Her eyes had a familiar sheen. Shock.

"What's wrong?" he demanded in the quiet but insistent voice he'd learned to use with the victims of violence. "Is it Ryan?"

"Kimbra just called. She's at the hospital. She and Dennis were attacked in the FoodPlus parking lot by four men wearing ski masks."

"They hit him with a baseball bat," Kimbra said, her voice shaking and her skin tone bleached to the color of aged parchment.

"I know, honey," Marca soothed, holding the girl's hand in hers. "They're monsters. Low-life cowards."

The waiting room adjacent to the OR at Bradenton General was only slightly more attractive than the average small-town bus station, with hard plastic chairs, anemic blue walls and worn linoleum. At one end of the shoe-boxlike space were the all-important double doors leading to the operating rooms.

Dennis Swenson was presently behind those doors undergoing surgery for a fractured skull. He'd been there for nearly two of the three hours since Marca and Ian had arrived.

After conferring with Ian, Detective Brandt and the sheriff's deputy who'd taken the 911 call had left a little more than a half hour ago. It was nearly six.

"There was so much blood," Kimbra cried softly, her voice thin with disbelief and exhaustion. "Everything was sticky with it. And the smell, like wet metal." She glanced down at her sneakers, which were coated with dried blood, some of which was her own. "I'll never forget it, will I?"

"No," Ian said quietly. He was seated on one side of Kimbra with Marca on the other. "But the memory will gradually blur until you'll go for long chunks of time without thinking about it."

"Promise?" she asked, her voice shaky.

"Promise," he said, taking her fine-boned hand in his. "Tell

me again about the van. You said the windows were tinted dark
blue?''

"Yes."

"Any idea of the make or model?"

"No, sorry. American cars all look alike to me."

"Did you notice the license plate?"

"No, Dennis and I were being silly. He was chasing me with
the grocery cart, and I was dodging out of the way. Like...like
the game of tag I play with the boys sometimes?''

Ian nodded. "Tell me again what happened next."

While Kimbra went through the story again, Marca leaned her
head back against the wall and let the lethargy seep through her
bones. Though she'd done little more than listen and offer a
strong shoulder, she was utterly drained.

Kimbra, too, must be exhausted, yet she managed to remain
relatively calm as she repeated her story over and over. How she
and Dennis were putting the groceries they'd just purchased into
the back of Kimbra's little Mazda hatchback and playfully squab-
bling over a candy bar he'd purchased when four men came spill-
ing out of a dark blue van parked in the next space.

They'd worn camouflage fatigues and ski masks, and they'd
spouted racial epithets and filthy obscenities as they'd surrounded
the young couple. Big hulking men with young-sounding voices.
Educated voices.

"Think, Kimbra," Ian ordered in a calm, but compelling voice.
"Did you notice anything unusual about any of the men? Their
clothing? An accent when they spoke? Some unusual physical
characteristic?''

Kimbra furrowed her brow. She had a bruise on her jaw and
around her wrist where hard fingers had all but broken the fragile
bones. Her eyelids were swollen from her tears, and a bandage
covered the cut on her head.

"One of them, the one who grabbed me, he had enormous
hands. I noticed because I was trying to pry his fingers from my

arm so that I could go to Dennis. But that man, he...he threw me across the parking lot, like I was no more than a child."

"The bastards," Marca muttered, outrage and disgust twisting inside her.

"Any distinctive marks on those hands?" Ian persisted. Marca knew that he was thinking about the story Ted Matsuda had told.

Kimbra started to shake her head, then frowned. "The little finger," she said suddenly, her eyes going wide. "There was no fingernail. And it was shorter than it should be. That's it! Chopped off. He was missing part of the little finger on his right hand."

Marca sat up quickly, her gaze meeting Ian's. His mouth slanted, but his eyes were steely as he looked back at Kimbra. "You're doing good, Kimbra. Really good."

"It's hard to get it all straight. It happened so fast."

Ian shifted. "Let's try something, okay? You close your eyes and when I tell you to look at something in your mind, you tell me what you see."

Kimbra glanced at Marca who smiled and nodded. "It's okay, honey. You can trust Ian. I know he's big and scary looking, but he's really just a big old teddy bear."

Ian snorted. "Hell, and all this time I was thinking of myself as a cross between Mel Gibson and Sean Connery."

Kimbra laughed, her face more animated than Marca had seen it since she'd arrived. "No, Clint Eastwood. Like in *Dirty Harry*."

Ian grinned. "Smart girl," he said to Marca, who smiled too.

"*Woman*. And she certainly is."

More relaxed now, Kimbra sat back in her chair and closed her eyes. Ian took her through her day one more time, this time focusing on only her sense of sight.

Head cocked to one side and her expression intense, Kimbra listened carefully to every question. Before she spoke, she seemed to consider her answer, as though actually touching each image.

"And next to the broken bottle of apple juice, what do you see?" Ian asked quietly.

"The rear wheel of the van." She knew the procedure now and after a short pause went on. "It doesn't have a hub cap, just lug nuts. The tire is extra wide. There's mud spattered on the side and packed in the tread. But it's not black dirt like the soil in Marca's garden."

"What color is it?"

"Rusty colored, like the mud in my father's village."

"Good, honey, very good." Ian drew a breath. "Do you see anything else?"

Appearing lost in thought, Kimbra furrowed her brow and pursed her lips. "Nothing else," she said, opening her eyes. "I'm sorry."

"You did great," Ian said, his smile gentle. "Better than most. You're an excellent observer."

"Kimbra was tops in her class in Johannesburg," Marca said proudly. "She's going to be a doctor someday."

"Hey, way to go."

Kimbra's smile was short-lived, as though it cost too much to sustain. "Dennis calls me 'Doc' sometimes." Her voice broke, and she bit her lip. "If you would excuse me please, I think I'd like to wash my face."

She rose with the disciplined grace of a dancer and left the small room. Having gotten to his feet, as well, Ian stood with his long legs braced and his hands on his hips, watching her until she disappeared into the ladies' room halfway down the corridor.

"Poor kid is worn out," he said, turning back to Marca. The thoughtful look on his face turned to a frown. "You don't look much better."

"It's the waiting."

"Yeah, I hear you." He shifted, then held out one hand. "Would a hug help?"

"Yes, please," she said, letting him pull her to her feet and into his arms.

They were a perfect fit, she realized. Her head settled into the hollow of his shoulder at just the right angle for his mouth to brush her temple. Or, if she angled her neck, just right for his mouth to cover hers.

At the moment, though, it was the warm security of those strong arms holding her close that she needed most. And the steady comfort of his heart beating quietly beneath a padding of powerful muscle.

Her eyes drifted closed, and she breathed in the familiar scent of her favorite soap on his skin. It was a wonderfully whimsical combination—English lavender and raw masculinity. One that made her smile.

"I was right, you know," she said, drawing back to look up at him. "You *are* a teddy bear."

He glanced around, then kissed her. Hard. "A teddy bear who has work to do," he said, stepping back. "Will the two of you be okay for an hour or so while I check out the scene?"

"We'll be fine." She adjusted his collar. "Don't forget to come back for me."

"Just like a woman. Take her to bed a couple of times and she can't bear to let you out of her sight."

"There's that certainly," she said with a grin. "But in this case, Agent MacDougall, you also have my van."

"Are you sure you can't force down a cup of soup?" Marca asked gently. "Or maybe some juice. I can leave word to have us paged in the cafeteria if there's any word."

"No, nothing," Kimbra said with an apologetic smile. "My stomach is one big knot."

Marca slumped back in her chair, her gaze fixed on the clock on the wall. The hands seemed frozen, and yet they eventually clicked off another second and then another. Ian had been gone a little over an hour, yet it seemed like a decade.

"Do you think the boys are all right?" Kimbra muttered, her lyrical accent muted by worry.

Marca and Ian had dropped Ryan off at the mansion on their way to town, along with PJs and a change of clothes for all of the boys. The plan was for them to spend the night with Carly and Mitch.

"I'm sure they're fine, sweetie. Tilly was planning to serve spaghetti and Lettie was lobbying her daddy for a Pooh Bear marathon when I left."

"What about Ry's medicine?"

"I gave Mitch detailed instructions. He wrote them down."

Since both Mitch and Carly were essentially their own bosses, they worked it out so one of them was home in the afternoon to be with the children. Mitch especially loved to have his girls with him while he watched game films. Her boys, too, were beginning to like "Unca Mitch's movies."

"Dennis respects Coach Scanlon a lot." Fighting back a sob, Kimbra wiped her lashes with an already-saturated tissue. "He's...he's like a father to Dennis," she added, when she had herself under control again.

"Mitch is like that with his players. I think that's one of the reasons his team is so successful." Marca handed Kimbra a fresh tissue from the box that some kind soul had placed on the waiting room table next to the outdated magazines and Gideon Bible. "He said to give you his love and tell Dennis to hang tough."

Kimbra smiled a little. "Dennis's father was very kind when I rang him. Very calm, like Dennis before a game." She bit her lip and fought back tears. "He...he said he would phone back with his flight information." She glanced toward the door. "Are you sure the woman on the switchboard knows to find us here?"

"Yes. I told her myself and made her write it down for her relief in case she was gone when Mr. Swenson called."

"Why is it taking so long?" Kimbra asked after a moment or two.

Suddenly the doors swished open, and they both tensed only to slump in disappointment when they saw that the patient lying so still in the bed pushed by a burly, redheaded orderly was an elderly female.

"He's going to make it, honey," Marca assured her with a calm confidence she was far from feeling. "Dennis's as tough as an old Nebraska corn cob."

"He's also flesh and blood." Her face crumpled. "This is all because of me. Just like in my country, people hate because of color."

Marca slipped her arm around the girl's fine-boned shoulder to give her a reassuring hug. "Only a small, ugly minority."

"Why does not this sheriff who is always in the newspaper doing something to stop this violence?" Kimbra asked suddenly, her gaze going once again to the doors keeping her from the man she loved.

"Because the idiots who belong to the Brigade are careful to cover their tracks. But sooner or later they'll make a mistake and leave a clue behind. Maybe the rusty dirt you mentioned. Or the mutilated finger. Something that will help Ian find them."

"I like your man, Marca. He has kind eyes and gentle hands."

Marca smiled. "He does, doesn't he?"

"He cares for you, also. I could tell by the way he looks at you."

"I hope you're right. But I'm not counting on it."

After that, they lapsed into silence. Marca was drifting toward a doze when she heard a gruff male voice call her name.

"What's wrong?" she cried, leaping to her feet to talk to the deputy. "Is it Agent MacDougall?"

"Uh, yes, ma'am. He asked my partner and me to bring you back your van." He walked toward her, her keys in his hand.

"It's parked outside the main entrance, second row to your right as you exit."

"Thank you," she said, slipping the key ring into the pocket of her jeans. "Where's Agent MacDougall now?"

"Back at his motel, ma'am, checking out."

Marca's heart gave a hard thump. "Checking out? Are you sure?"

"That's what he said."

"Did he say where he was going?"

"No, ma'am. And I didn't ask. A man like Agent MacDougall, he's not the kind you question real close like." After expressing the hope once again that the victim would recover, he turned on his heel and left.

# Chapter 12

The road was deserted and had been since Marca had turned off the main highway. In the last five miles she hadn't passed another vehicle. Too much like the end of the world, she decided as she automatically flipped on the blinkers to make the turn into the short lane leading to her place.

It was nearly midnight. After several hours in recovery, Dennis had been taken to a room down the hall from Ted Matsuda's, and Kimbra was spending the night on a roll-away, shoe-horned into a corner of Dennis's room.

Woozy from the hours of waiting and the stress of worrying every minute of those hours, Marca had given some thought to begging a bed for herself, but had opted for her own instead.

In fifteen minutes she'd be asleep. At most it would take five to park and unlock her back door. Another five to climb the stairs and strip off her clothes. Five more and she'd be burrowed under the covers, doing her best to forget the sight of Dennis's swollen face. The swastika etched into his cheek had been the worst, a blatant obscenity.

She saw the porch lights first, cutting welcoming arcs into the black night. Lights that shouldn't be blazing, she realized as alarm shot through the fatigue. Kimbra was the only other person who had a key to her place, and she was at the hospital. So who had turned on the lights?

Raw fear gripped her before reason returned. Why would the Brigade be after her? Even as she asked herself the question, the answer was obvious. Because she had a black woman living with her, of course. To their twisted minds that made her the enemy.

Maybe she *should* let Richard select a gun for her, she thought, braking hard at the cluster of rhododendrons at the edge of her front yard. Letting the engine idle, she peered over the wheel, then let out a huff of air. Ian's dark blue Cherokee was parked on the left side of her two-vehicle garage.

Conscious that her vision kept blurring, undoubtedly from exhaustion, she guided the van into the vacant space at a snail's crawl and killed the engine. Moving slowly, her muscles stiff from the hours of tension, with her keys gripped tightly in one hand, she crossed the short section of driveway from the garage to the house, only to freeze as a grotesque shape detached itself from the darkness and came bounding toward her.

She let out a shriek a split second before a shrill whistle cut the air. The shape slid into the patch of light, revealing four splayed legs, a mass of wrinkled dog fur and a canine face bearing a doofus expression. Marca burst out laughing.

"Mutt, you idiot!" she exclaimed, bending to scratch the ridiculous tuft between his floppy ears. Looking enormously pleased with himself, the dog lapped at the toes of her sneakers.

"Sorry about that," Ian said as he walked toward her. He'd changed into jeans and a sweatshirt and seemed larger than life in the eerie blue glow cast by the mercury vapor lamp. "He's not big on manners."

"I don't mind," she assured them both. "He has other redeeming qualities."

Ian squatted on his haunches and shot her a look that questioned her sanity. "Name one."

"Loyalty. Courage. I'll never forget the way he tried to protect me from those goons."

Ian grunted. "Probably figured you for a free meal. Dummy damn near eats up half my paycheck every month."

He ruffled the dog's fur, then held out a big hand to help her up. As she stood, she staggered a little, and he slipped his arm around her shoulders. It seemed natural to snuggle close, maybe even lean a little. Just for a moment or two, until her nerves stopped jangling and strength returned to her tired body.

"How's Swenson?" he asked as they walked toward the back stoop. Mutt trotted along next to them, his tail slapping the air.

"Asleep when I left. The surgeon thinks he'll make a full recovery."

"Score one for the good guys." Though his tone was laconic, she saw the flash of relief in his eyes and loved him for it.

"Kimbra didn't come with you?"

"No, she couldn't bear to leave Dennis alone. His father is flying in tomorrow morning at six, and I promised to pick him up at the airport in Medford. I'll take her a change of clothes and some toiletries when I drop Mr. Swenson off at the hospital."

"No airport. You're beat. You need sleep."

"But someone has to be there to meet the poor man and Kimbra—"

"Someone will be," he said, before ordering the dog to stay outside under pain of an early death.

"I don't mind if he comes in," she said, smiling down at Mutt who was gazing up at her with canine worship in his eyes. To sweeten the pot, he gave out with a piteous whine, then licked her hand. "It's okay, baby. Marca won't let you shiver out in the cold."

"Sucker," Ian muttered, before giving the adoring animal a nod. "Behave yourself," he ordered, as Mutt bounded up the steps and into the utility room.

Marca grinned as she followed. "The boys are going to be crazy about you," she told the dog as his tail thudded against the front of the dryer.

"He's not used to kids," Ian warned, his hands warm on her shoulders as he steered her into the kitchen where the rich aroma of simmering beef greeted her.

"You cooked?" she asked, her tone reverently hushed.

"Yeah." His gaze narrowed, and his chin jutted. "You got a problem with that?"

"Good gracious, no! Just the opposite. It's just that I'm, well, to tell you the truth, I'm just a little dumbfounded to find you here."

"Yeah, well so am I."

Looking grumpy and a little dangerous, with a day's growth of whiskers darkening his jaw, he eased the leather tote that did double duty as a purse from her shoulder, then frowned and gave it a couple of pokes with his finger. "Jeez, Marca, what are you packing in this thing, anyway? Gold bars?"

"With three toddlers a mom has to be prepared for anything— and I mean anything."

"No wonder you look whipped, lugging around a full field pack all day." With a flick of his wrist, he tossed it onto the counter and something clanked. She tried to recall if there was anything breakable in the tote, then gave up.

"Sit," he said, leading her over to the table, which was set for two.

After settling her into a chair, he walked to the stove and filled two bowls. She noticed a loaf of French bread on the table and a pot of honey.

"Is that chili I smell?" she asked, her stomach rumbling.

"Trail stew. Learned it from an old Navajo wrangler who worked for my uncle once. Mostly stuff from cans. I improvised." He returned to the table and set the bowl of steaming meat and vegetables on the mat in front of her. With the aplomb suitable to a five-star restaurant, he unfolded a paper napkin and placed it on her lap.

"Don't wait for me," he ordered, handing her the fork.

Bemused, she blinked up at him. "You're being bossy again, MacDougall."

"I'm being thoughtful, damn it, and I'm not real good at it, so don't push your luck." Because the worry in his eyes belied the surly words, she forgave him.

"Did I say I disliked bossy?"

He grinned a little. "Where do you keep your wineglasses?"

"Sideboard in the dining room. Top right."

He disappeared momentarily, returning with one of her wedding goblets. "You want red or white?"

"White. There's a bottle of Riesling in the fridge. I opened it Saturday when I got back from the game to celebrate the victory."

"Was Swenson still out of it when you left?" he asked as he opened the refrigerator door.

"Pretty much. Bless his heart, he was more worried about Kimbra than himself. Kept asking if they'd hurt her." She forked stew into her mouth, tasted, then sighed in pure bliss. "Is there any chance that old Navajo wrangler would consider hiring on at my little ranch?" she asked, closing her eyes to better savor the divine blend of rich flavors. "I'll take out a second mortgage to pay his salary if that's what it takes."

"Nope. He's dead. Got kicked in the head by a mean old mustang stallion he was trying to break."

She opened her eyes to find that he'd set the glass of wine in front of her and a glass of milk in front of his own place. "No wine for you?"

"Hate the stuff, actually." He sat down in the chair opposite her and put his napkin on his lap.

"I think I have some scotch—somewhere." She waved vaguely toward the cabinets before summoning the strength to take a sip.

"I'll pass."

"Bourbon? Or brandy?"

"I don't drink."

She frowned. He'd certainly been putting away the booze the night they met. At least three doubles. "Since when?" she asked, unable to stifle her curiosity.

His gaze flickered, then met hers. "Since I woke up one morning and realized a damned bottle had become my best friend."

"Is this a recent realization?"

"Nope." He took a bite of stew and chewed. His reaction was considerably less rapturous than hers. "Happened around the same time I realized I'd never be able to drink myself to death, no matter how hard I worked at it."

"I've heard it can be done if a person tries hard enough."

His mouth relaxed into a grin that was almost mischievous. "Trust me, sugar, I was putting my heart and soul into it. But every time I got a real good drunk going, I'd throw up and have to start all over again. It just plumb wore me out."

Marca glanced down at her stew. "Thank you so very much for sharing that, MacDougall."

He laughed. "You asked."

"You don't have to be so honest."

He put down his fork and took a drink of milk. "Yeah, I do," he said as he set the glass on the table again. "I don't want to hurt you, Marca. God knows, I've hurt too many people in my life as it is."

She felt a thud in her stomach. "It's been my experience that when a man says he doesn't want to hurt me, he's about to say or do something that will do just that."

His mouth slanted toward a smile, but his eyes remained somber. "You want me to leave?"

"I don't know. Maybe you'd better tell me why you're here first."

"The short answer is protection. For both you and Kimbra."

"You think the Brigade will come after us?"

Though he shrugged, she sensed a gritty determination riding below the controlled surface. "It's possible. I talked to the sheriff about assigning a deputy to you, but he's short staffed as it is."

She drew a breath and thought about the bruises on her young friend's arms. And the fragile bones in that small wrist. The man who had grabbed her could easily have crushed those bones—or worse.

"So far they haven't attacked women," she said in an attempt to reassure herself.

"Not here. Not yet. But they nearly killed a Latina in L.A. because she was walking down the street holding hands with an Anglo."

"I...see."

"You're the perfect target, Marca. A house in the country, two women alone with...with three little boys."

"I could buy a gun." She drew a quick breath and managed a grin. "An Uzi, maybe."

Instead of grinning back, he gave her a hard look. "Have you ever fired a weapon?"

"No, of course not."

"Ever loaded one, cleaned one? Pointed one at another human being and pulled the trigger, knowing that one of you is about to die?"

She shook her head. "I get the message. No Uzi."

He ran his fingers up and down his glass. His eyes were dark, his face controlled. Behind the control, however, she sensed an indefinable but powerful emotion.

"You're vulnerable, Marca." He raised his gaze to hers. "So are your children and your friends. I can't promise to keep you safe, but I can damn sure do my best."

She directed a pointed gaze at the duffel bag and worn leather briefcase on the floor by the door to the utility room. "By moving in?"

"That's the best way, yes."

She put down her fork and wiped her mouth. Her body was a bundle of nerves. "With or without my permission?"

The impatience was back in his eyes. And something darker and more dangerous. "In spite of what you think, I'm not a bully, Marca."

Her smile was designed to tell him that she knew that. "Is it your intention to share my bed as well as my board?"

"Yes, but maybe I read you wrong." His gaze narrowed, challenging her. "I've bunked on the floor before on a job."

A job? Is that all she was? Another potential victim he'd dedicated his life to shield from the insanity of maniacs like Renfrew?

Her first inclination was to refuse. But that was pride speaking. False pride, perhaps. The same false pride that had kept her in a failing marriage until it nearly destroyed her. Maybe she learned slowly, but she did learn.

Besides, she had to think of Kimbra and the boys. Because he was right, she realized. Hatred had no logic. And there was something else to consider. Something vitally important. Living here, sharing their lives as he invariably would, Ian could get to know his sons. And they, him.

Once he knew them, he wouldn't be able to keep himself from loving them. No matter what happened between the two of them, she wanted her boys to have a relationship with their father.

Marca picked up her wine and took a sip, holding the cold Riesling in her mouth for a moment before letting it trickle down her throat. It was funny how ordinary everything seemed, she realized. No blaring of trumpets, no dramatic drum rolls, nothing but the quiet ticking of the clock on the wall and the rapid thudding of her heartbeat to herald one of the most important decisions she had ever made in forty-three turbulent years.

"It would be silly of me to pretend I don't want to sleep with you," she admitted, looking directly at him over the rim of her glass. "And it would be foolhardy to refuse protection for those I love and for myself, as well." She managed another grin which he acknowledged with a nod. "But there are some problem areas I think we should discuss first."

His mouth flattened, and his eyes turned steely, offering a hint of the dangerous man behind the steady calm. "Your house, your rules?"

"You really are formidable, you know," she said, smiling. "One minute you're dazzling me with tenderness and the next you're ready to go for my throat."

He shoved aside the half-eaten stew and rested his forearms on the table. She felt the force of his personality reach across the table to buffet her. Fierce little licks of power, a subtle lash of savagery barely contained. Somehow she resisted the urge to sit back in her chair. "Suppose you tell me exactly what kind of problem areas we're talking about here," he said quietly.

"Logistics. Three adults and three children in one small house. Creating order out of chaos is hard work. It takes planning and attention to detail."

In what had to be some canine equivalent of ESP, Mutt chose that moment to give out with an impatient bark. Marca burst out laughing. "I stand corrected, Mutt. Three adults, three children and one pampered pet."

Toenails clattered on the tile as Ian's no-name dog came trotting over to her. With a delighted "woof" he rested his scarred snout on her thigh and looked up at her expectantly.

"I think I'm in big trouble here," Ian muttered, shaking his head as he leaned back.

She grinned as she rubbed Mutt's head. "This is just the beginning, MacDougall. Tomorrow you'll find out what it's like to live in the center ring of a three-ring circus."

It was after 1:00 a.m. when Ian wandered out of the master bathroom, expecting to find Marca sound asleep on the side of the bed she'd claimed as her own. Nonnegotiable, of course. One of the house rules she vehemently denied existed. Like ordering him to shower at night, since she and Kimbra already had dibs on morning showers.

Ian hated to shower at night.

He also hated to sleep in a heated room. Hers was nice and toasty. He figured he'd be sweating inside of five minutes.

Instead of sleeping, however, she was sitting up in bed, a large zippered day-planner propped against her knees, writing furiously. While he'd been in the shower, she'd changed into an oversize man's T-shirt with a stretched-out V neck that stopped just short of indecent. It was the dark outline of her nipples against the soft material that had him sucking in hard, however. Suddenly his tired old body wasn't as tired as he'd thought.

"Tomorrow is going to be really hectic," she said without

looking up. ''Kimbra will want to spend as much time as she can with Dennis, of course, so that means taking the boys to day care. Tilly will give them breakfast, so that's taken care of.'' She paused for breath, her pen tapping the edge of the planner as she considered. He told himself that only an insensitive jerk would be thinking about coaxing her out of that shirt after the kind of day she'd had.

''The campus day care center where I take the boys opens at seven-thirty, but I won't be back from the airport by then.'' She glanced up, a frown pleating her forehead. ''What time do you start gardening or...whatever?''

''Eight-thirty.''

''Great! That means you can pick up the boys at the mansion and take them to day care before you start work. I'll draw you a map.''

Handle three two-year-olds on his own? Little boys who didn't even know him? Ian felt a moment of raw panic before he wrestled it down.

''I'm handling the airport run, remember? You do the day care bit.''

''Hmm, I suppose that does make more sense. The boys don't really know you yet, and neither do the ladies at the center. Yes, that'll work.'' Returning her attention to the schedule, she made another note.

Ian rummaged through his duffel for a clean pair of briefs, then turned his back and unwound the towel he'd looped around his waist. He slept nude as a rule, but he figured he'd better wear U-trou until she got used to him.

He turned back and caught her stifling a yawn. In the soft glow from the bedside lamp, the shadows under her eyes were muted, but visible nonetheless. His heart stuttered a little at the fragile droop to her mouth.

''Lights-out in two minutes,'' he said, taking his watch from the pocket of his trousers to wind it. When he was finished, he put the Hamilton on the table next to his side of the bed and slipped between the covers.

It had been a long time since he'd shared a bed. A long time since he'd wanted to. A long time since he'd wanted anything as much as he wanted Marca. It scared him a little. Hell, it scared him a lot. Almost as much as becoming a dad again—and that flat-out terrified him.

Her smile was welcoming as he scooted closer, but the distracted look in her dark eyes told him her thoughts were somewhere else—on the schedule she seemed obsessed with mapping out in fifteen minute segments, he suspected.

"Enough," he said, plucking the thick book from her fingers before tossing it onto the floor. He did the same with the pen, earning him an indignant look. "No arguing, sweetheart. You're exhausted. And so am I."

The anger he'd seen gathering like storm clouds behind her eyes dissipated, and she sighed. "You're right. It has been a long day."

She sat up and turned off the light, then rearranged the pillows before settling down again. "Do you sleep on your back or your stomach?" she asked after a moment of silence.

Hell, he thought. Now she's organizing our sleeping habits.

"Stomach," he said after thinking about it. "How about you?"

"On my side." As though to illustrate her point she shifted to face him. There was just enough light coming through the loose weave of the curtains to outline her body under the quilt. Her hair smelled like roses and tickled his arm.

"This is not going to work," he said, turning to face her. "Either one of us is going to have to change or we buy a king-size bed." He flattened his palm over the cap of her shoulder and rubbed gently. To soothe her into sleep he told himself, even as the one part of his well-disciplined body that was not under his control gave an unruly jerk.

"You could sleep on your side, and we could cuddle spoon fashion," she said after a moment's thought. "You know, front to back."

"Only if it's your front to my back," he said, feeling decidedly uncomfortable. "Otherwise, we're doomed."

She gave a little gurgle of laughter. "Maybe I like doomed."

He closed his eyes. "Marca, I'm trying really hard to be a good guy here. You've had a stressful day. You're worn out."

"Much as I hate to admit it, you're absolutely right." She ran her fingers over his arm. "I wouldn't mind a hug though," she said softly. "Yours are pretty special, as I recall."

She spoke lightly. Casually, even. He thought back to the night on the beach. The way she smiled and laughed in the bar. She'd made jokes about the blood on her jeans and the bruises on her arm. He'd had to look deep into her eyes to see the terror. His brave lady was mostly bluff and all heart.

"I think we can manage a hug," he said a little gruffly as he turned onto his back. "Come here, sweetheart."

With a soft little sigh, she settled over him like a blanket, her head on his shoulder and one leg splayed over his thighs. Her breasts were soft, her body warm.

"Nice," she murmured, drowsily. He felt her lips curve against his neck as she kissed him. Two minutes later she was asleep. And he was as hard as a rock.

Way to go, MacDougall, he thought, inhaling the rich, warm scent of woman—and peace. Welcome to chaos.

# Chapter 13

Marca had just finished fending off an inquiry from UPI about a rumored attack on one of the T-wolves when Winston ushered Carly into the office the next morning at a little past nine.

"I got your message you wanted to see me, but if you're busy, I can come back," Carly assured her, her gaze skimming the organized chaos that was Marca's desktop.

"No, stay, please," Marca said, waving her to a chair. "I need one of those executive decisions you get paid big bucks for issuing."

"Uh-oh," Carly said, exchanging rueful looks with Winston. "I think I hear my phone ringing."

"Sit," Marca ordered, opening a folder tagged in red, indicating highest priority.

"Only because you asked so sweetly." Carly settled into the chair opposite the desk and, as was her habit, slipped off her spectator pumps.

"I'm leaving for the printer's in ten minutes," Winston told Marca when she glanced up again. "Is there anything you need from town?"

"Dog food," Marca said with a grateful smile. "That kibbly kind—or whatever. Ian brought a bag with him, but I can tell by the way Mutt goes through the stuff that we're going to need more."

Ever efficient, Winston made a note on his pad. "Twenty-five pounds?"

Marca flashed back to the huge mound of dry chunks that had disappeared before she'd had time to take more than three sips of her morning coffee. And then the opportunistic hound had come begging for a piece of her bagel.

Ian had already left by then. She'd been sleeping so soundly she hadn't heard him leave. But he'd made a pot of coffee before he'd gone, and left a note next to the coffeemaker asking her to feed the "dumb animal." Dumb like a fox, Marca figured. The wily canine had obviously been pampered within an inch of his charmed life.

"Better make it fifty. And get some dog treats, too. The boys are going to love their new pet."

Winston shared a knowing look with the woman he loved to call Madam President. "Does that man work fast or *what?*"

"Apparently at warp speed," Carly agreed, her lips twitching.

Marca sighed. "You are dismissed now, Winston," she said with a pointed look at the door.

"Don't forget to catch the phone while I'm gone."

Marca winced. "Do me a favor and switch it to voice mail."

"You got it, boss," he said as he left and closed the door.

"So what was it like, sleeping in the same bed with a gorgeous ATF agent?" Carly asked when they were alone.

A smile bloomed in Marca's mind. For better or worse, the man was back in her life. For how long was a question she refused to consider. "Like cuddling up to a blast furnace."

Carly clucked in sympathy. "Why is it that men get the great metabolisms and we get cellulite?"

Marca swiveled her chair to the side and reached into her tote for the chocolate Kisses she'd stuck in at the last minute before leaving home. "I live for the day cellulite is declared the ultimate in female beauty,'' she muttered as she ripped open the bag and dumped a goodly number of the foil-wrapped pieces onto the desktop. Both she and Carly reached at the same time.

"Ian's also a sprawler, like Trev. When I was kicking off the covers, I was dodging arms and legs. I ended up clinging to ten inches on the edge of the mattress most of the night."

"Mitch can't sprawl because of the paralysis, but somehow he manages to control the space, anyway." Carly smiled, and her eyes softened. "No matter how we start out, I always end up in his arms. He claims he can't get a good night's sleep until I'm on top of him."

"A fate worse than death, of course."

"Of course!" Carly eyed the dwindling pile of Kisses longingly, then shrugged and dove in. "You realize, of course, that you could be badly hurt if he doesn't fall in love with you and the boys."

"Are you telling me I should throw him out?"

"Not me. I stopped trying to tell you what to do about five minutes after you barreled into our dorm room, appropriated the bottom bunk and began compiling your list of 'dos and don'ts for room 2A.'"

"I didn't!"

"You did and you know it."

Marca had been the first person in Carly's life to yell at her, the first to argue with her, the first to tell her she was being a self-centered jerk. Instead of deferring to her every whim as nearly everyone in her life but Tilly had done for eighteen cosseted years, the black-haired dynamo from Henderson, Washington, had sat her down at the end of their first stormy month as roommates and given her a lecture on Marca's rules for survival.

Now, as Carly peeled foil, she wanted to warn her friend to be careful. But she was afraid to spoil Marca's happiness.

"What?" Marca asked, leaning forward to pin her with a piercing look. "You've got that prissy look again. Something's bothering you."

Carly sighed. "I just don't want you to get hurt again, that's all."

"I'm a big girl, Carly. My life was very nearly perfect without Ian in it. I don't need a man to make me feel fulfilled or valued or attractive."

"I guess that means you won't be accepting Richard's offer of marriage, then?"

Marca's mouth popped open, and she shot a glance at the fading roses. "Oh, my goodness, I'd completely forgotten about that."

Carly collected the discarded bits of foil and rolled them into a ball. "Somehow I doubt that Richard has," she said as she lobbed the foil over the desk toward the wastebasket.

"He's coming to dinner Friday night. I'll...talk to him."

Carly grinned a little. "Take a memo, Ms. Kenworthy," she said, holding up her hand. "Number one, don't you think it might be a trifle awkward talking to Richard with Ian sitting at the table, too?" she asked, ticking off one finger. "And number two, are you or aren't you going to marry Richard?" Down went the second finger.

"Aren't," Marca said, before Carly could come up with number three. "Seeing Ian again has made me realize that a relationship without passion would never last. Not if I'm one of the parties of said relationship, anyway."

Looking relieved, Carly lowered her hand. "I always said you were a bright girl, Marcella Frances."

"Not bright enough to figure a painless way to keep from hurting Richard." She chewed her lip, first listing her options in her mind, then narrowing them gradually until there was only one. "Much as I'd like to, I just can't turn him down by phone. As you pointed out, dinner at Chez Kenworthy as planned is *not* a good idea. I'll call him and invite him to a late lunch."

She picked up her pen and made a note on her desk calendar. At the same time Carly checked her watch. "I have exactly fifteen more minutes. Now that the important stuff is out of the way, you want to tell me about this executive decision you need?"

Marca glanced down at the forgotten notes in front of her. "I think we're going to have to issue a press release about the attack on Dennis. The 'jackals' as Mitch so lovingly refers to the brothers and sisters of the media are hot on the scent."

Carly sighed. "It'll be like setting a match to the parents, especially those of minority students. Not to mention the furor it's going to cause on campus."

"The news is already spreading. My phone hasn't stopped ringing." To illustrate her point she tapped the console with her pen. All six lines were blinking. "So far Winston is handling most of them with a 'no comment at this time,' but that's not going to work for very long. If we don't issue a statement, it might look as if we're not doing anything about the problem."

"God, I hate that Renfrew person and cretins like him." Carly sighed. She and Mitch had stopped by the hospital around eight the previous night to see Dennis, but he'd been in the recovery room.

"How's Dennis this morning? Have you talked to Kimbra?" Carly asked, concern lining her face.

Marca let her head fall forward while she tried to massage away some of the tightness at the nape of her neck. "She called about an hour ago. She and Mr. Swenson had gone down to the cafeteria while the doctor was with Dennis."

"How's she getting along with Dennis's father?"

"She said he was a nice man. Big like Dennis. She said to thank you and Mitch for the flowers and the phone call this morning. Dennis was very pleased to hear from the coach."

"The least we can do," Carly said, frowning as she ran her fingers through her chin-length bob. Marca recognized the sign. Her friend was worried and trying hard not to show it.

"Apparently Dennis was awake when Ian arrived with Mr. Swenson, but according to Kimbra, he couldn't tell Ian much of anything about the attackers."

"You're the PR expert, Marce. What do suggest we do?"

Marca glanced down at the list of callers she'd promised to contact before she went public. Not for an exclusive, because she almost never promised that, but to return the courtesy to those who'd agreed to hold off on public speculation for twenty-four hours. Favor for favor, one of the unwritten rules of her trade.

"We have to issue a statement. That's a given. I've offered the nurses on Dennis's floor a steak dinner at Gallagher's in exchange for keeping a lid on it for just a few more hours. But their co-operation won't be much help."

Carly absorbed that, mulled it over and nodded. "Agreed. So what do we say?"

"That's the rub. I'd like to consult with Ian before I decide what kind of spin to put on this." She drummed her fingers against the list of journalists and sportscasters, sorting through possible scenarios in her mind. "I'm better at generating publicity than downplaying it," she admitted when her thoughts refused to narrow. "When we were trying to generate alumni support for the Wolves I knew exactly what to do. The downside risk to creating hoopla and uproar was negligible. But in this case, it all seems like the downside."

"You're saying you think Ian might be able to suggest the right slant to take?"

"Yes. Or at the very least, tell me what to do to avoid making a terrible situation worse." She drew a breath. "The last thing I want to do is to make Renfrew so mad he retaliates against some-one else at Bradenton. Or anywhere else."

Carly ground her teeth. "It's like being blackmailed," she mut-tered. "We can't do what we want, what's *right,* because it might hurt someone."

"And yet, where do you draw the line between protecting oth-ers and perpetuating a great wrong?"

Carly's expression turned sad. "It appears that Ian drew a line—and will spend the rest of his life suffering for it."

Marca drew a breath. "God help me, I hope I never have to make a choice like that."

"You probably won't. Nor will I, simply because we *do* have people like Ian."

Marca reached for another of the foil-wrapped treats, then realized with a sharp jolt of surprise that she'd lost her taste for chocolate.

According to the numerals carved in the gray granite lintel over the main entrance, the building housing Bradenton's athletic department had been erected in 1915. Constructed of Oregon granite, the rough gray facade had the same weather-beaten, slightly sinister look of a medieval dwelling as the rest of the buildings on campus.

The stadium was within a stone's throw of the wide double doors, squatting like a steel and concrete mountain in the midst of a huge parking lot. "The Home of the Timberwolves." The team Mitch Scanlon had built, and in the process—according to the head gardener, who was clearly a fan of the charismatic retired quarterback—saved Bradenton from the auctioneer's gavel.

Scanlon was in the building. Ian had seen him arrive a little past nine, right after he had started in on the leaves that had fallen during the night. As he'd worked, he'd kept an eye peeled, and Scanlon's silver Jag sedan was still in its slot next to the rear entrance.

As he raked, he'd let his mind sift through the information he'd amassed. A punk who spoke good English. Expensive sneakers. A powerfully muscled hand missing the tip of a little finger. In a building full of jocks, a small detail like that was easy to overlook. In the close confines of a locker room, men seldom gave each other more than cursory glances. Ian knew it was a long shot, but he might get lucky.

The last of the stragglers heading for their ten-o'clock classes had finally disappeared. Still, Ian waited another five minutes before propping his rake against the side of the building and slipping inside.

The foyer was deserted when he entered. Inside were thick, lath-and-plaster walls, marble floors and high ceilings. According to the directory affixed to the wall by the wide staircase, Scanlon's office was on the ground floor. A quick look at the numbers on the nearest doors had him turning to his left and heading down the deserted corridor.

Senses on alert, the way they had to be when he went into an unfamiliar territory, he checked out names, noted exits, kept his hands free. Most of the office doors were closed. He heard muffled sounds from some, music from others. According to the directory, the basketball courts were in the other wing, and the classrooms were upstairs. There was even a swimming pool in the basement.

He heard Scanlon's voice a split second before he reached the open door. "Yeah, I know, honey. Marca's already phoned and laid down the law. Refer all calls from the media to her."

Holding the phone to his ear with one big hand, Scanlon was seated behind a large oak desk piled with notebooks and file folders. A half-dozen or so picture frames took up the rest of the space, and a pair of obviously well-used, brown, forearm crutches were propped against one edge.

Dressed very much as he appeared on the sidelines, in a pale blue polo shirt with the T-Wolves insignia emblazoned across his massive chest, he was listening to someone on the other end as he flipped through the pages of a thick blue notebook of what looked like play diagrams.

Other than the glasses with thin gold frames sliding halfway down the considerable length of his nose and the silver in his thick, dark blond hair he looked very much like the all-pro quarterback he'd once been. In fact, if Ian didn't know better, he would swear Scanlon could take the field with the team he'd built and do a damn good job of holding his own against twenty-year-old bruisers.

As soon as he caught sight of Ian, Scanlon flashed that familiar grin and waved him into the room. Instead, Ian propped a shoulder against the jamb and waited. At the same time he noticed the position of the windows and swept the room for places a man his size could take cover.

It wasn't a large office, but it had a quiet dignity, like the man who occupied it. Though trophies lined the shelves, all were for

Timberwolves feats, and Timberwolves players. The pictures, too, were of his players and former T-wolves coaches.

"No, the nurse I spoke with around nine gave me the 'resting comfortably' bull. I figured I'd stop by the hospital around lunch time and check out Dennis's condition myself. Besides, I want to make sure his dad knows the college is picking up the tab for his plane fare and lodging."

He paused, listened. Smiled. "I love you, too, sweetheart." He hung up and offered Ian a rueful look. "Something I can help you with?"

"I hope so, Coach." Because caution was as familiar as breathing, Ian checked the corridor before stepping inside and closing the door.

"I'm Ian MacDougall," he said as he crossed to the desk. "I figured your wife has filled you in."

Scanlon leaned forward and offered a hand as big as Ian's own. He had a solid grip and a steady way of meeting a man's eyes. A cop who lived or died by what he read in an enemy's eyes tended to evaluate a potential ally the same way. Disabled or not, Mitch Scanlon was a man Ian would trust to guard his back anytime, anyplace.

"How can I help?" Scanlon asked as he sat back.

"First off, have you seen this man?" Ian pulled Renfrew's photo from his pocket and handed it to Scanlon.

"Afraid not," the coach said after studying the side-by-side poses intently. "Carly said he looked like the guy who does our taxes. She was right."

Disappointed, but not surprised, Ian returned the photo to his pocket. "Nice thing for the college to do, paying for Mr. Swenson's visit."

Though Scanlon's gaze never faltered, Ian would lay down heavy change that Scanlon would be the one writing the check to cover Paul Swenson's expenses. "Old Brady's a special place, Agent MacDougall. Anyone who walks through the gate is considered family."

"Call me Ian, okay? Since I'm family now, too—at least temporarily."

Scanlon grinned, then suddenly winced in obvious pain. His jaw tight and his gaze narrowed, he encircled his left thigh with those big hands and massaged rhythmically. After a moment the jagged look of pain around his eyes eased.

"Sorry about that," he said with just enough of an edge to his voice to forestall any sympathy Ian might be tempted to offer. "Crossed wires in my back."

Ian acknowledged that with a nod. It was evident that embarrassment didn't sit well with Scanlon, but he was handling it well. A result of living twenty-four hours of every day with a visible handicap, Ian figured.

"Yesterday, when I was talking with Professor Matsuda, he remembered that one of the men who attacked him was missing the tip of his little finger. He also said that the man was very large and moved like an athlete. He might also have a tatoo of a spider web someplace on his body. Probably in the left or right armpit. To bastards like him it's a sign, like a badge of honor, that he's participated in a beating." He paused to give Scanlon time to digest that, then asked, "To your knowledge, do any of your players fit that description?"

Scanlon's jaw clenched, and one hand plowed furrows in his thick hair. His eyes glittered with a steely anger that Ian understood all too well.

"His name is Will Peterson," he said in a voice lashed with frustration and disgust. "Plays right tackle. Told me he shot off the tip of his finger playing with his dad's gun when he was five."

Scanlon's hand slowly fisted on the desk. "He was late for practice yesterday. Had a cut on his cheek and a couple of scrapes on the back of his hands. Told me he'd had a fender bender with his van."

Ian felt a savage punch of excitement. Maybe they just got lucky. "Any idea where he lives?"

Scanlon nodded. "All my players live on campus. It's one of my rules. Peterson lives with a guy named Krauss. Rolfe Krauss.

They'll both be on the practice field this afternoon. Two o'clock sharp.''

Marca took a sip of iced tea and waited for the busboy to clear away her half-eaten shrimp salad. Normally one of her favorite entrées, the salad had all but stuck in her throat.

Instead of eating, she'd talked. About her plans to add a room to the house. The upcoming football game. The boys' birthday party next month. Forestalling the inevitable, she knew, yet she hated to inflict pain on a friend.

Across the table Richard was meticulously spreading butter on a poppy seed roll. In some unsettling coincidence, they'd been seated at the same window table she'd shared with Ian.

"I must tell you how pleased I was to get your call this morning," Richard said with a smile as he cut the roll into precise halves. Wielding the knife with the dexterity of a surgeon, he sliced the halves into half again. "I'm taking it as a good omen."

She waited until the busboy was out of earshot before saying quietly, "I'm sorry, Richard. I asked you here so that I could tell you I can't marry you."

His face froze, and for an instant he looked almost stupefied. His eyes had a strange cast to them, she realized. They seemed lighter to her as well. More gray than brown. Or perhaps she was simply becoming accustomed to gray eyes.

"I see," he said at last.

"I never meant to hurt you, Richard. I hope you believe that."

"Of course." He took a moment to select a bit of roll, then conveyed it to his mouth with an almost feminine delicacy. His gaze remained passive and unreadable on hers as he chewed and swallowed. Then lashes dipping, he blotted his mouth with his napkin before returning it to his lap.

"I assume your decision has been prompted by the return of the man we spoke about yesterday," he said, bringing his gaze to hers again.

"Yes."

"A faculty member, I presume?" His color had heightened,

giving his face a sunburned look she found surprisingly unattrac
tive.

"No, we met at a conference."

"Oh, so he's in public relations."

"Something like that, yes." A woman at the next tabl
laughed. The man with her joined in. A couple passed, followin
the hostess to a table in the back.

"With one of the Madison Avenue firms?"

"No, he's with a smaller...agency. In Florida."

"Ah." He took another bite and went through the ritual o
chewing and blotting his mouth. Those fussy mannerisms ha
never bothered her before. Now they made her want to giggle
Pressing her napkin to her mouth, she pretended interest in th
view beyond the window.

"I've some close friends in the business community in Miam
An old army buddy, in fact, who owns a string of sporting goo
stores and does a great deal of advertising in the area."

Marca returned her gaze to Richard's face. "Yes, well—"

"What's your...friend's name? Perhaps I've met him at th
country club or at the marina."

Marca took another sip of iced tea and fervently wished sh
could fast forward through this entire conversation to the en
where they parted amicably as friends. "I don't think he's th
country club type actually."

"You never know, my dear. But if you'd prefer not to tell me
I understand."

The hurt underlying his words said just the opposite, adding t
the guilt that seemed to be piling up exponentially. "His name i
Ian. Ian MacDougall."

His expression remained set. "No, I've never met the ma
socially."

"He's from California originally. Fresno." She reached for he
tea, then realized there was nothing left but melting cubes. Glanc
ing around, she caught the busboy's eye and held up her glass.
He nodded and disappeared into the kitchen, returning almos

immediately with the tea pitcher. After filling her glass, he reached for Richard's salad plate with his free hand.

He bobbled it, almost dropping the salad fork in Richard's lap before he caught himself. Eyes narrowed, Richard hissed out a warning that had the boy's eyes goggling.

"Beg pardon, sir," the hapless student muttered, backing away. Clearly Richard was more upset than she thought.

Marca realized she was staring and shifted focus, smiling a little as she sought to reassure him. "I've treasured your friendship, Richard, and I hope we'll continue to be friends."

"That goes without saying, my dear." Leaning forward, he reached across the table to cover her hand where it rested on the table. "I just hope this fellow MacDougall treats you right." He squeezed her hand, his well-manicured fingers pinching a little too tightly into her flesh. At her wince, he murmured an apology and withdrew his hand.

"Of course I...we will still expect you to come to dinner Friday night," she said, resisting the urge to rub her stinging fingers.

"'We' meaning you and your betrothed?"

Marca blinked. "We're not engaged," she hastened to clarify.

"I see. Merely sleeping together." His voice was smooth, his expression placid, giving no hint of censure. Yet there was no question that she'd just been crudely insulted.

"That's none of your business," she said, chilling her voice.

"Sadly, that's true," he said, sitting back. "I'm afraid I'm not a gallant loser, Marca. In fact, I hate losing almost as much as I hate making a fool of myself—especially over a woman."

He was hurt and trying not to show it, she realized, and her earlier anger dissipated in a flood of regret. "Richard, please believe me, if you're referring to me, you did not make a fool of yourself. Just the opposite. I'm humbled by your offer, but I can't in all honesty accept one man when I'm in love with another."

His face was stony, his body rigid, and then, suddenly, he seemed to shake off the anger and the hurt, and was his charming self again.

"My dear, you are a prize any man would move heaven and

earth to win. I tried my best, but obviously it wasn't enough. Still, we've enjoyed some lovely hours together. For that I thank you. I do believe I'll pass on dinner, though. I don't relish sitting across from the man who bested me.''

Had his speech always been so stilted? she wondered as she smiled in response. ''You'll always be welcome.''

He nodded. ''And your friend. MacDougall? I take it he's staying with you?''

''At the moment, yes.'' Relieved that the worst was over, Marca glanced around until she caught the eye of their waiter. She mimed writing out a check and he grinned, coming forward immediately.

''Would you care for anything else?'' he asked each in turn. Marca declined, expecting Richard to do the same.

''I'd like coffee now,'' he said, ''and a brandy.'' His smile was congenial as he added, ''Too bad cigars are no longer allowed in restaurants.''

Marca cleared her throat. ''I'm afraid I'll have to get back to the office,'' she told him after the waiter retreated. ''I have meetings scheduled.''

''Of course, my dear. Run along. I'll take care of the check.''

''I invited you, remember? I'll sign for it on my way out.'' She slung her tote over one shoulder, then stood. For an instant she thought he would remain seated before he got slowly to his feet. ''Take care,'' she said, extending her hand. He shook it briefly, then smiled.

''I suppose it's no use to ask you to reconsider, and yet, that's exactly what I'm doing,'' he said in a low voice that only she could hear.

Surprised, she shook her head. ''No, I won't reconsider. It wouldn't be fair to either of us.''

He nodded slowly. ''Well, I told myself I'd give you two chances to accept me, and that's what I've done.'' His grin flashed again. ''I won't say goodbye, Marca. I'm sure we'll cross paths again.''

"I look forward to it," she said, giving him another quick smile as she left.

"I think not, little bitch," Hutch Renfrew murmured as he reseated himself in the high-backed chair.

*MacDougall.*

Renfrew was beyond rage, he realized as the waiter returned with the coffee and brandy.

MacDougall couldn't possibly have found him. He'd covered his tracks and disguised his identity too well. No, this had to be an act of divine providence. Another indication that his cause was just and right.

Still, it was unsettling, he thought, dismissing the waiter with an imperious nod of his golden head. Even as a child Hutch had hated surprises. As an adult he both despised and distrusted the unexpected. Surprises almost always caused disruptions. Nothing good had ever come from chaos. Failure to plan for the unforseen led inevitably to disaster. Such was the lesson he'd taken from studying the downfall of the Third Reich—and one he'd learned in his own life.

His mother had remarried without notice, and his stepfather had been a monster. A godless, brutally bestial man of the worst kind, which was no less than could be expected in cases of racial mingling. A mulatto who'd forced Elsa Renfrew to abandon her only son to a welfare system set up to perpetuate the proliferation of mongrels.

The United States was decaying from within because of such muddle-headed, left-wing garbage. The government had no cohesive leadership. The infrastructure was decaying. It was Germany in the twenties all over again.

Adolf Hitler had understood. Just as Hutch understood.

A smile shimmered in his mind as he brought the snifter to his lips and inhaled the smell along with the rich flavor.

Life was meant to be ordered and precise. Breeding must be rigorously controlled, not left to some sort of hormonal crapshoot. Order created calm from chaos and separated the ruling elite from the vermin fit only for manual labor. Irrational impulses had to be controlled, the reining genus kept pure. Nothing could be left to chance.

Yet, paradoxically, this surprise was welcome. Even relished.

Slowly unclenching the fingers that had tightened around the balloon glass, he fought down the excitement that shimmered like a red veil in front of his eyes. In some exquisite twist of fate, MacDougall had come to him.

Hutch sat back in his thronelike chair and took a moment to savor the feeling of power that rose in him. This time he would take MacDougall's woman as well as his children. They would be the bait. MacDougall would be the prey.

Once he'd been lured into the trap, Hutch intended to mete out punishment with exquisite slowness. His blood pumping hot in anticipation of the kill to come, he thought about the weapons at his disposal—from the most powerful of shotguns to the thinnest of filleting blades. And in the secret underground room beneath his house were the assault weapons the government crybabies tried to ban.

For a time he'd been fooled into thinking Marca was a worthy mate. He knew better now. She was as stupid as the rest of the liberal intelligentsia. An advocate of the mongrelization of this country. Worse, she'd cohabited with his worst enemy. For that she would have to die.

It was a shame to lose prime breeding stock, but it couldn't be helped. Now that he knew MacDougall had had her, Hutch was no longer interested. The children were MacDougall's, of course. The resemblance was strong, now that he knew the sire. Hutch could scarcely contain his glee. At the trial MacDougall had called him a hatemonger and a monster and his soldiers vicious sociopaths who preyed on the innocent. It was a lie, of course. A product of liberal brainwashing and ignorance.

Fighting to contain the sudden spike of hatred, he lifted the snifter of brandy to his lips and took a sip. Oh, yes, he would have his revenge. And soon.

He would have to make his plans carefully, with a meticulous attention to detail that was his genius. When he was ready, he would act. MacDougall would be as helpless as a buck caught in his sights. A trophy worthy of Hutch Renfrew's superior skills.

His death would be messy and prolonged. He would die by inches, in deepest agony. Renfrew could scarcely wait.

## Chapter 14

It had been a long time since Ian had come home to a house that was more than just a stopover with a bed, a fridge and a place to keep his clothes when he wasn't out prowling the gutter for low-life scum or sweating out a stakeout in a smelly, government-issue sedan. It had been even longer since he'd been greeted by the sound of bluegrass blaring from a boom box on the kitchen counter and a woman in stocking feet with a laughing toddler on her hip. She was holding the phone in her hand and biting her lip.

"Thank God," she said as she caught sight of him. "I was getting desperate."

He fought down a rush of feeling he wasn't ready to sort through. "What's the problem?" he asked as she turned down the volume.

She'd been in his head all day. Her smile, the way she'd clung to him in the night. The sweet sigh she made in her throat right before he kissed her.

He hadn't realized how much he was looking forward to seeing her again until he was driving up her lane. His hands had gotten slick on the wheel and his gut had developed a nervous tick at the thought of taking her to bed tonight. Anything beyond that had his mind closing down hard.

"I teach reading at the Women's Resource Center on Thursday nights. Kimbra is usually here to sit, but Mitch and Carly have invited her to dinner with Dennis's dad, and my usual sitter has the flu. Winston can usually fill in, but he's practicing for a wrestling meet. I've gone down the entire list, and you're my last hope."

Panic clawed his stomach lining. He fought it back. "How about the Scanlons' housekeeper? Uh, Tilly?"

"She's got Nan and Letty already, plus Letty's coming down with a cold. With Ry still fighting off a bug, I'd just as soon not deal with another one."

"Yeah, right." He raked his hand through his hair, caught himself and shrugged. "Okay, sure. I guess I can handle it."

Her smile blazed, stirring his blood. "I knew I could count on you," she said, leaning up to give him a kiss. His mind clouded and his body hungered, but before he could get more than one arm around her waist, sticky fingers were tugging on his hair.

He reared back to see the kid grinning. "Who're you?" the boy asked with a kid's bright-eyed curiosity.

Ian caught Marca's expectant look. He knew what she wanted. What she deserved. He was still trying to get a handle on the best way to handle his responsibility toward this little one and his brothers.

"Call me Ian," he told the kid as he stepped back. Away from the promises a better man would already have made.

"Ian," the boy repeated. "I'm Twevor."

Ian managed a decent enough smile. A tight knot was wedged in his throat. "Yeah, okay. Trevor."

He was being strangled. He needed air. And please, God, a cigarette. Just as he stepped back, the boy lunged. Ian barely had time to get his arms up when the boy hit his chest with a solid thunk. Sure of his welcome, the little boy took a stranglehold on Ian's neck and squirmed around to get comfortable. Ian felt his heart tumbling toward love and pulled back hard. People died if he let himself love them.

"I need a smoke," he said, shoving the boy into her arms again. He caught the anguish in her eyes right before he got the hell out of there.


A half hour later Marca had just finished changing Sean's diaper and was buttoning the straps of his overalls when she realized Ian was standing in the nursery doorway. He'd shucked the worn denim jacket and rolled the sleeves of the maintenance department shirt to his elbows. His hair was windblown, his hard cheeks ruddy from the cold, and yet he looked more haggard than healthy. His expression was that of a man unsure of his welcome, but determined to accept whatever came his way.

"I, uh, figured I'd do the cooking since you're pressed for time." It was an olive branch, as close to an apology as she suspected he could get at the moment. But then, how did a person frame an apology for refusing to love?

She battled back a need to plead with him to let go of the past, and formed a smile instead. "There's frozen lasagna in the freezer. I figured we'd nuke it and add a salad."

"Sounds good." He shifted, tucked his hands into his back pockets and watched her hug his child. Through the narrowed lashes she saw the slow burn of a yearning so deep it seared her.

Oh, Ian, can't you see what's waiting for you? she cried silently, averting her gaze. Can't you try?

"'Sesame Street,'" Sean cried, arching to look over her shoulder toward the door and the familiar sound of the theme song she sometimes heard in her sleep.

"Hurry or you'll miss the beginning," she said, setting him on sturdy little legs already churning.

Ian stepped back and let the little boy streak past. "Ryan?"

"Sean. His hair is a little curlier."

He watched until Sean disappeared down the stairs, then stepped warily into the bright nursery. She could see the instinctive withdrawal, the lonely line of his broad, brave shoulders, the stark aura of guilt.

"Ian, it's all right," she said, going to him. "No one's judging you. Or asking for more than you can give."

"You deserve better," he said, his jaw hard enough to splinter steel. "Your...our sons deserve better."

There was so much pain, she realized. Such terrible grief. And yet she sensed he was poised on a knife's edge. Instinct told her he wouldn't accept pity, so she fell back on the old standby.

"That's probably true, but what the heck? Sean Connery's married, and Mel Gibson already has, what...seven kids? So what's a pear-shaped forty-three-year-old woman to do?"

His mouth quirked, and something like stark relief silvered his gaze an instant before his face relaxed into a grin. "Honey, I love every pear-shaped inch of your figure. In fact, I've spent a large chunk of these last few days trying to figure out how to get you naked."

A slow, sweet thrill ran through her. "What a lovely idea," she murmured, running her hands over the hard contours of his chest. "Hold on to it until eight thirty-five."

He settled his hands on her waist and dropped his gaze to her mouth. "Why eight thirty-five?"

"My class is over at eight. I can be home by eight-twenty. The boys go to bed at eight-thirty. I leave you to figure out the rest."

He narrowed his gaze and let out a heartfelt groan. "God, woman, you do test a man's willpower."

"Good," she whispered as his mouth came down hard. She strained upward, her hands in his hair, her fingers anchored in the silken thickness to draw him closer.

He slipped his thigh between hers, spreading her until she gave into the need to rub against him like a cat. His breath caught, and he slipped his hands lower to cup her buttocks. His own desire was blatantly evident, a hard ridge of flesh straining against her abdomen.

This time she was the one who groaned. She drew back, breathing hard, her eyes glittering. His face was flushed, his eyes hungry and hot. He dragged in air, his struggle for control painfully obvious. Her own control was hanging by the thinnest of threads. Only the obligation she felt to the hardworking, dedicated women in her class kept her from pulling him into her bedroom. Stepping back, she managed a creditable grin.

"So it's a date?" she said. "Eight thirty-five, in my sexy brass bed?"

"Not a chance," he said, tucking a lock of hair behind her ear. "Anything past eight thirty-one and you'd better be prepared to do it on the kitchen table."

She burst out laughing. "There is that," she said as she gave him a gentle shove toward the door. "I'll have to give it some thought."

The kitchen reeked of wet dog and worse. Trevor had messed his diapers, the second time in two hours, and Ian had been too busy trying to coax Ryan into taking his medicine to change him.

"This isn't a circus, it's a madhouse," Ian muttered as he sidestepped sixty pounds of galloping dog. One of the triplets in hot pursuit—Sean, he thought—barreled into Ian's knees, and would have fallen if he hadn't grabbed the kid by the back of his overalls. His brother, the stubborn one in the red shirt who'd spilled orange juice all over the kitchen floor, shot past, screaming something unintelligible.

"Careful, sport," he said, holding fast until Sean found his legs again.

"Get Mutt!" the boy shouted, racing out of the kitchen after the delighted hound.

"Watch the—"

The sound of a crash interrupted him, followed by Mutt's frenzied barking and Sean's giggles. "Lamp," Ian finished, only because he was a man who prided himself on seeing every job through to the end, no matter how gritty or frustrating.

On the other hand, there came a time when a man had to fold his cards before he lost it all—in this case his sanity or his temper. He wasn't sure which would blow first. Probably both, he thought as he took the small white bottle of antibiotic from the fridge. From the corner of his eye, he saw Ryan streaking toward the back door.

"Oh, no you don't!" Ian lunged, his hand closing over the seat of the kid's pants.

"Ry get down!" the furious toddler screamed, flailing his arms and legs as Ian plunked him like a still-wriggling fish on the kitchen counter.

"Take my advice, kid. Never push a desperate man to the wall!"

Ryan glared at him, his little black brows drawn into an ominous line. "Want Mommy!"

"So do I, but until she gets home, it's just the three of you against old dad." *Old dad* was barely hanging on. The last one hundred and twenty minutes had been the longest in recent memory. He hadn't sat down once, and as for cleaning up the kitchen the way he'd promised, forget it.

Controlling the boy with one hand, he tried to draw up the right amount of antibiotic into the eyedropper with the other. Marca's instructions had been clear. A dose of antibiotic, a dose of decongestant, both in easy-to-administer liquid form. Ha!

It had taken him ten minutes, and a lot of fast talking, to get one teaspoon of decongestant down the boy's throat. It had left Ry spitting and screeching.

"No med-cine," Ryan declared, turning his head away while at the same time beating the heels of his sneakers against the cabinet.

"Listen, Ry, your mom ordered me to give this to you at eight. It's quarter past, and she's due home soon, so give me a break, okay?"

"No med-cine."

Ian said something pithy and, okay, maybe a little too loud, but that was no reason for the kid to take a punch at him. Got him a slap in the eye with a sharp little fist. Letting out a bellow, Ian jerked backward, his hand sending the medicine bottle flying.

At the same time he heard the thudding of little feet and the sharp clatter of canine toenails on the dining room floor. An instant later Mutt raced past him heading for the utility room with two screaming black-haired hooligans neck and neck behind.

"Come back here, you two!" he shouted, grabbing Ryan off the counter and tucking him under one arm as he took off after boys and dog.

He'd just gotten a hand on the ungrateful mongrel's collar when the back door opened and Marca walked in. Her jaw dropped, and her eyes widened.

"What on earth—?"

"Mommy!"

Ian felt a stab of guilt. "Now, honey, it's not as bad as it looks."

Eyes widening, her mouth working silently, she stared at the tangle of boys and dog, overturned laundry basket and muddy paw prints before shifting a disbelieving gaze to the harassed forty-six-year-old, presumably competent male who'd been in charge.

Ian had the same urge to bolt he'd once had at the academy when he'd messed up during weapons training and darn near shot himself in the foot. The instructor had reamed him a good one, and he'd been convinced his face would be red for the rest of his life. He felt the same sting in his cheeks now.

"Uh, Marce, are you okay?"

Her mouth twitched. "The four of you have exactly ten minutes to get this place in shape again, or I swear I'll send all of you to your rooms for the rest of your natural lives!"

With that she picked her way gracefully through the mess into the kitchen, gave a strangled gasp when she saw the destruction spread like the aftermath of a tornado from one end of the house to the other and disappeared upstairs.

"Uh-oh, Mommy's mad," Trevor said with a grin that was anything but repentant.

"Uh-oh," Sean echoed.

Ryan was too busy trying to pull out his father's hair by the roots to say much of anything at all.

* * *

It was nearly eleven. The boys had been settled since nine.

While Ian cleaned up the debris, she'd gotten the boys ready for bed. She'd finished first and taken a long, soothing bubble bath. For good measure she'd washed her hair and blown it dry, then slathered on lotion and dabbed on perfume. Feeling daring, she wore the silk and lace gown she'd bought years ago, when she'd still believed in Cinderella.

Her blood singing with anticipation, she'd been in bed reading when he'd sidled into the bedroom with a sheepish look on his face and a glass of wine in his hand. A pathetic attempt at bribery, she'd told him, but she'd been thirsty, so she'd grudgingly accepted.

While he'd showered, she'd sipped, anticipation building. He had come straight from the shower, unabashedly naked and slipped into bed next to her. He was fully aroused.

"Sleepy?" he asked, as she set the empty glass on the bedside table.

"A little." Giving in to a need to touch him, she traced a lazy figure eight in the soft black hair around Ian's flat nipple. Beneath her finger the thick chest muscles jerked, and she curved her lips in a smile that felt deliciously smug and wicked. A siren's smile, she thought, created on the sixth day along with Eve herself.

"I wish I'd had a camera handy," she said when his hand came up to capture hers. "You looked so adorable with Ry tucked against your side, a big, tough cop standing in the midst of chaos with this befuddled look on your face."

"Befuddled, hell. That was raw panic." He lifted her hand and nipped at her index finger. "If you have an ounce of womanly compassion in that sleek little body of yours, you will never, *ever* leave me alone with your brood again."

"Don't worry. I can't afford any more imitation Tiffany floor lamps." She stretched up to feather a series of soft kisses over his tense jaw until the tight muscles relaxed.

"Did you know you have a bruise under your right eye?" she murmured, inhaling the clean scent of his skin.

He looked endearingly sheepish—and a little proud. "Ry slugged me."

Marca bubbled a laugh. "He did what?"

He sighed. "Doubled up that little fist, hauled off and cracked me a good one. Seems he's not all that crazy about that pink stuff the doc prescribed."

"I guess I forgot to mention his temper."

His lips quirked. "I guess you did, yeah."

"He's also the shyest of the three." Marca turned her hand in his hand, intertwined their fingers. "Now Sean, he's the most serious. Sometimes he gets this broody look on his face, like he's off in space somewhere."

His chest rose and fell in a ragged breath. Then tension touched his jaw again. "My brother was like that. I remember my mother calling him her little space cadet."

"What did she call you?"

"'Ian Connors MacDougall,' which was usually followed by 'stop that this instant or I'll tell your father!'"

Marca laughed, and he kissed her temple. "That's Trevor," she murmured, testing the waters. When he didn't stiffen, she took that as a sign to continue. "He's my climber. Furniture, drapes, the bushes outside. He even managed to fall off the bureau in the nursery when he was fifteen months old. He has a little scar on his chin, and another on the back of his head when he tumbled off of Letty Scanlon's jungle gym."

His mouth relaxed a little more until a smile hovered in the corners. "I collected my share of stitches when I was a kid."

"Is that when you hurt your wrists?"

"No."

She felt him tense and rubbed her cheek against his warm shoulder. "I'm not prying, Ian. Simply interested."

He shifted on the pillow, pulling her closer. Soap from the

shower still lingered on his skin. "My uncle was a bigot like Renfrew. Hated blacks and Jews and especially the Mexicans who worked the fields in the valley. Used to spit on them and cuss them out in two languages." She felt him tense. "When I was thirteen, he took me to this meeting with him. Turned out Uncle Angus was the Grand Wizard of the local chapter of the Klan. He expected me to ride with them."

Marca tilted her head and looked up at him. "What did you do?"

"I did what he wanted and joined up. Repeated this sick oath. My cousins were already members, and I had this dumb idea that beating up helpless farm workers would make them accept me as part of the family."

"Did it work?"

"For a while. And then one night we were on this raid. The Gonzales family had moved into an old line shack on government land bordering my uncle's. He couldn't evict 'em, so he decided to scare 'em off. I had my hand cocked back, ready to smash into this old guy's face." He stopped and drew a breath. "All of a sudden I just couldn't do it. I let go of that poor old *abuelo*, grandfather, and just stood there, watching my uncle and my cousins taking out this sick rage on old men and young boys."

Marca realized she was ice cold and inched the blanket closer to her neck. He smiled a little and pulled her closer. "Pretty sick, huh?"

"Yes, it is," she said simply. "I had no idea."

"It's not something I advertise."

"What changed you?"

He shrugged. "I have no idea. I think I went a little crazy then, and just waded in, trying to do to my uncle what he was doing to the Mexicans. I broke his nose and busted his lip. Someone smashed a baseball bat into my skull, and I woke up the next morning with my head exploding. Angus had me tied to a post in this old tool shed he had, and every so often he or one of my cousins would drop by to plant a fist in my gut."

He lifted their entwined hands and looked at the puckered skin. "Angus had coated the rope with tar to make it irritate my skin. Claimed it was an old Indian trick. It was months before I regained full use of my hands. I can't stand anything tight around my wrists. Makes me feel trapped." His tone was rueful, his face taut.

Marca flinched. "How did you get away?"

He shrugged. "I kept butting against this post, trying to loosen it. One night when they were out on a raid I managed to knock it down. I just took off running. Well, staggering. Buck naked. I ended up at that old line shack, and the old guy whose face I nearly pulverized lent me some clothes, then hid me under a tarp in this beat up old pickup and drove me into the sheriff's office."

She lifted his hand and kissed his wrist. The puckered skin was rough against her lips. "You're not like Renfrew, Ian. Maybe you got off track, but there's no evil in you."

"Maybe in your world, honey. In mine, it seems sometimes like there's nothing *but* evil." His face creased into bitter lines. He didn't deserve this pain, she thought. Or the steady lash of shame he inflicted on himself. She wanted to pull that proud head to her breast and stroke away his agony, but she knew him well enough now to be certain he wouldn't accept that from her.

"What happened to your uncle?" she asked instead.

"Nothing. The sheriff had a sheet and hood hanging in his closet, too."

Marca sighed. "What did you do? Where did you go?"

Restless, he shifted on the pillow. "Went to live with relatives of Señor Gonzales in Fresno. They had a bakery in the barrio. I worked nights and went to school during the day."

"You can bake?"

His mouth relaxed into a self-conscious grin. "Nope. But if you need pans scrubbed or ovens scoured, I'm your man."

Marca laughed, even though her throat ached for that bruised, guilt-stricken boy. ''You've been paying penance all these years, haven't you? Trying to make it up to the people you hurt.''

His jaw flexed. ''Wrong. I'm just a blue-collar guy doing a job that pays lousy and makes me rotten relationship material.''

''Uh-oh, that sounds like a warning.'' She traced the roped network of veins on the back of his hand with her fingertip.

''It is.''

All that was able to hope in Ian's sorry soul longed to let her keep her illusions of him. To bask in that idealistic image she'd created of this noble guy in the white hat. But he'd had a lot of sleepless nights to examine the choices he'd made and the motives that had driven him. Instead of admirable, they'd been disgustingly shameful. Nothing more than a selfish need to feel important to someone. He didn't deserve her admiration, or the unconditional acceptance she offered.

Because he wanted it so desperately, he knew he would have to leave soon. Before the need to be different from how he was weakened him. But not yet. Not until he stored up memories for the dark nights.

Ian shifted so that she could see the face he'd earned over the years. The weary eyes, the hard cynical lines that had begun to form before he'd been old enough to take his first legal drink.

''Marca, I can't give you more than I'm giving you now,'' he warned in a voice he tried to make harsh enough to count. Instead it came out as a gruff plea.

''All right,'' she answered with the gentlest of smiles as she caressed the flat expanse of his ridged belly, firing a hunger in him. For her touch, her warmth, her love.

''You make me crazy, wanting you,'' he grated. ''I can't think straight when you're touching me.'' He trapped her hand, and she pouted beautifully.

''Coward.''

''More than you know, honey,'' he whispered, his need savage.

Because he needed to feel the silk of her skin against his, he nudged her legs apart and began stroking her inner thigh. She shivered and sighed, her eyes warming and turning sultry.

"You always do that, you know," she murmured, her voice breathless.

"Do what, honey?"

"Start making love to me whenever the conversation gets intimate."

She was right. He couldn't say the words she deserved. Words that represented feelings he was incapable of handling. And yet, at this moment she was *everything* to him. All he'd ever wanted in a woman, all he'd always known he couldn't have.

She was his heart. His salvation.

"Want me to stop?"

"I'll kill you if you dare," Marca cried when his hand stilled.

His laughter was rich and relaxed. "Can't have that, sweetheart." His hand resumed the lovely stroking and as the tension built she began to move. She was consumed, adored, filled with feelings and pleasures.

He was so tender, so absorbed, drawing shuddering sighs from her, kissing her moans into his mouth, stroking and kneading. Finding all the sensitive spots on her body, watching her. Responding to her cues. Worshiping her.

His hands skimmed and searched, while he measured, gauged, responded, and then when she knew she was about to beg, satisfied each sweet yearning, each wild hunger.

Controlled by his hand, she writhed and arched, her hands clutching at those wide unbending shoulders. Eyes open, she saw his yearning, his awe, the deep, abiding love he couldn't express in words.

"Come inside me," she begged, needing to be a part of him. To feel his heart beating as hers, his breathing meshing in the same rhythm as hers.

His mouth took hers, his urgency a wild and anguished cry as e positioned himself, his thighs rough against smooth, his heat nveloping her. And then there was only his heat, his hard slick esh, the searing possession of his mouth.

Again and again he filled her until she felt pure pleasure, mindss, desperate, straining toward the soaring escape. He was hers. he was his. But even as she let him take her away, she knew it vouldn't last.

They had only now. This moment. And though it was wonerful, it wasn't enough.

## Chapter 15

While Ian prowled the cubicle Deputy Brandt called an office
the detective studied the nearly identical publicity photos lyin
on his blotter. Ian had done the same a few hours earlier i
Marca's office watching her work, finalizing arrangements fo
Mitch's press conference scheduled for Friday morning. Pres
people were already showing up. Ian himself had passed a satellit
truck on his way into town. Scanlon was fighting mad, and thoug
he said little, Ian had seen the fierce spirit in the man. He had
feeling Mitch would go head-to-head with the devil himself t
protect one of his own. Ian knew the feeling.

Still, he had strong reservations about going public with a
ongoing investigation. Publicity could send Renfrew back into hi
hole for more months of hiding, during which Ian was sure to b
pulled off the case. On the other hand, publicity might jog a fe
memories or scare up a decent lead or two.

Renfrew might be an egotistical, homicidal bastard, but h
wasn't stupid. Ian's instinct told him the fascist son of a bitc
would call an immediate halt to the attacks until media interes
cooled. Maybe, if they got lucky, the lull would give Ian time t

care up enough evidence for an arrest, if not of Renfrew himself, then of the goons that had done his dirty work. That had been the deciding factor—for himself and for Carly Scanlon whose abiding concern was the safety of students and college employees.

Since they had a high-profile name like Mitchell Scanlon, why not use him, Ian had told her senior staff at an emergency meeting. In spite of his aversion to personal scrutiny, and to his credit, Scanlon had agreed immediately. He'd even called a few of the biggest names in sports to personally invite them to Bradenton.

Though Renfrew's name would not be mentioned, nor the name of the NAFB, facts like the drawing of a swastika on three of the victims and the racial epithets thrown at all of them would be carefully listed. Renfrew's incendiary statements and views on white supremacy were well-known and documented. The public would be able to draw their own conclusions.

In the meantime Ian was concentrating on the two leads Mitch had given him. Neither of the players looked like the average person's image of a thug, which made them all the more dangerous. Rolfe Krauss was blond, blue-eyed and clean-cut—an honor student majoring in political science. William Peterson had the same preppy look about him, his grin a marvel of parental diligence and orthodontic skill.

While the team had been suiting up for practice yesterday afternoon, Ian had wandered into the locker room with a bucket and a mop. Keeping his head down and his ears open, he'd managed to stay within earshot of both Krauss and Peterson.

He'd gotten a bellyful of bull about their sexual conquests and heard enough muttered racial slurs to convince him he was on the right track, but nothing he could hang an arrest on.

Early Thursday morning Marca had contacted the photographer who routinely took publicity shots of the T-wolves players and asked for the proofs on this year's team to be messengered to her office.

They were stock poses, action shots, the usual. Ian had waded through a stack an inch thick, until he'd found one of Will Peterson gripping a football. His mutilated digit was clearly visible.

Matsuda was willing to swear that Peterson's hand looked very much like the hand that had carved the swastika into his chest. It wasn't much. In fact, in legal terms it was damned close to worthless, but it was a place to start.

"Dang it, MacDougall, these boys look like they just walked out of church on Easter Sunday." Leaning back, the easy-going detective rubbed his hand over his thick belly, doubt stamped into every line of his pleasantly homely face. "You think we can make a case on the professor's testimony?"

"Not a chance." Ian took out a stick of gum and shoved it in his mouth. Marca hated smoking. Though she didn't say anything, he sensed her dislike of kissing him after he'd had a cigarette. Giving up booze had been tough, but giving up cigarettes was pure hell. Giving up kissing Marca would be far worse. He'd made it through the past four hours with only two cigarettes—and three packs of gum.

"You think your boss would okay a tail on both boys for the next couple of weeks?"

Brandt tugged at his earlobe and considered. "Budget's tight these days. Sheriff screams over extra paperclips." His sigh was heavy and familiar. Ian knew what it was like to chafe at restrictions. He had a couple of reprimands in his personnel file for insubordination because his sense of justice had mattered to him more than the system.

"How about you and me go see him together?" he proposed, careful to keep his tone offhand. "Maybe tickle his vanity, drop a few hints about the benefits of a high-profile arrest during an election campaign."

Brandt narrowed his eyes, his lips twitched. "Done your research, I see."

Ian shrugged. "Man does what he has to."

"Yeah, sometimes he does, at that." Brandt's gaze slid sideways to rest on the photo of his family. "For what it's worth I'm damn sorry about your ex-wife and daughters."

Ian took a breath. How long would it be before he stopped

feeling gutted every time someone mentioned the past? "Guess I wasn't the only one doing research."

"My daddy taught me to hunt when I wasn't much taller than the old .22 I was shooting. Told me never to go into the woods with a stranger unless I trusted him to walk behind me with a loaded gun. Guess that stuck." Brandt shoved the photos into the folder Ian had brought and handed them back before pushing back his chair.

"Sheriff's in his office," he said as he stood. "Why don't we go see if we can bag us a favor?"

Hutch sat frozen in front of the TV screen, his new Winchester Model 70 cradled lovingly in his hands. The frigging reporters were going ape, shouting questions at that lying bastard, Scanlon. Hanging on his every word like he was some kind of a god instead of a has-been cripple.

*A despicable act of cowardice by pathetic excuses for men...animals with no sense of decency...common thugs... failures.*

The very words made Hutch's blood boil. And yet, it was only to be expected. Peterson, Krauss and the others had warned him about Scanlon. The man actually went to the houses of his black players, sitting down with them like they were his equals. He even had those subhuman mongrels to his house where his daughters lived.

Hutch muted the sound, then reached for the phone, his gaze riveted on the woman in the neat purple suit seated to Scanlon's left. Marca had introduced the liberal pinko coach first, and then, when Scanlon was finished with the lies, turned the microphone over to the buffoon of a sheriff who'd been so nervous he stuttered like Porky Pig. Marca had finally come to his rescue by calling for questions.

MacDougall hadn't been anywhere in sight, but Hutch knew he was there. He could feel it, a burning in his gut and a tingling in his spine. Like the anticipation of the kill right before he squeezed off a shot.

Hutch hated mistakes. He took pride in rarely making them, and the few he'd made were rarely his fault. Trusting MacDougall had been one. Failing to see Marca's true colors had been another. That, of course, had been purely sexual. As with many great leaders, he'd allowed his superior virility to overrule his intellect. It was the curse of a man as well-favored as he was, he thought as he punched out the number of Jackson Smith's office.

"Professor Smith's office." The voice on the other end of the line was young and perky. Another of Jackson's student "protégés."

"Good morning. This is Richard Hartson. May I please speak to the professor?"

"Oh, sure, Mr. Hartson. Just one sec."

Jaw clenched, Hutch drummed impatient fingers on the desk.

"Are you watching the sports network?" Smith's voice was edged with panic, and Hutch frowned. He'd long thought that the professor's avowed desire to participate in the actual raids was little more than the posturing of a weakling, a man who talked of conquest but hid when the shooting started. Now he realized his instincts had been sound. Smith didn't have the guts required to be a soldier.

"Calm down, professor," he soothed. "This is simply a minor diversion, easily handled. There'll be the usual furor for a few days, then the press will go on to something else. All we have to do is lie low for a few months and then return to the master plan."

"What about this 'evidence' the sheriff claims he has? Jack, Jr., participated in both those raids. He could end up in prison instead of the NFL."

Hutch covered his impatience with a chuckle. "Nothing but a smokescreen, Jackson. I promise you, if they'd had anything, they would have made arrests."

There was a pause, then Smith sighed. "You're right, of course. I apologize for my apprehension."

"Perfectly understandable." Hutch all but choked over the words. Smith would have to die, of course. He was the only one who could link the man known as Richard Hartson directly to the beatings. As far as the others knew, Smith had been the mastermind. The man issuing the orders. Gunsmith Richard Hartson had simply been a believer in the cause who provided a place for the young recruits to gather together.

It would appear to be a suicide. Like the one he'd arranged to eliminate the man who'd rigged the bomb in MacDougall's car. A squeeze of the trigger, and a potential turncoat was eliminated. A leader had to be ruthless as well as efficient.

"Professor, I called because I have need of your assistance in recruiting a couple of Brigade members for a small errand."

It was raining, a heavy drenching rain. A soggy, dreary Sunday afternoon. The first day of October. The Timberwolves had played mud ball yesterday, winning against Portland College by one wobbly field goal. Marca had cheered herself hoarse. Even Ian had a scratchy throat. He'd made her a hot toddy to soothe hers and was sucking on lemon drops for his.

The boys were at the Scanlons for their regular Sunday afternoon play date, a ritual Carly had initiated as a way of getting a few hours alone with her workaholic husband every other Sunday. Next week Nan and Letty would be at Marca's house from one until five.

Until Ian had come back into her life, Marca had spent her stolen hours soaking in a tub of fragrant bubbles, reading about knights or Scottish lairds or hard-bitten cowboys. Ian's kisses were just as thrilling, his words just as stirring. His honor as steady and true. Real life was definitely better than fiction.

Because of the lousy weather Ian had had to put in a call to the Portland office of ATF and cancel the chopper scheduled to take him up for another search of the hills. So far he'd found two sections of terrain containing red dirt. Neither had provided any clues.

After four days in the hospital, Dennis had flown home with his father to recuperate, and Kimbra had resumed classes. Ted

Matsuda was at home, as well, being pampered by his wife and daughter, yet chafing to return to his teaching duties.

As Ian had predicted, there had been no more attacks or incidences of vandalism since Mitch's press conference. Though relieved, the campus had an air of breathless anticipation that had minority students looking over their shoulders and Carly negotiating with the board for more money to hire extra security guards.

Ian still posed as a maintenance man, hanging around the practice field, scrubbing the locker room floor, helping the equipment man repair helmets and pads, and generally slipping into the fabric of the players' on-the-field life.

He had been in Marca's life now for two hectic weeks. Lovers who were sharing a bed and the household chores, if not a life. A few days ago he'd started roughhousing with the boys, rolling around on the floor like a big disheveled kid, letting them pummel him with their pugnacious little fists, in turn tickling them until they dissolved in laughter. He could tell them apart now, too. And had let them help while he'd built a doghouse for Mutt. The one dim spot on Marca's bright mood was Ian's edgy refusal to participate in the boys' bedtime ritual.

Marca knew why. That's when the hugs and sloppy kisses were exchanged. And "I love yous" aplenty. Words he'd never said. Words he wasn't ready to hear, although they were always there on the tip of her tongue. Still, he *was* trying, she reminded herself as she brought up one knee and slid it over his heavy thigh. He sucked in, and she giggled.

"Are you trying to get me all heated up again, sugar, 'cause if you are, I have to tell you, it's working."

She walked her fingers over the wide forearm now draped over her thigh.

"Forty-four more minutes and counting before Kimbra brings the boys back from their play date," she murmured, arching upward to offer her mouth. He took it with a greedy hunger that never failed to send waves of love running through her.

"You taste like bourbon." His smile was lazy. "Gets me a little drunk, just kissing you."

"You taste like lemon sherbet," she murmured, sliding her tongue over her lips. "I'm passionate about lemon sherbet."

"Guess you like that better than cigarettes, huh?"

"Much better. I especially like it that you don't disappear every half hour or so to have a smoke. I love having you around."

His face went still. "I kinda like being around."

They were speaking of more than proximity, she realized. Her heart beat faster as she realized they were both edging closer to saying the words she felt in her heart. But Ian was still wary, still very controlled whenever she mentioned some future event. Even now, the tension he'd been slowly losing was back, tightening his face and hardening his belly, as though he'd braced himself to repel a blow.

"Ian, the boys and I are part of you, but that doesn't mean we want you to feel trapped when you're with us." She touched his scarred wrist with the tips of her fingers. A pained look crossed his face, and his eyes were bleak. She could feel the loneliness in him, bunching in his muscles, radiating from him like a fever.

"Be patient, okay?" He folded his hand over hers and rested their entwined hands on his chest. Did he know he was holding her over his heart? she wondered.

"Hey, I have three almost-two-year-olds. I'm an expert at patience."

He lifted her hand and kissed her wrist. "I can't believe you haven't kicked me out." There was a rumble of rueful humor in his voice, but his eyes closed her out.

Reminding herself that she couldn't force love, or even permanence, she snuggled closer. Now was enough. This moment. And at this moment she wanted to feel him inside her again.

"How's that forty-six-year-old body feeling?" she murmured, trailing her fingers lower.

"Hopeful," he answered, then gasped as she embarked on an intimate exploration.

"Hmm, yes, I can detect a definite stirring of interest, here." She withdrew, teasing him the way he'd teased her earlier with his tongue.

"You're enjoying this," he accused, his breath coming faster.

"It's a woman thing." She made lazy circles on his abdomen, causing the muscles to jerk spasmodically. "We love to reduce a big, tough male to a mass of panting jelly."

"Men don't pant," he muttered, tracing the curve of her body, his hand lingering on the generous contours of her hip. "And we don't turn to jelly." He cast a pointed glance down the length of his body. She followed his gaze, then laughed.

Gently she ran her fingers over the ridge of scar tissue on his belly. Her fingers burrowed lower, into the thatch of tightly curled hair below his navel. He sucked in, his hips arching upward. Her hand closed around him, feeling the pulses of returning hardness against her palm.

"Does that feel good?" she asked, echoing the words he'd used earlier as he'd slipped two fingers into her, testing her readiness.

"Yes," he grated, his eyes closed, and his face taut. His body quivered and bucked as she stroked. Sweat glistened on his forehead, as he bared his teeth.

She smiled slowly, seductively, reveling in the potency of her femininity. Ian had told her in a dozen different ways that he loved her body. Her small breasts seemed as voluptuous as any centerfold playmate when cupped in his callused hands, the slick sheen of his passionate kisses still glistening on the dusky skin surrounding her nipples.

She purred as she closed her eyes and gave herself up to pleasing him as he'd pleased her earlier. Her fingers were caressing, stroking the hard length of him, absorbing the heat and the fierce need as her other senses absorbed the shudders running under the skin and the pleading moans issuing from his throat.

Her body heated from within, fueled by the love she was pouring into her touch. As though sensing the power of that love, he went stiff, a harsh cry emerging from his parted lips.

"I need you," he cried as he rolled over her. His hand swept down her body, his fingers easing into her, stroking. Eagerly she parted her legs, feeling the dampness pouring over his fingers.

He groaned, then positioned himself. She gripped his shoulders and arched upward. He plunged, filling her.

"I love you," she cried out as the pleasure exploded inside her. "I love you," she repeated as his hot release pulsed into her. "I love you," she whispered as he slumped against her and buried his face in her hair.

She'd fallen asleep. A cramp in the arm she had wound around Ian's neck woke her. Drowsy and sated with love, she was listening to the sound of Ian's relaxed breathing and reluctantly thinking she needed to wake him, when the phone rang, doing it for her.

As she reached for the portable she routinely carried with her whenever the boys were out of the house, she glanced at the clock. Alarm ran through her as she realized it was almost six. They'd overslept.

A frown creased her forehead as she realized she didn't hear the boys. Kimbra probably had them corralled in the family room, she thought as she fumbled for the right button.

Ian yawned, then gave her a drowsy grin as she cleared her throat. "Uh, yes, hello?" she managed finally.

"Ms. Kenworthy, this is Deputy John Brandt. Is MacDougall available?" The detective's voice was too controlled, she realized as she handed the phone to Ian.

"Detective Brandt," she mouthed.

His eyes changed instantly, going from lazy to hard. "Yeah, John?"

Marca sat up, then froze when she realized he'd gone stark white. She touched his arm, drawing his gaze.

"What?" she cried, stunned by the anguish in his gray eyes. His hand reached for hers and gripped hard.

"Is she all right?" he grated, his voice harsh and dangerous.

Marca heard the rumble of Brandt's voice as he spoke at length. With each word, Ian seemed to grow more remote. More and more the deadly agent trained to kill.

"Ian," she pleaded, but instead of answering, he signaled for her to wait. Fear seized her throat and accelerated her heartbeat.

"I'm on my way. Twenty minutes." He punched the button, then threw down the phone and pulled her hard against him. He was rigid, his breathing tortured. A tremor ran through him. *"Please no!"* he cried against her neck.

"Ian? What is it? Ian?"

He drew a ragged breath, then put her at arm's length, his expression fierce. "I don't have time to make this easy, honey, so hang on, okay?"

"Something's happened to Kimbra?" Her voice rose in concert with her terror. "The boys? Something's happened to our boys?"

The anguish racing over his face had her crying out. "Apparently, when Kimbra was driving back home with the boys, there was a pickup angled over the road where it narrows for the bridge over Frenchman's Creek. When Kimbra stopped the van, two men in ski masks came up from the shoulder and pulled her out of the driver's seat. One of them jumped in and drove off the way she'd come while the other knocked her around. The boys were still in their seats."

"Oh, my God," she whispered. "Is she—?"

"She's hurt, but not critically," he hastened to assure her. "She pretended to faint, and when the man drove off, she started running down the road. A log truck came by and she flagged him down. He put in a call to 911. The deputy who rolled on the call alerted Brandt as soon as he heard Kimbra's story."

Marca felt the hot lick of panic and fought for composure. Her babies were in danger. Her worst nightmare come true. "I'm going with you," she cried as he made to leave the bed. He grabbed her arm and held fast.

"Someone needs to stay here, Marca. In case he...whoever did this calls."

She tried to steady her breathing. Her racing heart was beyond her ability to control. "You mean Renfrew, don't you? He's behind this. He stole the boys to punish me for opening my house to a black woman.''

''We don't know that.''

''Yes, we do. It's him. And I know why. It's because I set up the news conference. That's it, isn't it? It's my fault. I...*oh, God, Ian!*''

He took both her hands and pressed them together between his. His were icy, frightening her even more than his words. ''Sweetheart, listen to me. I need you to stay calm. The boys need you to stay calm. Okay?''

She gulped air and fought to center herself the way she'd learned to do in meditation class. ''I...yes, calm.'' She concentrated on the air going in and out of her lungs until the need to scream receded. ''I'm so scared,'' she whispered in a terror-shredded voice. ''I can't think.''

He nodded. ''That's okay. I'll do the thinking.''

''Oh, Ian...''

''Do you trust me, sweetheart?''

She blinked, then realized tears were running down her cheeks. ''Yes, I trust you, but—''

''Okay then, this is what I want you to do. Get dressed and put on a pot of coffee. Call Carly and Mitch and have them come here to be with you. Keep the phone line clear, and if anyone calls here with a message about the boys, take careful notes, then call me at the sheriff's office. And don't, repeat *do not* let anyone in here you don't know. In fact, don't do anything without checking with me first, okay?''

Marca drew a shaky breath. Putting herself under someone else's power went against her instincts and her inclinations. If it were anyone else but Ian asking this of her, she would already have refused. In fact, she wouldn't even be having this conversation.

She saw understanding come into his eyes. Eyes that had seen his daughters die. Eyes that never really lost their haunted look, even when he smiled. Would her eyes look like that someday? Full of regret and guilt and a pain that went beyond expression. A shudder ran through her, and she felt her face crumpling.

"Ian, please." She clutched at him with desperate fingers. "They've never known anything but love and kindness. They...Ry needs his blankie or he can't fall asleep and Trev gets cranky when he's hungry and...and Sean gets scared sometimes when strangers come too close."

He wiped the tears from her cheeks with the pads of his thumbs. His gentleness calmed her more than the words. "Sweetheart, they're tough little guys...as tough as their mom."

"And their daddy," she whispered, her voice shaking.

"Marce, I wish...damn!" He shot a look at the clock, then pulled her against him hard. She felt his heat, his urgency, the solid strength in him. She clung, trying to absorb some of that strength for herself. Too soon he pushed her away.

"I have to go." He left the bed, throwing on his clothes with a quick efficiency she doubted even she could have managed, though she tried. She was still pulling on her jeans when he disappeared into the closet. She was fumbling with the buttons of her flannel shirt when he returned.

Just that quickly he had become a different person. A hardbitten, steely-eyed, dangerous stranger with an ugly black gun tucked into a holster clipped to his belt and an air of deadly intensity surrounding him. In his hand he carried another gun, a semiautomatic small enough to fit easily into his palm.

"This is a .32, not an Uzi," he said with a fleeting smile as she stared down at the weapon, "but it'll have to do. It's loaded, but the safety's on. See the red dot? Click this and it turns to white. That means it's ready to fire. Understand?"

She drew a breath. Now wasn't the time to be squeamish. "I understand."

"It's accurate for the length of the hall outside this room. If someone's coming after you, point it at their heart and fire. Don't think. Don't pray, just pull the trigger until the gun's empty. You got that?'' His gaze bored into her. She sensed the coiled tension in him and the terrible impatience held under rigid control.

''Yes, point at the heart and fire.'' Her voice wavered, and his face softened into a quick, reassuring smile.

''Think about the boys if you have to. If you get yourself killed, who'll take care of them?''

She grabbed him, her fingers trying to find purchase in the hard muscles of his forearm. ''Please, please be careful. Promise me you won't get killed, either. I love you so much.''

He closed his eyes and pulled her into his arms. He buried his face in her hair for a long, ragged breath, then drew back, grabbed one of her hands and pressed the gun into it. ''Stay strong for me, Marca. And for our boys. I'll let you know what's going on as soon as I can. In the meantime trust me.'' And then he was gone.

Five minutes later Marca was tying her sneakers when the phone rang. Her heart raced as she grabbed the receiver. She'd heard Ian's Jeep roar off down the lane, but she ran to the window anyway before she punched the button. Instead of the black Cherokee, she saw only Kimbra's hatchback.

The phone rang again for the fourth time. She drew a trembling breath and answered.

''Hello, Marca.''

She closed her eyes and sagged against the window frame. The hope drained from her, leaving her limp. ''Oh Richard, I...forgive me, I can't talk now.''

He laughed softly, a sinuous sound that reminded her of a viper's hiss. ''I see that MacDougall has left you alone in your hour of need.''

Her heart was racing in her throat now, making it difficult to speak. ''How...what are you talking about?''

''He did seem in quite a hurry. Is something amiss?''

"How did you know...?"

"A telescope, my dear. Trained on your lovely house. Over the last months I have amused myself quite often watching over you. It was especially pleasant this summer when you were working in your garden." His laughter hissed out again. "I did enjoy those cute pink shorts."

Marca gasped. "You were spying on me. Like...like a Peeping Tom?"

"Tsk, tsk, my dear, you wound me. But no matter, I forgive you. And now to the purpose of my call. I have someone here who wants to talk to you."

Marca froze. Her face was icy, and she could scarcely breathe past the constriction in her chest. "Richard? What are you talking about?"

"Mama, Ry hungwy."

Fear tore through her. "Ry, baby—"

"Listen carefully, Marcella." Richard's voice came on the line again, cold and harsh. "Do you have a clock where you are?"

Her gaze darted to the clock radio by her side of the bed. "Yes."

"It takes me exactly twenty-three minutes to drive to your house from mine. But I'll be generous and give you twenty-four. If you fail to arrive on time, I shall shoot one of your children."

"Oh God, no! Richard, please." Calm. She had to be calm. She closed her eyes and summoned Ian's steady eyes. *Be strong for me and our boys.*

"You're wasting precious time, my dear. But that is your choice, of course."

"Richard, listen to me—"

"My name is Hutch. Hutchinson Renfrew to be specific."

"Oh my God."

"Another word of caution, Marcella. It would be a mistake to recount this conversation to MacDougall—or the authorities. If I

ee anyone with you when you arrive, or if I see anyone on my
roperty uninvited, I will kill all three of your sons.''

"I won't call him. I swear I won't, but please let me talk to
y again.''

Instead of her baby's sweet voice, she heard an odd metallic
ound come across the line. "In case you didn't recognize that,
ıy dear, that was the sound of the cocking mechanism on a
articularly fine Glock 9 mm.''

The line went dead.

# Chapter 16

Night had fallen while Ian had been at the hospital, talking with Kimbra. As soon as the Jeep's headlights flashed over the empty carport, the terror that he'd managed to beat back by sheer will returned full-blown.

Where were the Scanlons? Or Kimbra's Mazda. Or the light that should be blazing from the windows?

He parked where Kimbra's car had been when he'd left four hours earlier and took off running. Mutt greeted him halfway, barking wildly, his scrawny tail for once still and his actions frenzied.

Ian's heart pounded, but as he reached the back door he managed to ice his mind. He ordered Mutt to stay, then slipped inside and flipped on the interior light. He held his breath and listened, the instinctive action of a man accustomed to dodging hostile fire. It was so silent he could hear the quiet hum of the refrigerator in the kitchen beyond the mudroom.

"Marca, are you here?" he shouted, more to vent some of the vicious tension burning in his muscles, he realized, when only emptiness answered.

The kitchen was dark. Comfortable now in the house, he hit the light switch first try. Already pulling his wallet from his back pocket, he crossed to the wall phone. After extracting Carly Scanlon's card from the small collection tucked into one of the pockets, he punched out the private number she'd written on the back.

Mitch answered, laughter in his voice. The man would never walk again, and yet he acted as though he were the happiest guy on the planet. The love of a good woman, Marca had told Ian, when Ian had mentioned that once. But she would think that. A woman who believed in wishing stars had to believe in miracles.

"Mitch, it's Ian. Is Marca with you guys?"

"No, why? Did you tick her off?"

If only, Ian thought. Quickly, efficiently, he filled Mitch in, then warned him not to tell anyone but Carly.

"Jeez, Ian. How badly is Kimbra hurt?" A deep concern had replaced the laughter in Mitch's voice.

"Cuts and bruises. A broken wrist and some bruised ribs. The doctor is going to keep her overnight for observation."

"And the boys? Any sign of them?"

"No. Nothing."

"What can we do to help?"

"Stay by the phone in case Marca calls. If you don't hear from me in the next twelve hours, send someone over here to feed the damn dog."

"You got it."

"One more thing, did you tell anyone who I was or why I'm here? Maybe some offhand comment?"

There was a pause. "No, I'm sure of it. Hang on, and I'll ask Carly."

Ian heard the rumble of Scanlon's deep voice, the sharp cry of anguish as Carly absorbed the news, the unintelligible sound of her answer.

"Carly said the only one she told was Mike McNabb so that he would hire you without any hitches. She also swore him to secrecy and says to tell you she can vouch for him. So can I. He's an upright guy."

Ian drew a ragged breath. The maintenance man had seeme
like a solid citizen. As Ian had instructed, he'd introduced Ian t
the foremen and the other guys on the crew as Mac Connors. Ia
intended to have Brandt run a check on the head of maintenanc
anyway.

"Let me know if you think of anything that might give me .
place to start," he said, his mind already clicking back throug
the days he'd spent on campus, looking for clues he'd overlooke

"I'll do that." Mitch cleared his throat. "Good luck, and...kic
a little butt for us."

Ian smiled a little as he hung up. "Kick butt" was a mild terr
for what he intended to do, something he suspected Mitch kne
very well.

One by one he went through the rooms, sweeping a now
suspicious gaze over the familiar furniture, the floor, the corners
In the kitchen the crispy squares Marca had made while he'd fixe
a busted plug on her toaster were still on the counter, safe unde
the plastic wrap, waiting to be doled out with kisses for the boys
dessert.

Even while he'd told himself not to hope, he searched for a
note on the counter, on the table, even stuck to the fridge wit
one of the happy-face magnets kept in readiness for proudly presented artwork made with stubby little hands.

He found toy trucks and puzzles with giant pieces strew
through the dining room and living room and a stack of folders
on the desk in the small den. No messages on the answering
machine. No note in that impatient ladylike scribble that was becoming as familiar as his own backhanded scrawl. He found
traces of her everywhere, but no laughing woman with starry eyes
and a heart as majestic as the Cascades themselves.

His gut tight, his mind ruthlessly focused, he continued the
search upstairs, taking the stairs the way he'd once taken hurdles.
Kimbra's room was closest to the stairs, the door closed. He'd
never been inside. Resisting the urge to knock, he turned the knob
and eased open the door.

He flipped the light, his gaze narrowed against the glare. The room was empty. Tidy and neat, like Kimbra herself.

The nursery was next. Bright walls, generous shelves filled with books and toys and stuffed animals. A room he avoided, if possible. He gave it a thorough search, saw Ry's blankie was draped over the horse, Trevor's favorite truck half-hidden under his pillow, Sean's moth-eaten bear. His chest constricted, and he fought back a need to plead with whatever deity protected the innocent.

The bed in Marca's room was still rumpled, the faint musk of their lovemaking in the air. Ignoring the burning in his gut, he checked the closets, the bathroom, behind the door and under the bed. A smile lit his mind as he withdrew one purple sock. It was the one Mutt had stolen a few days earlier and refused to give back. One of his socks was there, too, and a shirt of the boys'.

Marca would get a kick out of that when he told her. He could hear that tinkling laugh of hers now. He could see her now, grabbing the miserable hound by his face. Putting her nose to his, she would issue a stern lecture while at the same time grinning that gypsy grin that made him go weak inside.

He closed his eyes and fought back a wave of emotion too strong to handle, even for a man who'd been to hell and back. Twenty-one years of channeling his thoughts, ignoring his feelings, disciplining his body, clicked in, and he felt the powerful grip of panic receding.

Shoving the sock in his pocket, he retraced his steps around the room, this time with an eye to what was missing. Her ubiquitous tote bag, the sneakers with the plaid laces that had been on the floor, the .32 he'd given her.

There were no signs of a struggle, nothing to indicate she'd been taken by force. The phone she carried everywhere was lying on the pillow that still bore the imprint of her head.

He had a damn good idea what happened. Renfrew had called, and she'd gone. In spite of Ian's request that she trust him, she hadn't. Bile rose in his throat, burning like acid.

Trust *him?* The same selfish man who'd taken all the warmth and compassion and love she'd had to given, then walked away?

A smug self-important, over-confident son of a bitch who'd messed up, and gotten his family massacred. Why should she think he'd do better now? Why did *he* think so?

Scrubbing hard at the ache in his belly as though he could erase the guilt as well as the pain, he walked to the window and looked out. The rain had ended with the daylight, but the overcast blocked the stars. Only a few lights dotted the darkness. In the hills, mostly.

She and those little black-haired rascals she adored were up there in that darkness. He felt it. Scared and trying hard to be brave, trapped with a monster bent on revenge.

Hurting in every muscle, every tendon and sinew, as though he'd been kicked by a half-dozen iron-shod mules, he reached into his pocket and withdrew the folded sheet of paper the kidnapper had shoved into Kimbra's bra. The kidnapper had done other things, too. Crude, ugly things Kimbra didn't deserve. Obscenities it would take time to put behind her. The look in her eyes had told him she would bounce back. He wasn't sure *he* would.

He unfolded it with numb fingers and looked down at the grainy photograph of his own face, taken as he'd left the cemetery. A message had been lettered across the newsprint in red:

"*Promised I'd make you pay, MacDougall. Unlike you, I always keep my promises.*"

"This time I'll kill you, you frigging bastard. I swear it." He took a moment to let the images of Renfrew's bloody death imprint on his brain, then spun around and grabbed the phone. He would call Stebbins first, then the Portland agent-in-charge. By the time the first fingers of dawn clawed through the blackness, he would have a dozen trained men and dogs scouring those hills.

"Hold still, you mangy mongrel." Ian grabbed Mutt's collar and ran the brush through the silky coat. It was just past midnight. CNN was on the tube in the family room, muted to a low drone.

Ian sat on the floor with the dumb creature who seemed determined to lick the whiskers from Ian's jaw. Grooming the sorriest dog in history was a waste of time, but it was a habit he'd gotten into when he'd been giving up the booze. Because it had worked, it stuck. When he was concentrating on the tangles in the butt-ugly coat, the knots in his mind seemed to ease as well.

He'd done all that he knew to do. Cleaned his weapon and slipped extra clips of ammo into his boots. Filled Eddie in, rejected his advice to let another agent handle the rescue attempt once he found the compound, checked with Brandt to make sure the men manning the roadblocks knew not to force Renfrew into a shoot-out.

The chopper pilot would meet him at the small municipal airport at first light. He'd be bringing heavy firepower with him—as heavy as the government allowed, that is. Which was piss-poor compared to Renfrew's armament.

*Armament.*

The brush stilled as Ian nursed the niggling thought into full flame. Marca had mentioned a friend who lived on Daily's Mountain. A gunsmith. Someone who knew the area. Ian had called the number she'd given him, one day, and gotten a machine telling him the shop was closed. He'd tried again the next day. Same message.

In the aftermath of the attack on Dennis, and Ian's moving into Marca's house, he hadn't followed up. He thought back to the baritone voice on the machine. It wasn't Renfrew, Ian was sure of that. Hutch's voice was a clear tenor which sometimes rose into feminine registers when he went into one of his diatribes.

"It's a long shot, Mutt." The kind of bizarre coincidence that solved more cases in real life than cops wanted civilians to know. He put down the brush and pulled the tattered notebook from his pocket.

"Richard Hartson," he read after scanning his own all-but-illegible shorthand. "Hartson's Antique Guns."

Renfrew had used aliases before. This wasn't one of them. He glanced at the number again, then the phone on the floor by his thigh, balancing the risk of tipping his hand against the need to know.

The more he debated, the stronger his hunch. Somehow, Renfrew had found out he was here. In some unknown way he'd discovered that Ian MacDougall and Marca Kenworthy were connected. A game of cat and mouse was right up Hutch's alley. Hell, he'd like nothing better than to see Ian MacDougall sweating buckets and chasing his tail.

His gut soured, and the pieces clicked into place. The guy with the roses. More than a friend. Someone Marca trusted. Someone she might have told about Ian MacDougall.

"Son of a bitch!"

Mutt whined and glanced up, the one eye that could see questioning.

"Compared to me, you're a damn Einstein," he grated, his voice rasping like ground glass through his suddenly tight throat.

Whining in sympathy, Mutt licked the fist Ian had clenched on his thigh. "Yeah, you're right. Focus on the present, not the past."

He took a deep breath, settling his heart rate and his nerves before snatching up the phone and punching the number. If Hartson was innocent, the man would lose a little sleep, that's all. If not, Renfrew already knew enough to be two steps ahead. What was one more?

"Hartson's Gun Shop."

Ian's blood ran cold. It was Renfrew.

"Renfrew, you son of a bitch. If you hurt her or the boys, no place is safe."

Renfrew's laugh was smug. "I'm impressed, MacDougall. I thought it would take you longer to find me."

The thought of that bastard putting his hands on Marca had his gut churning and his mind hazing. Ian forced his mind past the emotion. "You want me, you can have me. Let her and the boys go."

"Oh, I'll have you, all right, but *I'll* make the rules of this exercise."

Ian took a tighter grip on the phone. Renfrew's training exercises had been more like cockfights, with each side encouraged to kill and maim. One recruit had been nearly blinded, another had lost a hand. A man who'd bested Renfrew in hand-to-hand combat had ended up as prey in a hunt. Ian had saved the stupid bumbler with some fast talk and a lot of ego-massaging bull, but it had been a near thing.

"I'm listening," Ian said, chilling his voice.

"Take County Road 52 to Daily's Mountain Road. Go east five miles and turn left at the fork. Two miles up you'll see a graveled road going due north. The gate will be open. Take the road to the end where you will see a log house on your left." Renfrew chuckled. "Perhaps you should repeat that back to me, MacDougall. I'd hate for your whore to die simply because of a stupid misunderstanding."

Refusing to allow himself to rise to the bait, Ian repeated the instructions, seeing the terrain in his mind as he did.

"Excellent. Park next to the Mazda and van you'll see there. Don't leave the key in the ignition. Got that so far, Ian?"

"Go on."

"Tsk, tsk, so impatient. But of course you want to see your woman. I don't blame you. She's quite spectacular looking."

Ian closed his eyes and struggled past the wave of fear and rage surging like a wild thing inside him. "Park next to the van, take the key," he repeated coldly while his hand clung to the dog's fur. As though sensing his distress, Mutt pressed closer, but remained mercifully quiet.

"Come alone. Unarmed, no jacket. Sunup is at five forty-six. I know how accurate that watch of yours is. If you come a minute before that time, all bets are off. If you come one minute late, your whore is dead."

Renfrew flashed the thin blade in front of Marca's stinging eyes, his lips pulled back in a feral grin. "You will do exactly as I've instructed, or I will use this knife on one of your sons. Is that understood?"

"Yes, Richard, I understand. I know exactly what you want me to do." Marca was terrified. Her stomach was leaping uncontrollably, and her heart was beating so fast she was amazed she hadn't passed out. Somehow, though, she had managed to keep reasonably calm.

They were alone in the house. In fact, she hadn't seen anyone but Hutch since she'd arrived. At first, when he'd met her outside, every inch the courteous, kindhearted man she'd thought of as Richard Hartson, she'd allowed herself to think this was some kind of bizarre mistake.

His voice had been gentle when he'd apologized for causing her distress. But when he'd taken her down to the basement room and let her glimpse her children sleeping like angels on a pallet on the floor, she'd known what it was to hate. How had Ian stood it? she wondered. Knowing what this man had done, knowing that in the eyes of the law he was innocent and therefore untouchable.

That hate had grown until she was consumed with it. She was also terrified. During the past twelve hours she'd spent in the surprisingly comfortable log house in the woods, she'd schooled herself to think of the man parading around in combat fatigues as Richard Hartson, gentleman gunsmith, instead of Hutch Renfrew, vicious amoral terrorist. Reducing him to titles had helped keep the terror at bay. Thinking about the three innocent babies in the vaultlike room below this one helped buoy her courage when it flagged. She was prepared to do what it took to keep her children alive.

"MacDougall is going to die today, Marca. I'm willing to be merciful because in his way he's as much a soldier as I am. But if you interfere or do anything at all to help him, I'll make sure that his life bleeds out in agonizing inches. I will also make those sons of yours watch."

Marca managed an admiring smile. "I thought Ian was the strongest man I knew, but I realize now, of course, that he's no match for you."

She watched arrogance war with suspicion in his eyes. "Yet you chose him over me."

"Ah, but you see that was before you let me see your power.

I fully understand your need for a disguise, of course, given your status as an enemy of the government, but I wish you had trusted me enough to reveal your true spirit and genius.'' She managed a creditable smile. ''Now that I know you as you really are, I have come to realize how superior you truly are.''

His eyes glittered with a preening pleasure. ''You flatter me, my dear.''

''Richard, I deal in fact, not flattery.'' She made a broad gesture. ''Didn't you get me here, when I promised MacDougall I wouldn't leave the house?'' She snorted a laugh. ''You were so clever not to give me time to make even one phone call. It was ridiculously easy for you to outsmart him.''

''I regret the death of his daughters,'' Renfrew said, setting aside the whetstone he'd been using to hone an edge on the filleting knife. ''The bomb was meant for him. Like the führer himself, I'm extremely fond of children.''

''I know that, Richard. It's one of the reasons I'm so fond of you. And of course, the boys adore you.''

''As I adore them, my dear. Such strong young males. Prime examples of Aryan blood.'' He chuckled. ''MacDougall makes a fine stud.''

In the hours he'd spent posturing and orating for an audience of one, she'd conceived the idea of flattering him into believing she actually admired him. While pretending to be cowed, she'd been studying him, searching for those small subliminal cues that she could use to manipulate him as she'd once manipulated the secret desires and weaknesses of the public. With Richard, as with the public, however, she had to be careful not to be too obvious.

After some initial anger and a sickening arrogance, Renfrew was beginning to respond. He'd even kissed her in the wake of the phone call from Ian. As though, somehow, he had to show her that he was the superior of the two men.

Pleading menstrual cramps, she'd managed to avoid going to bed with him. But the strain of walking that fine line—added to her lack of sleep and worry over Ian and the boys—was beginning to sap her strength.

"Richard, would you mind if I made us some coffee?" She trilled a laugh. "I think I'm going through caffeine withdrawal."

"Of course not, my dear." He walked closer and lifted his hand to her throat. With his thumb he massaged the pulse that beat there. "I apologize for slapping you earlier. Such a terrible shame to bruise that perfect skin."

She forced herself to rub against his touch as though she really liked it. "I was hysterical. You had no choice."

His smile flashed in a blaze of white teeth. Caps, she realized now. "What a remarkable woman you are, Marca. So brave in the face of superior force. Coming here alone. Fighting for your children. I must admit to a certain reluctance when I think about passing you on to men who haven't the sensitivity to appreciate you."

Marca prayed she wouldn't be sick. "But why should you do that, Richard," she all but purred. "When I can make you so very happy."

"An interesting thought, my dear. I'll think about it while you make that coffee." He released her, and it took all of her will to keep from recoiling. He'd searched her tote bag first thing and found the gun. The rest of the things—the diapers, her wallet and makeup bag, the toys and wipes and granola bars were in the basement room where he'd made her leave them after the one visit he'd allowed her.

"I have a better idea," she said, gesturing toward the cozy conversation pit in front of the fireplace. "Why don't you build us a fire and pour brandy to accompany our coffee. I'll just be a minute."

A sexual gleam settled in his eyes, buoying her hopes. "I think not, my dear. Leaving you alone would be a mistake. And I abhor mistakes." He linked his arm through hers and escorted her to the kitchen. The night was dying, and a new day was stirring. It would be dawn soon.

Please keep us all safe, she wished on the star she couldn't see. Please, please, keep my family safe.

* * *

Ian pulled out his watch and stared at the face. Five forty-four. After replacing the Hamilton, he released the brake and accelerated upward, covering the last half mile at a crawl.

Renfrew had cleared the brambles from the land bordering the driveway, giving him a clear view of the area. Fresh gravel had been spread over hard-packed dirt the color of rust. The clearing ended in a thicket of brambles that seemed to surround the house on three of four sides. A narrow break wound through an otherwise solid wall of canes and thorns. Beyond the brambles the land sloped upward at a gentle angle. The trees were thick enough overhead to hide the area from a cursory look from above. Ian suspected that an obstacle course was secreted someplace under those trees. If Brigade members were hidden in those brambles, Ian couldn't see them.

Jaw tight, he parked next to the Mazda, removed the key and got out. He'd seen no one on the drive. It was setting up to be a clear day, but the air was cool. He was wearing a flannel shirt tucked into tight jeans, both designed to show Hutch he wasn't carrying a weapon.

His eyes stung from the sleepless night. Tension rode his shoulders and clawed his spine. But his mind had the crystal clarity of a seasoned pro. He'd been on raids before, but never alone. Never unarmed. But the service weapon that was his best friend was under the Jeep's seat. He'd given Marca the .32 that normally rode in the top of his boot. Where was it now? he wondered.

The house was a long, low log structure in the shape of an L. A covered porch ran the length of the shorter leg. Two tall Douglas firs flanked the house, forming an arch of branches overhead. Ian let out a slow breath when he saw that Marca was standing on the porch near the steps, her arms folded over her chest, watching him. She was dressed in the same jeans and lemon-colored sweatshirt he'd peeled her out of yesterday afternoon, and her hair was tumbled, as though she'd just gotten out of bed.

Ian brought his mind back to the plan he'd cobbled together during the long, sleepless hours he'd spent pacing Marca's living room, chewing his way through three packs of gum and thinking longingly of the days when he could numb the unbearable pain with scotch.

He'd run a dozen tactics through the filter of his training and experience—and rejected them all as unworkable, and worse, a risk to Marca and the boys. Renfrew held all the cards. All Ian had going for him was a knowledge of Renfrew's hot buttons. He figured maybe he could find a way to push one or two. If Renfrew exploded, the power would shift for an instant, maybe two. Long enough for Ian to improvise. As a course of action, it was damn thin. It was all Renfrew had left him.

He took a careful, cleansing breath and walked forward, his hands in plain sight. Marca didn't smile as he approached. Her face was drawn and terribly pale. Framed by purple shadows, her eyes pleaded with him an instant before she let out a little huff of air.

"I was praying you wouldn't come."

"You know better than that," Ian said, but his attention was focused entirely on the man standing behind her, using her body as a shield. In his hand Hutch Renfrew held a rifle. A 30.06 Winchester Model 70. A sniper's rifle. And about as deadly as they come. It gave him an idea, one he shoved to the back of his mind so that he could concentrate on the man himself.

Dressed neatly in camouflage fatigues, he was clean shaven now instead of bearded, his naturally brown hair bleached blond. Brown-tinted contacts covered eyes Ian knew to be a watery blue. He looked tanned and fit and triumphant. Ian would not have recognized the man in a crowd, which made him all the more dangerous. Like the shape-shifters of legend, Renfrew had the ability to change his appearance at will.

"Right on time, MacDougall. What a good boy you've become."

Ian walked into a patch of brighter light. Overhead the sun was struggling to burn through the early-morning haze. He kept his gaze on Renfrew's face as he approached the steps.

"Hold it right there, MacDougall. Drop your keys on the ground there."

Ian halted, let his keys drop by his boots. Waited.

"Keep those hands where I can see them and give me a slow 360. Any quick moves and I'll cut you in two."

Ian extended his hands and turned a slow circle. As he turned, his gaze swept the perimeter. Nothing moved. His hopes nudged up a notch. Maybe Renfrew was playing this out alone.

"What's that sticking out of your back pocket?" Renfrew asked sharply, his eyes glittering with suspicion.

Ian waited until he faced Renfrew again before answering. "It's Ryan's blanket." He heard Marca utter a small sound, but kept his gaze trained on Renfrew's eyes. "He can't sleep without it."

"Throw it on the railing there. I'll take it to the little fellow later, when I tell him I'm going to be his daddy from now on."

"You, a family man?" His face impassive, Ian walked up the steps and draped the tattered scrap over the cedar rail.

"I admit to a certain fondness for the lady. Of course, she's not the kind of slut a man marries. But every company of soldiers needs a camp whore." Renfrew stood up and Marca flinched. With his gaze fixed on Ian, Hutch reached out a hand to fondle her breast. Her flesh crawled at the thought of the man she'd learned to detest touching her ever again, but Renfrew had warned her to submit. All part of his plan to make Ian suffer.

"Tell me, Ian. Does she scream your name when she comes, the way she screamed mine?" Renfrew's fingers dug into her flesh, and though she forced herself to remain wooden and unresponsive to the blatant lie, bile roiled in her stomach. The face she'd once thought handsome now seemed a mask of evil. All that was in her longed to claw at him with her nails until he was writhing in agony. Instead, she thought of the boys and manufactured a smile.

Renfrew's gaze glittered with triumph directed more at Ian than at her. "Don't be impatient, my dear. As soon as I take care of this inconvenient nuisance, I'll remind you how it feels to have a real man inside you."

Ian snorted, his eyes filled with contempt. "In your dreams Hutch."

"Jealous, MacDougall?"

"Not much sense being jealous of a pathetic wimp who can't get it up," he drawled, deliberately diverting Renfrew's attention.

Rising to the bait, Renfrew released Marca and stepped forward. Quick as a rattler's strike, he jammed the rifle barrel into Ian's belly. Marca screamed as Ian doubled up. He came up fast, but Renfrew had already stepped back, the rifle pointed directly at Ian's groin.

"Try it, MacDougall," he said, his lips peeled back in a feral grimace.

"Richard, let him go," she pleaded, trying to quell the violent trembling of her knees. "He's not worth the trouble."

"I beg to differ, my dear." He moved again, slamming the barrel into Ian's ribs. This time Ian cried out as he folded up.

"Bastard," he grated through clenched teeth. Sweat had broken out on his forehead, and his face had gone white.

"Stand up, MacDougall." Renfrew's voice was a vicious snarl.

"Leave him alone, Richard," Marca begged, grabbing Renfrew's arm.

"Shut up, bitch!" He shook her off, and she stumbled. Off balance, she slammed into a porch upright. Her head cracked, and Ian charged. Renfrew was ready. That lethal barrel slammed again and again into Ian's mid-section, sending him stumbling backward. Marca cleared her head and moved forward. With a triumphant cry, Renfrew grabbed her by the hair and spun her toward Ian who managed to catch her.

"Don't worry, sugar," he managed to drawl in spite of his breathing that was harsh and rapid. "Renfrew here talks a good game, but when it comes to backing up the boasts, he's nothing but smelly gas."

Renfrew's eyes flashed, and he took a step forward before he visibly checked himself. "Brave words, liberal scum. But notice who's in charge here."

Ian pushed her behind him. "Yeah, you're a big man, all right.

'ut hey, who couldn't be with a rifle in your hand.'' He lifted
is hands higher. Marca heard the rasping of his breathing, but
he subtle aura of unquenchable strength that always emanated
om him seemed undiminished. "Me, all I've got are these two
ands. But that's what you're afraid of, isn't it, Hutch? Afraid
'll beat the crap out of you in a fair fight?"

Marca saw the insult splinter the smug confidence in Renfrew's
yes and felt her hopes rise. She rushed to press the tiny advan-
age Ian had created. "He's right, Richard. Throughout history
varriors fought in single combat to determine the strongest and
est."

"Don't waste your breath, Marce," Ian told her with a sneer.
"Hutch here is all talk and no action. I'm stronger, smarter and
an shoot better than Renfrew any day of the week."

Renfrew kicked out with his heavy boot, catching Ian in the
,roin. He went down, and Marca tensed, a hair's width from
eaping at Renfrew. Only the expectant gleam in his eyes stopped
er.

"Help your lover to his feet, Marca," he ordered, his face
wisted into madness. "I've decided to accept the challenge."

Ian's face was taut with pain, and he was gasping for breath
s she bent down to wrap her hand around his biceps.

"Hurry it up," Renfrew shouted, drawing back his leg to kick
an in the head. Seeing the blow coming, Ian twisted, taking the
orunt of the blow on his shoulder. He groaned, then rolled, al-
owing Marca to help him up.

From the rasping sound of Ian's labored breathing and the dif-
iculty he had in standing erect, she suspected that one of the
olows from the rifle barrel had bruised his ribs. Or worse, splin-
ered the fragile bone.

She felt her emotions fray, but somehow held herself together
s she slipped her arm around Ian's waist, using her body to
support his. As he let her take his weight, he glanced down at
er, and for a moment an urgent message flashed in his eyes. She
owered her lashes, trying to figure out what he was trying to tell
er.

Looking ecstatic at having Ian under his power, Renfre⟨w⟩ shifted, bracing his booted feet wider in a bizarre posture rem⟨i⟩ niscent of Mussolini at his most preposterous. Without the mu⟨r⟩ derous rifle, he would be nothing more than a pathetic madma⟨n⟩ posturing and posing. A madman with blood lust glittering in h⟨is⟩ eyes, she realized with a sinking heart.

"First the rules," Renfrew said, his gaze never leaving Ian⟨'s⟩ face. "You can go in any direction, but I must tell you I've clos⟨ed⟩ the gate and switched on the current, so I suggest you head up⟨-⟩ ward." He jerked his gaze toward the hills. "Because I'm ⟨a⟩ sportsman and not a butcher, I'll give you a thirty-minute hea⟨d⟩ start."

"What are you talking about?" Marca demanded, fixing h⟨er⟩ horrified gaze on Renfrew's face.

"Why a hunt, my dear. It's a hobby of mine, you see. An⟨d⟩ I'm good at it. The best, if I might be permitted a moment ⟨of⟩ immodesty. So good that I'm bored with the usual game."

A hunt? Marca could scarcely believe her ears. "You...yo⟨u⟩ can't be serious."

"I assure you I am." Taking care to keep a safe distance be⟨-⟩ tween himself and even the most powerful lunge Ian might mak⟨e,⟩ he glanced toward the hills. "There's a clearing on the other sid⟨e⟩ of that ridge, in plain sight of the main highway. It's not mor⟨e⟩ than ten miles as the crow flies. Unfortunately, it's heavil⟨y⟩ wooded between here and there, and there are several ravines tha⟨t⟩ will slow you down. However, if you reach it you'll be safe. N⟨o⟩ even I would risk shooting you in sight of witnesses."

Marca took a breath.

"At least give him a weapon," she pleaded. "You were tellin⟨g⟩ me you're a fair man. Fine. Give him something to even th⟨e⟩ odds."

Renfrew's eyes glittered. "Ah, but I am, my dear. I'm givin⟨g⟩ him you."

## Chapter 17

Ian didn't waste time arguing. He grabbed Marca's hand and took off running toward the break in the brambles, praying Hutch wouldn't back shoot them. Behind him, he heard the Winchester's bolt action click a cartridge into the firing chamber.

"The boys," Marca shouted as she ran with him.

"Later," he shouted back, throwing up a hand to push aside the encroaching canes. At the same time he concentrated on the clock ticking in his head.

They could go a long way in thirty minutes, but they couldn't escape. The best they could hope for was a bolt-hole where he could keep Marca safe while he tried to come up with a plan.

The grass was damp, and twice Marca's sneakers slipped. He caught her the first time. The second time she went down on both knees, bracing herself on her hands. He heard her cry out as the impact with the hard ground thudded through her. Conscious of the seconds ticking down, he grabbed her by the back of her shirt and hauled her to her feet, very much as he'd done with Ryan. Every instinct urged him to put his body between her and a bullet, but he also knew what those thorns could do to her delicate skin.

"Stay behind me," he ordered, already moving forward again.

Without a sound, she followed, racing in his wake, her breathing labored. He took a hard left, knowing that Renfrew would assume they'd unconsciously turn toward their dominant hand—which for the majority of human beings was the right. As he quickened the pace, he hoped to God Renfrew wouldn't remember that he was left-handed.

He set a punishing pace, praying she could keep up. He chose a serpentine course, keeping to the hard ground as much as possible.

Time, he thought as the clock in his head ticked. Any second now. Two beats later firing erupted, sending bullets spraying the brush a hundred yards or so to their right. Lead slugs whistled overhead, ricocheting off tree trunks and splintering branches. Bastard had enough firepower to bring down an army, he thought as he scanned the terrain ahead. They were in dense brush now, which whipped at their already lacerated skin and slowed their progress.

They had to go to ground, and soon. Marca wasn't in any shape for an extended run, and his bruised ribs couldn't handle much more pounding. Still, they had to put distance between them and Renfrew. And since they were leaving a trail a child could follow damn near blindfolded, they had to double back, to create a maze of tracks. As a way of putting him off the scent, it was downright pathetic, but it was the best he could come up with.

The ground grew rougher, and tree roots crisscrossed a narrow deer track. Behind him he heard Marca cry out and felt her lurch forward. Twisting, he managed to catch her before she went down.

"Tripped," she gasped out, holding her side. Her face was fiery red, and leaves and sticks from the thatchlike underbrush were caught in her hair. He'd never seen her look more beautiful.

"Take deep breaths," he ordered, rubbing her back while he looked around. To the east the ground was too soft for good footing. The area to the north offered almost no cover. The rocks to the west would have to do.

"Ready or not, here I come," Renfrew shouted, his voice booming off the hills that formed a natural bowl. The sound was still echoing when he let loose another fusillade. Bullets whined overhead, and Ian realized he was shooting at random, hoping to panic them into bolting from cover.

"Oh, God," Marca cried softly, her hands pressed to her ears.

He bent to kiss her hard, then jerked his head toward the boulders. "We go that way, okay?"

Her eyes were huge, the terror hovering in their depths, but she nodded. He managed a grin, then led the way.

By the time they reached the rocks, Marca's lungs were burning and her legs were leaden. Blood dripped from the scratches ripped into her flesh by the thorns. Ian shoved her into a crevice between two craggy chunks of granite and tumbled in after her. It was cramped, no more than an irregular space approximately four feet by six. The ground was trampled and wet. The air smelled of rotting vegetation.

Ian helped her to the ground, then slumped down next to her, his back to the boulder, his long legs outstretched. "Be...safe here for now," he said, his hand pressed to his side as he gulped air. His face was a mass of crisscrossing scratches. Some were still oozing blood. Others had caked over, the dried blood appearing nearly black.

"How long before he finds us?" she asked between shuddering breaths.

"Hour, maybe longer." He pulled out his watch and blinked to clear the blood and sweat from his face. He frowned, then returned the timepiece to his pocket.

"I'm so sorry," she said when her breathing eased. "This is all my fault. I never should have mentioned that stupid idea of single combat." She swiped her sleeve over her face, then flinched at the mix of dirt, sweat and blood that clotted the yellow sweatshirt fleece.

To her utter amazement, his grin flashed. "Honey, it was sheer genius."

She blinked at him. "It was?"

"Yep. In fact, it was the only chance I could see, and I'd bee
running through a damn long list while trying to keep that basta
from busting my ribs." Wincing with the effort of moving, I
tugged the tails of his shirt free, then unbuttoned it. The effo
seemed to tire him, and he closed his eyes.

She moved closer. Now that some of the strength was returnin
to her burning muscles, she was anxious to do something—an
thing—but sit and wait to be slaughtered. "Ian, I've been thin
ing. Maybe, if I distracted him, you could sneak up behind him.

He opened his eyes and looked at her. "No."

"I could make a lot of noise—"

"Marca, that Winchester of his has a range of eight hundre
yards, easy, and a sniper's scope. One glimpse of that yellow shi
and he could pick you off anytime he wanted."

"Yes, but that's the idea, isn't it? I could run in and out of th
trees, and while he's playing mighty hunter, you could circl
around." She grabbed his arm, her enthusiasm mounting. "I'v
seen you run, Ian. I know you're fast and—"

"On the flat, Marce. On these hills I'd be like a bear crashin
through the woods. And even if I could cover ground withou
being seen, I'd have to get within a few feet to take him dowr
Hell, the way I'm sweating, he'd probably smell me coming
good fifty feet away."

She recognized his attempt to ease her anxiety and blessed hir
for it. "I think you smell very manly," she responded, but he
heart was racing, and it was an effort to keep even a semblanc
of calm. "You could keep, uh, downwind, or upwind. Which
ever."

He touched her face with his fingertips, and she leaned agains
him for a moment. "Downwind. With my ribs the way they are
I'd be about as effective in hand-to-hand as you would."

"Would a knife help?"

His gaze narrowed, and she felt the excitement thrum throug
him. "You have a knife?"

She nodded. "I keep it in my makeup kit for emergencies."
She shifted, then brought up one foot and unlaced the sneaker

"You're not the only one who keeps a lethal weapon in your shoe." Triumphantly, she drew out the small white knife and displayed it on her palm. "It was a freebie from my broker. See, it has the brokerage house logo on the handle."

His mouth twitched as he took the knife and flicked it open. "How'd you manage this?"

"When I first got to his place, Renfrew let me see the boys—" Her voice faltered, and she had to take a moment to regroup. If she let herself think about losing her babies, she would shatter. "He'd searched my tote and found the gun. But he just tossed my makeup kit and the other things back in. I talked him into letting me diaper the boys, especially Trev. He'd messed his pants, and...and you know how smelly that is."

His face softened and he laughed. "Yeah, I know."

Tears came to her eyes. Determined to be strong, she reached up to dash them away, but Ian beat her to it. His callused fingers were gentle on her cheeks, and she trembled. Now that the flush of exertion had faded, his skin had turned a sickly gray beneath the blood and dirt, but the look in his eyes was fiercely protective.

"Easy, honey," he said in a gruff tone. "It's going to be okay. You'll see your babies again."

She nodded, and he withdrew his hand. "Renfrew let me have the tote back, and while I was getting out the wipes, I managed to get the knife from the makeup bag."

He tested the blade with his thumb, then glanced up. "Not exactly a razor's edge," he said when she lifted an eyebrow.

"I was thinking I could shove it in his eye and then knee him in the groin, but he watched me so closely, I couldn't figure out a way to get the knife out of my shoe."

He used his free hand to pick twigs from her hair. "My little warrior," he murmured, his tone husky. "I'm glad you're on my side."

"And I'm glad you're on mine."

She offered her mouth and he took it hungrily for a deep, but brief, kiss. "So you like my plan," she said eagerly, watching his face.

"I'd like it a lot better if this were a commando knife. Or even a paring knife, but—" He stopped, his face going utterly still. "Damn, it might just work—with a few suitable changes."

It had been nearly an hour since he'd conceived his plan. After showing Marca how to hone the edge of the puny blade against the granite, he slipped from the crevice and went in search of the raw material to make a javelin.

Finding an oak sapling had been a stroke of luck. Scraping off the branches and whittling a point had been a test of patience.

Renfrew had come close once, following one of the trails a good hundred and fifty yards below them. He'd made a good target, but the javelin wasn't finished. They would have only one chance. Ian didn't intend to blow it.

"Is it ready?" Marca asked, glancing away from the opening where she was crouched, keeping watch.

"Yeah." Ian tested the point and bit off a sigh. It was sharp enough to break the skin if he pressed hard enough, but had little hope of killing Renfrew with it. Or of even injuring him. But if he could surprise him into letting go of the rifle, he just might have a chance to sprint for it in time.

Timing was everything. And luck. Though he hated to admit it, he figured it was the luck that would make the difference between life and death for him. And for Marca.

"Ready?" he asked when she looked back at him.

"Ready." She smiled, her eyes liquid with trust, and his heart did a slow tumble.

"It's a good plan," he said, moving to crouch next to her. "You'd make a great agent."

"You're pretty great yourself," she said in a voice that trembled. "And I love you so much."

He groaned and hauled her against him. Please, please let her make it, he prayed, with his mind and with his heart. Keep this brave, dear woman safe. He kissed her, wanting a lifetime of soft, lingering kisses and cuddles.

He drew back, then groaned softly when he saw the tears. "Don't, honey. Please don't."

"Ian—"

Rifle fire erupted, pinging against the trees on the other side of the small ravine. Marca winced but managed to keep from crying out.

Ian pulled his watch from his pocket and put it into her hand. "Remember, give me ten minutes, then go into your act."

"Promise me you won't get hurt," she whispered fiercely, curling her hand around his arm.

"I'll do my best."

"Because your sons and I will never forgive you if you do."

Ian managed a smile. He knew all too well what lay ahead for her and his boys if he failed. No, he thought. *No!* Not this time.

"I love you," she whispered.

Ian took a ragged breath. "I love you, too. I think I fell in love on the beach that night when I saw you take a swing at that bruiser who had you by the hair."

"I know." She reached up to touch a finger to the corner of his mouth. "You couldn't help it."

He loved her smile. And the militant light in her eyes. And the way she had of leaning forward and grabbing his shoulders when she wanted to make a point. "I couldn't?"

"Nope. I wished on a star for you. All my life I wished. And then one night, there you were."

"Hold that thought," he said as he kissed her hard, then grabbed the javelin. "Ten minutes."

Her lips trembled as her hand closed over his watch. "Good luck."

"You, too."

He paused at the entrance to their bolt-hole to survey the terrain. Renfrew was nowhere in sight, and he headed into the watery early-morning sunshine.

Marca watched him go, her heart in her throat. She didn't expect him to look back, and he didn't. The warrior facing a dragon alone couldn't afford to mix emotion with the single-minded concentration on his mission.

Keeping her gaze riveted to the watch, she tried to calm her jittery nerves. She didn't dare think of the boys or the fact that they might be waking up alone and hungry and wet. Ian was right. They were tough. And they were hers. Hers and Ian's.

No way in hell was that monster Renfrew going to get his hands on them. Ian wouldn't let that happen. And neither would she.

*Five minutes. Four.* She crept closer to the opening and looked out. It was a perfect fall morning. A light breeze and sunshine. Temperature in the fifties. Nothing stirred.

*Three minutes.* Ian was counting on the man's need to pump his ego to keep her alive long enough for him to act. She was counting on Ian.

*Two minutes. One.*

After slipping Ian's watch into the pocket of her jeans, she stood up, took a couple of bracing breaths and let out a shout that sounded exactly like a scalded cat.

Crouched behind a stand of salal, the makeshift javelin balanced in his hand, Ian heard the sound echo across the clearing, and grinned. God, she was magnificent, he thought, his gaze roaming, looking for his prey.

"*Hutch! Can you hear me?*" Her voice was shrilled and shaded toward hysteria.

A shot resounded, followed by Renfrew's shouted answer. "*I hear you.*"

"*There's something wrong with MacDougall, and I don't want to do this anymore.*" She should be an actress, Ian thought, scanning the brush bordering the open space. Renfrew would wait before he acted, to make sure he wasn't walking into an ambush. Ian was counting on the bastard retracing the path he'd taken earlier and had positioned himself to get a clear shot. He would be angling his shot downhill, putting all the weight and power and lingering skill into his throw.

"*Hutch, did you hear me? I want to make a deal.*"

He saw a blur of movement below and to his left, just a subtle shift of color. He tensed.

"What kind of a deal?" Renfrew wasn't shouting now.

"I'll be your mistress if that's what you want." Marca stepped out into the opening, wearing the yellow shirt again, the way they'd planned. She was holding Ian's shirt in one hand and had a look of weary defeat on her face. For good measure tears were streaming down her face.

"What's wrong with MacDougall?" Renfrew sounded both wary and excited.

"I'm not sure, something inside," she said moving forward. "I think you broke his ribs and one of them must have punctured a lung. He couldn't breathe and then he coughed up blood."

She spread his shirt in front of her, the one Ian had bloodied for this purpose by nicking a vessel in his arm with that silly little knife of hers. Renfrew's laugh resounded—a shrill, almost feminine sound.

"Come down here so I can see you better," Renfrew ordered.

"Promise you won't shoot," Marca cried, her voice trembling. "I'm so s-scared."

Ian tensed, his gaze focused. He heard the rustle of leaves beneath combat boots, saw the brush sway, then part, and then Renfrew was there, the Winchester pressed to his shoulder in a firing stance. It was pointed directly at Marca.

Ian's mind clicked into slow motion, and he waited. Trusting her.

"Come down here, Marca," Renfrew ordered, his rifle aimed at her heart. "I won't hurt you."

"I c-can't move," she said, her voice rising. "I...please." She sank to her knees, the picture of abject defeat.

Renfrew drew back from the scope but kept the rifle against his shoulder as he scanned the area. A crow flew overhead, its raucous cry chilling Ian's blood almost as much as the sound of Marca's piteous sobs.

Put down the Winchester, you son of a bitch, Ian begged quietly.

Finally, with a slowness that had Ian's muscles burning, Renfrew lowered his weapon. In the fluid motion he'd learned as a kid chucking rocks at crows, Ian reared back and threw the javelin directly at Renfrew's heart. At the same time he sprinted forward.

The spear caught Renfrew dead in the stomach, embedding deep. With a look of utter shock, he went down, both hands clawing at the protruding shaft. Ian poured on speed and reached the struggling man just as Renfrew wrenched the spear free.

Blood gushed as Renfrew scrambled for the gun. Ian reached it first and jerked it up. Instinctively he whipped it into firing position and drew a bead dead center on the bastard's face. Rage and grief rose in him like a violent tremor, and he knew he was going to kill the man.

"This is for my girls," he said, his voice low and lethal, his finger tightening on the trigger.

*"No, Ian. Don't do it. Please don't do it."*

He froze, his blood pounding. Through the lens of the scope, he saw Renfrew's mouth open and close silently in a rictus of terror. Overlaid on the reality was the image of his Camaro dissolving into a thousand pieces.

"Ian, he lost." Marca's voice was low and intense, penetrating the madness like a warm touch on a cold heart. "You won. You saved the boys. You saved me."

"He killed my babies, Marca," he grated, but the savage rage was receding.

"And he'll be punished." She touched Ian's arm, letting her hand linger. Slowly, reluctantly, he lowered the rifle. Renfrew closed his eyes and let out the air trapped in his lungs in a keening moan. His hands clutched the hole in his belly. Ian hoped the bastard bled to death, but the oozing had already slowed.

Damn.

Using his belt, Ian tied up Renfrew for the authorities. Then, looking down into Marca's eyes, he let his shoulders slump. "I love you," he said with his heart in his voice.

Tears spilled from her eyes and ran down her cheeks, making little tracks in the grime. "I love you, too."

He lifted a hand to catch a tear that trembled on the curve of at stubborn jaw. "Marry me?" he asked gruffly.

She gnawed her lip, then nodded. "Can we collect the boys st? I have a feeling Trev will need changing again." Her voice asn't quite steady. Neither was his pulse. "And this time, it's ur turn."

Ian felt a suspicious dampness stain his eyes as he scooped her to his arms. "I can't wait," he said before he kissed her. "Now, oot on up to the house and call Brandt. Tell him to send in the oops." But instead of letting her go, he pulled her close for other hug. "I'm going to need some help, Marce. Being a dad ain..." He drew a jagged breath. "Be patient, okay?"

"As long as you're patient with us, too," she said, lifting her ce to invite a kiss.

He brushed his mouth over hers. His ribs ached, he was muzzy om lack of sleep, he was filthy and smelly. He felt wonderful. ut that's the way it was when a man came home, he realized. ome to his family.

# Epilogue

Marca stood in the doorway, her arms folded and her foot tapping. Soap-scented steam swirled like mist in the close confine
of the bathroom and clouded the mirror.

"All right, which one of you MacDougall males is responsib
for this?"

Closest to the door, Trevor looked and grinned. "Loo
Mommy, we're giving Mutt a shampoo!"

"I see that, sweetie."

Covered in soapsuds and looking miserable, yet stoic, Mu
thumped his tail, sending suds flying. Ryan giggled, his bare boo
slick as a little seal's. "Daddy said Mutt's gonna be the prettie
dog at the graduation."

Marca somehow managed to keep a straight face. "I thi
Daddy owes me big-time for this little escapade."

Ian drew back the shower curtain, a sheepish grin on his tann
face. "Now, honey, don't get your panties in a twist. Mitch a
Carly were here ragging me about having to wear a cap and gov
for the ceremony, and I lost track of time."

Her husband of twenty-three months and two days was bu

aked and half-covered in soapsuds himself. Her heart gave a little stutter. His year as an impatient, grouchy graduate student had frayed her temper more than once, but it hadn't diminished the love she felt for him.

"Eddie's plane is due in two hours," she said, coming forward to snatch a towel from the rod. "If you're going to meet him, you'd better be moving those sexy buns, MacDougall."

Sean peeked around his father's legs and grinned. "Daddy said we can have ice cream 'cause we're celebraving him being a masser's degree now."

"*Having* a master's degree, darling. Daddy's going to be a professor." Marca wrapped Trevor in a towel, rubbing him down while he giggled and squirmed.

Ian had put in his resignation on the day Renfrew was senenced to a long stretch in prison. Dr. Smith and the others involved in the attacks were also serving time. Ian would begin teaching classes in law enforcement when the winter term began in two months.

"Okay, guys, listen up," he said with a grin. "Mommy needs our help here. We have to be dressed and looking handsome in twenty minutes max."

All three boys looked toward their daddy. "'Kay," Sean said before ducking his head under the spray.

"Your clothes are laid out on your bed," Marca told Trevor after giving him a hug. "Start getting dressed."

The boys were potty trained now—and learning to be regular little gentlemen. Most of the time. During those other times, Ian had been the soul of patience, handling the little hooligans with good-natured amusement.

Ian stepped from the tiled stall, then lifted Sean out, as well. "Not so fast, scout," he ordered when Sean started to take off. While the almost-four-year-old shifted impatiently from foot-to-foot, his daddy rubbed him dry with those big, gentle hands Marca loved. Completely at ease with his sons now, he dropped a kiss on Sean's damp, curly hair, before giving the little guy a gentle swat on the bottom.

"Go get dressed, tiger," he ordered gruffly. With a whoop Sean took off running.

"Ryan, you and Mutt get in the shower and rinse off," he ordered sternly.

The dog let out a bark, glanced at Marca, then shook violently, sending suds flying. Marca yelled, then leaped out of the way as the dog went racing from the bathroom with Ryan at his heels.

"I can't stand it," Marca muttered, trying very hard not to laugh.

"Admit it, sugar, you love it." He took her in his arms and rubbed his wet, clean-smelling body against her. "And I love you."

He angled his head and captured her mouth, just as she'd captured his heart. Her arms circled his neck, and she arched against him, uncaring that his damp body was ruining her new silk dress.

"I love the way you glare at your men, honey."

"My men deserve it," she said with a laugh.

"Of course, I love your body most of all," he murmured, running his tongue over her lower lip until it relaxed into that sweet gypsy smile that never failed to stir his blood. "You make me drunk on loving you."

She rubbed her silk-clad breasts against his chest. "I'm crazy about you, too," she murmured, her voice catching, warming his heart.

He'd kissed her countless times before and it was always thrilling. The sweet satisfaction of finding safety after a long lonely struggle. The peace of coming home after a lifetime of desolation and loneliness.

He took her mouth again, and it felt right. "My sweet gypsy," he whispered gruffly. "You make me humble."

Her smile was beautifully wild and free. Her heart was in that smile. "And you make me strong," she whispered. "My wonderful perfect hero."

\* \* \* \* \*

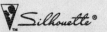

# Take 2 bestselling love stories FREE

## Plus get a FREE surprise gift!

---

## Special Limited-Time Offer

**Mail to Silhouette Reader Service™**

### 3010 Walden Avenue
### P.O. Box 1867
### Buffalo, N.Y. 14240-1867

**YES!** Please send me 2 free Silhouette Intimate Moments® novels and my free surprise gift. Then send me 6 brand-new novels every month, which I will receive months before they appear in bookstores. Bill me at the low price of $3.57 each plus 25¢ delivery and applicable sales tax, if any.* That's the complete price, and a saving of over 10% off the cover prices—quite a bargain! I understand that accepting the books and gift places me under no obligation ever to buy any books. I can always return a shipment and cancel at any time. Even if I never buy another book from Silhouette, the 2 free books and the surprise gift are mine to keep forever.

245 SEN CH7Y

| Name | (PLEASE PRINT) | |
|------|----------------|--|
| Address | Apt. No. | |
| City | State | Zip |

This offer is limited to one order per household and not valid to present Silhouette Intimate Moments® subscribers. *Terms and prices are subject to change without notice. Sales tax applicable in N.Y.

UIM-98        ©1990 Harlequin Enterprises Limited

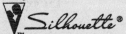

**For a limited time, Harlequin and Silhouette have an offer you just can't refuse.**

## In November and December 1998:

BUY **ANY** TWO HARLEQUIN
OR SILHOUETTE BOOKS and

# SAVE $10.00

off future purchases

OR BUY ANY THREE HARLEQUIN OR SILHOUETTE BOOKS
AND **SAVE $20.00** OFF FUTURE PURCHASES!

(each coupon is good for $1.00 off the purchase of two
Harlequin or Silhouette books)

..................................................................................................

JUST BUY 2 HARLEQUIN OR SILHOUETTE BOOKS, SEND US YOUR
NAME, ADDRESS AND 2 PROOFS OF PURCHASE (CASH REGISTER
RECEIPTS) AND HARLEQUIN WILL SEND YOU A COUPON BOOKLET
WORTH **$10.00 OFF** FUTURE PURCHASES OF HARLEQUIN OR
SILHOUETTE BOOKS IN 1999. SEND US 3 PROOFS OF PURCHASE AND
WE WILL SEND YOU 2 COUPON BOOKLETS WITH A TOTAL SAVING OF
**$20.00.** (ALLOW 4-6 WEEKS DELIVERY) OFFER EXPIRES
DECEMBER 31, 1998.

..................................................................................................

I accept your offer! Please send me a coupon booklet(s), to:

NAME: _____

ADDRESS: _____

CITY: _____ STATE/PROV.: _____ POSTAL/ZIP CODE: _____

Send your name and address, along with your cash register
receipts for proofs of purchase, to:

In the U.S.          In Canada
Harlequin Books    Harlequin Books
P.O. Box 9057       P.O. Box 622
Buffalo, NY         Fort Erie, Ontario
14269              L2A 5X3

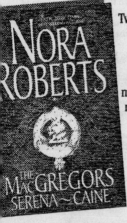

INTIMATE MOMENTS®

™ Silhouette®

# COMING NEXT MONTH

**#895 CHRISTMAS LONE-STAR STYLE—Linda Turner**
*The Lone Star Social Club*
Christmas was coming, and Phoebe Smith needed a place to stay with her
orphaned niece and nephew—pronto! The solution? Handsome bachelor
Mitch Ryan offered her a job—and a place to live—with him. Mitch found
his sassy secretary pretty darn irresistible, but how could this confirmed
cynic admit to his heart's deepest desire?

**#896 IT CAME UPON A MIDNIGHT CLEAR—Suzanne Brockmann**
*Tall, Dark & Dangerous*
"Crash" Hawken lived for danger, and not even the sweet temptation of
beautiful Nell Burns had deterred him from his duty. But when a conspiracy
posed a deadly threat, Nell offered the intense navy SEAL a safe haven for
the holidays—and more. Now Crash wasn't just fighting for *his* life—but
for that of the woman he cherished....

**#897 HOME FOR CHRISTMAS—Patricia Potter**
*Families Are Forever*
Legal eagle Julie Farrell would always be grateful to Ryan Murphy for
rescuing her and her son. Now, in a twist of fate, the amnesiac police
detective's life was on the line. As Julie fought to prove Ryan's innocence,
she envisioned spending every night in his arms. But had she invited a
murderer home for the holidays?

**#898 FOR CHRISTMAS, FOREVER—Ruth Wind**
Just as Claire Franklin was settling in for another uneventful holiday, a
compelling secret agent brought passion—and danger—into her safe, secure
life. She knew that Zane Hunter was bound to protect her from a killer, but
then she found herself risking everything to be with him this Christmas—
and forever!

**#899 ONE SILENT NIGHT—Debra Cowan**
*Men in Blue*
Although gorgeous Dallas Kittridge had lived to regret it, officer
Sam Garrett couldn't forget about the night of love he'd shared with his best
friend's widow. Now, as they worked together to track down a killer, Sam
ached to hold Dallas close again. Would the magic of the holidays inspire
Sam to bare his soul to the elusive beauty?

**#900 A SEASON OF MIRACLES—Christine Michels**
*Try To Remember*
It was a Christmas miracle when Devon Grayson discovered that her
presumed-dead husband was alive! A mysterious plane crash had erased all
of Geoff's memories, but Devon wasn't about to lose her beloved twice. Or
allow his intended killers to finish the job. Now she had to convince Geoff
that their love was worth fighting for....